We all know Sprawlburg Springs, with its countless chain stores, its heat, the intense need of its teenage vandals for a savior. Here we have a sort of best-case scenario in The Enchanters, the greatest band to never cut a record. Brian Costello, whose refreshingly hilarious and beautiful work I've had the great fortune to edit and publish a good bit over the years, has created a strong American satire with more than a small vestige of the romantic, the perfect combination.
—**Todd Dills**, editor of THE2NDHAND and *All Hands On*

With this book, Brian Costello has done the nearly impossible: He's managed to document the secret world of a rock n' roll band in hilarious, satirical detail. *The Enchanters...* is as important as *Moby Dick*: the song by Led Zeppelin, not the book. His prose wields the same immortal bombast and ferocity as a John Bonham drum solo.
—**Joe Meno**, author of *Hairstyles of the Damned* and *Bluebirds Used to Croon in the Choir*

This audacious debut novel leaves us with as much hope as it does despair. This is not just a story about a Protomersh band out to fiercely protect its iconoclastic identity; it's about a generation's brave, coming-of-age struggle to define itself in a jaded America that punishes any attempt at originality.—**Shawn Shiflett**, author of *Hidden Place*

What Brian Costello has accomplished with *The Enchanters vs. Sprawlburg Springs* is the literary equivalent of Peter Criss hitting the gong at the end of the drum solo on *KISS Alive II*. This rock 'n' roll epic is loaded with brass, balls and a good measure of hilarity. A delight to read.—**Sam Weller**, author of *The Bradbury Chronicles: The Life of Ray Bradbury*

This hilarious, hyper-observant debut novel defies category and concerns itself with, among other things: rock 'n' rollers who wear football helmets and Cheeto-hued makeup, beer and brawling, pizza sandwiches and love, squid, and places like Latent Republican Hipster Music Club World and the Perimeter Square Circle Centre Mall. Why would you not read it?—**Elizabeth Crane**, author of *All This Heavenly Glory* and *When the Messenger is Hot*

# the ENCHANTERS
## vs.
## *Sprawlburg Springs*

a novel by
## Brian Costello

illustrations by
## Mark Dunihue McKenzie

## *featherproof* BOOKS

Parts of this book have previously appeared in *F Magazine* and *Ink Stains*, to whose editors grateful acknowledgement is made.

Author photo: Rob Karlic.

Published by
*feather*proof books
Chicago, Illinois
www.featherproof.com

First Edition

10  9  8  7  6  5  4  3  2  1

Library of Congress Control Number: 20005931561

ISBN: 0-9771992-0-7
ISBN 13: 978-0-9771992-0-4

Set in Bookman Old Style

Printed in the United States of America World

# part one: forming

"...and the drummer, he's so shattered
...trying to keep up time."

**The Rolling Stones**

# chapter one

I sat out there on the diving board for a long time, looking at the stars and drinking foamy Buck Urine Lite keg beer from a red plastic cup. Mosquitoes drained my arms. Tiny lizards scurried around my feet. Hundreds of frogs and crickets droned the adult-contemporary hit *Sometimes When We Touch.* I didn't care where the other Enchanters were hiding. I just wanted to be alone with my recurring thought: *Why bother playing drums for these assholes?*

Soon the screened-in porch, the "Florida room," was packed with emasculated indie-rock kids in nerd glasses and facetious thrift-store tees. There were twelve of them. I was far enough in the darkness of the back patio to observe without being seen. While the magical beer cured me of my ahhhhngsty yearnings over Renee, it didn't give me the insight to see how these kids were on the verge of reinventing themselves and our town—however briefly—into something exciting.

There they were, just moments before The Enchanters inspired them to start their own bands. Some paced around the green and white vinyl lawn furniture. Some just sat around. Others stood staring at the wine bottles reserved for The Enchanters.

"How the fuck are you supposed to open this fuckin' wine?" said a nice girl with a stinky clove cigarette and black eye makeup made up intentionally like two black eyes. Her dress was long and black, and she had short whitish yellow hair and skin like a bowl of cream with floating pieces of burnt pepperoni. She stood in the middle of the room holding one of The Enchanters' wine bottles, inspecting it for any secret to its opening. How was anybody to know this Gothic Faerie Princess would be the same Melissa who taught herself guitar and formed the legendary neo-no-new-old wave group Chloroform? Sure, she's always said The Enchanters were a huge influence on her frenetic, kinetic, spasmodic songwriting, but we were none of those adjectives, and to say we were just because we had traces of that stuff would be like saying your favorite cereal tastes like rodent poo since there's probably traces of rodent poo inside every box you buy.

"Fuckin', I think you need a corkscrew and shit," said the

unwashed fat kid with the torn, black Exploited T-shirt sitting in the corner staring at Melissa's almost nonexistent ass. That was Red Head Ted, who became Ted Pungent, the driving force behind Verdant Iceberg. It's boring shit if you ask me, but lots of people—twelve-year-old mallrats mainly—enjoyed their "stark Teutonic depression." Ted always mentioned The Enchanters as a "major influence," but that's nonsense.

"I'll just get a knife and force the cork down the hole," said blond, long-legged Cathy as she rose from her slouch in a lawn chair and poked the wine bottle. As she stood there in her black miniskirt and fishnet stockings I wondered if she maybe had a thing for drummers, and, if so, was she legal? I certainly wasn't predicting she would change her name to Mia Culpa and play the lead bass guitar for everybody's favorite art-damaged four-guitar, three-bass and two–drum set assault noise ensemble The Picnic.

None of the bands these twelve went on to form after we gave them the little shove they needed were very "high concept," especially at the beginning. Some were content just using "rock" like the verb it is, like the effusively pensive Bryan, seated across from Cathy, mumbling voice-cracked worries about what the night would bring.

"I'm wearing my favorite pants, and I don't wanna shit in 'em," he whined in his cracking voice through his bad orange dye job. "I heard that's what The Enchanters make you do. Shit."

It was hard to believe that this was the same schmuck who became the guitarist and singer for The Sherilyns, whose song *Sweaty Hands* somehow made it onto volume #72 of *Thrilled by Death*, a serial compilation of hard-to-find Moron Rock. Regardless, Bryan always credited us for getting him started, but we were never the punk rock/classic rock hybrid they were. Not only that, but we definitely weren't a "garage" band like the Smoking Corvairs, formed by Jonathan, who stood there lanky in a black-and-white–striped cartoon criminal shirt, wide-eyed at all the girls, pacing, running his hands through his short black hair, talking to himself all like, "Nugget! Renee! She's such a nugget, dude!" Jonathan even claimed a song he wrote called *I Love Renee But She's So Reclusive* was about Renee Eisner from The Enchanters, and I believe him!

There was a boom box playing the Buzzcocks' *Singles Going Steady*, and hirsute Sally danced by herself next to the keg to the left of the room, singing "reality's a dream/a game in which I seem/to never find out just who I am...." This was the same Sally who started the hardcore militant feminist band Castration Nation. She too said we influenced her, but we weren't political, and Renee never screamed like Sally screamed. Renee never screamed.

"That wine's not for us anyway. It's for The Enchanters. Leave it alone. I'm sticking with the keg," said Tommy, whose big moussed-up hair was a desperate attempt at looking like, of all people, Morrissey.

"I'll pump it for you," giggled Andy. He wore black eye shadow, a black Bauhaus T-shirt and black pants with black boots. Andy and Tommy would pair up and start the gay folk-singing duo Adam and Steve. In interviews around town, they always spoke of the "profound influence" of The Enchanters, but we never used acoustic guitars and we weren't gay, and we didn't convey an aggressive heterosexual stance either, so I don't know what they're talking about.

Alison, with long black hair and a red thrift-store T-shirt emblazoned with the fuzzy white-lettered slogan, "I'M PRETENDING TO LIKE SOMETHING I DON'T REALLY LIKE" across the front was there, the same Alison who started the band Noon Wine. "So how did Scott get The Enchanters to play his house?" she asked, sitting on the plastic green outdoor carpeted Florida room and holding her boyfriend Norman's hand.

"Donald's his boss at Good Time America Family Restaurant World, and Donald kept bugging him and begging until Scott finally gave in," said Balding Norman, who at 18 was already losing his thin blond hair. He started the band Rubber Gone Bouncy Bounce.

I laughed when I heard bald Norman say that. Donald was the only person to respond to the handwritten fliers I taped all over town that read:

DRUMMER LOOKING FOR BAND
INFLUENCES: GERMS, MINUTEMEN, THE WHO, STOOGES,
BUTTHOLE SURFERS (OLD SHIT), AND NOTHING ELSE.
I'M GOOD. CALL SHAQUILLE AT...

When I picked up the phone and said hello, this pushy,

curt, and arrogant voice barked, "Hey, Drummer. We want you to play with us for a concert tomorrow. We like the same bands you do. Just meet us at our house to load up the shit."

"But I don't think I can play the songs without any practice."

"That's for us to decide, Drummer. You drum, we'll think. Here's how to get to our house..."

Things moved fast with The Enchanters, as I would soon learn. One moment, you're sitting in your living room after work laughing at a rerun of "Sanford and Son," and the next, you're playing songs you've never heard at a concert in some suburban living room for disaffected teenagers.

"It's very important we play this show," Donald told me on the phone. "It's a golden opportunity for us we cannot pass up. Promoters are begging to give us this shot." *What a tool*, I thought as I stared at the underwater lights stretching back and forth over the spleen-shaped pool's choppy turquoise waves, breathing in the humid air while the pool-cleaning machine floated around like a plastic angular octopus. *I bet he's a shitty guitar player. What does Renee see in him?*

"Well I just hope they're good. I have a calculus test on Monday I need to study for," said Mark, with the big brown afroed hair and silver sequined shirt, the progenitor of the Sprawlburg Springs's neo-glam-boogie movement. Mark even acknowledged me as the one who inspired his spaced out rhythms, but that's something Mickey, Donald, and Renee found laughable. My drumming was never something they admitted—at least not for a long time—as being anything but unpredictable at best, and careening at worst.

I enjoyed sitting outside and watching this dumb scene unfold, and maybe I would have stayed all night if frizzy-haired Scott, the concert's host and our self-proclaimed biggest fan, hadn't stumbled into the Florida room from the house in his white Minutemen T-shirt and red pants, yelling, "Hey is the drummer still out by the diving board?"

Twelve pairs of eyes stopped what they were doing to look my way. I waved with my red plastic beer cup and yelled, "I'm over here."

They just stared at me. Finally, hirsute Sally said, "I thought he moved to Atlanta."

"That was their old drummer," Scott answered, pulling up his red pants only to have them fall again. "This is the new one. He joined yesterday." He then yelled across to me, "They're waiting backstage for you!"

"Backstage?" I asked, stumbling toward the screen door.

"It's my room," Scott said. "They wanted a backstage before the show, but since I don't live in a house with a backstage, my room's the best I could do."

I laughed, and nobody else did. I couldn't believe what I was hearing, and everybody else in the room just accepted this "backstage" horseshit as a matter of course. When I walked through the clangy screen door, twelve jaws went slack, and twelve pairs of eyes stared in shock. It was a little awkward. I mean, I made my living as a Squid Cutting Technician for Cleveland Steamerz Good Time Bar and Grille World. I came from humble peasant stock. Just folks, really.

Despite my avocation, it was a little flattering, all this attention. My bad mood from before had worn off, especially when blond Cathy looked at me, eyes sparkling, cheeks flushed, long fishnetted legs shifting and crossing toward me. "You're the new drummer?" she asked.

"Yup," I smiled, extending my hand. "I'm Shaquille Callahan." Oh good: Cathy does have a thing for drummers, I thought. *Renee, shmenee.*

"Oh, um, Shaq?" Scott stammered like a personal assistant, left hand on my back. "The...the...other Enchanters? Um, they wanna see you man, um, backstage? In my room? They say it's real important that you're back there with them man...really."

"Nope," I said, pumping the keg and filling my cup with more ice-brewed Buck Urine Lite. "I'll be in your room—oh, I mean, *backstage*, sorry—in a minute." I said "backstage" with all the sarcasm I could muster in my voice, all the sarcasm I thought the word deserved. "I wanna stay here and, fuckin', meet some folks." I turned to blond Cathy and smiled like a horny idiot.

The beer was working and I was relaxed enough to try and make everybody around me relaxed—Enchanter or not—because I wanted to make friends. I fired off a bunch of "Whachername-whereyafrom?" type questions, and they just stared at me. Hirsute Sally turned down the Buzzcocks, and I smiled and nodded at their nervous answers.

I sat down with my hands pushing against the plastic roughness of the fake green lawn floor. They kept staring at me; then they fired off all these questions about the band and my role in it. It started with Bryan asking, cracked voice and all, "Are y'all gonna make me crap my pants?"

"No," I laughed. "Why would we do that?"

"It's what I heard."

"We heard y'all are crazy," blond Cathy said, looking at me like some animal in the zoo notorious for biting off people's heads.

"Did you shit your pants when you practiced with them?" Mark asked, picking lint from his afro.

"Nope. Shit free!" I announced, smiling like not being moved to defecate while I played with them was some kind of proud accomplishment. They just looked at me. Starstruck.

"So. What do you guys do for fun?" I asked, trying to change the subject away from pooping and this band that I didn't even think I'd stick around with after the night was over anyway.

Nothing. It was like I asked them some deep, dark personal question. The pool's gurgles entered the patio, then wide-eyed Jonathan shook his head from side to side and said, "Renee is such a *nnnnugget*, dude!" and everybody nodded or said "Oh yeah, totally." Then, it was back to the Enchanter questions:

"So what's Renee *really* like?"

"Is Donald really that much of a jerk or is it like an act or something?"

"And what about Mickey? Can he even talk? I heard he was retarded..."

These questions were fired at me at once, not really asked so much as demanded. It was all too weird, their blank stares, the slack jaws, the obsessiveness of it. I looked up at Scott. He was frizzy and nervous, wanting me to go backstage.

"Hey, um, they like really want you backstage and shit," he said, looking to his right, to the general direction of his bedroom. I jumped up, all too eager to get away from these weirdos. "Nice meeting y'all," I said in parting, which wasn't followed by a "Nice meeting you too, Shaquille," but instead, wide-eyed Jonathan stood up and grabbed the sleeve of my baby-blue oxford shirt and pleaded, "Wait wait wait wait wait!"

"What!" I yelled, creeped out and ready to leave.

"OK," he said, nervously, looking at the ground. "Does Renee have a boyfriend?"

"Yes," I lied. "Sorry."

"Uhhhhh!" Jonathan sighed, stomping off to pout in his lawn chair, to be consoled by Alison with the long black hair and Bald Norman, and I left them to their weird silence. But the moment I left, as Scott led me through the kitchen shortcut to the "backstage," I looked through the small window above the sink out to the Florida room. The party stopped having all the liveliness of an insurance seminar. The Buzzcocks were turned up again, singing "Everybody's happy nowadays..." and everyone talked excitedly. Mark and Bryan pretended to wrestle professionally. Jonathan paced, hands on his heart, repeating "Renee" over and over again until pimply Melissa walked up to him and yelled "Shut up!" while tweaking his left nipple.

I barely had time to admire the kitchen's pineapple motif— pineapple ashtrays, pineapple hors d'oeuvre trays, pineapple canvases, pineapple magnets, and so on—before Scott led me down a dark hallway to the last bedroom on the right; err, I kept forgetting, "backstage." Scott knocked.

"Go away!" Donald yelled like a petulant teenager, and Scott answered, "It's me, man..."

"Come in!" Renee sang cheerfully, as if nothing was wrong, and Scott opened the door.

Donald and Mickey Alexander sat on the bed in the far corner of Scott's bedroom, on green and white blankets decorated in the team colors of the Hessians, our professional sports team. The mattress was weighed down on Mickey's side like some kind of seesaw. He stared straight ahead, drool dripping off his wide tomato face. The rest of his big-lug body sank into the mattress like he was in a beanbag. He wore a white T-shirt that said "PLEASE KILL ME," with the "KILL" crossed out and replaced with "KISS" in black permanent marker.

On the lighter side of the seesaw mattress was Mickey's big brother Donald, but he didn't look bigger. Actually, they didn't look like brothers at all, but they were. Donald was a beanpole version of Mickey, with a moon head in place of the tomato. He wore lime-green polyester pants, and he also had on a white T-shirt, only his handwritten slogan was "oh sprawlburg springs... so much to answer for." I hated Donald. He flirted with Renee nonstop while I drove them to the party. It's why I went out to the diving board to brood. Both Mickey and Donald had bad clipper-shaved, short black hair with large and random patches of hair growth across the scalp missed either by accident or by design.

Renee sat cross-legged on a swivel chair, hunched over a desk to the immediate left of the doorway, scribbling on a piece of paper. When her hair bounced in thick black coils and her glazed green eyes looked up at me and that dimpled smirk formed around her red and green lips (red lipstick for the top lip, green for the bottom), my insides felt like I was jumping out of a turnip truck at 100 mph. On the desk to her right was an old 1940s brown leather football helmet.

"What the fuck were you doing, faggot?" Donald hissed; dark round eyes staring like he wanted to kill me. So far, nobody in the band had called me anything but "drummer," "douchebag," "faggot," or "Blowjob the Roadie." This was the thanks I got for driving them to a party in their dying purple shag van. I was deputized Chauffeur because they spent the day preparing for the show by drinking bottles of wine chased with cough syrup.

"I'm goin' back to the party and shit," Scott announced, stepping out and shutting the door. He was ignored.

I sat down in the middle of the room, staring at all the Ramones and Clash posters on the wall. "I was just hanging out," I said, "Seeing how it's a party and all. Who cares?"

"Concert. It's a concert," Renee corrected, speaking in a deliberate snob tone, like the alumnus of an exclusive New England Boarding School. She didn't turn away from the paper in front of her. Mickey burrowed deeper into the bed and stared at the ceiling, repeating, "A concert, that's right, a concert."

I jumped off the floor and yelled, "They're twelve seventeen-year-olds! They're not fans! And this house is not a venue, and this room is not a backstage!" They also insisted on calling the house a "venue," correcting me anytime I called it what it really was: a bad high-school party. "And who drinks cough syrup after age 13 anyway?" I continued, one hand on the doorknob, ready to just go home. "Even crackheads laugh at that high."

"We think it's *grooooovy, maaaaaan!*" Donald said, weighing down the words "groovy" and "man" with as much irony as possible. "And what the fuck do you care? Blowjob the Roadie here drinks, of all things, Buck Urine Lite from St. Louis, Missouri, and he thinks he's something special. Sheesh, whatta douche."

"The point is," Renee cut in, primping her giant black coiled hair in the turned-off computer monitor in front of her. "We are here to put on a performance." She wore an orange shirt with a drawing of a little kid licking his lips and saying "I WANT PIZZA NOW!" in yellow and black lettering. She crumpled up the set list she was trying to write and tossed it into the brightly-colored Marvel Comics trashcan at her feet. "I can't concentrate under these conditions," she sighed, then continued. "We're here to entertain our fans, not befriend them. If we did that? What you were trying to do? Our mystique would be tarnished."

"Mystique?! Mystique?!" I flailed my arms and jumped up and down for twenty minutes, just arguing semantics like "venue," "concert," and "backstage," trying to get them back to Planet Earth, but, as they just stared at the ceiling or their fingernails or the black computer screen, I wondered if they were right. Maybe using those terms was good practice for whatever it was they wanted to do with what they had created, but I couldn't think about it that much, so I just yelled, "Fine! I'm leaving! You people are fucked! Really fucked! Really! Extremely! Fucked!"

But I didn't move. They just stared at me. Mickey smiling out of his fat dumb tomato face, Renee wincing at the language (she never swore), Donald frowning from his stupid horse asshole moon face, and finally, Donald said, "See? I told you he wasn't one of us."

"I guess you're right," Renee said. "And I thought he was so nice, but gosh! What a temper, huh?"

"Maybe he'll learn eventually," Mickey said.

"Will you STOP referring to me in third person?!" I yelled, still not moving, hand back on the doorknob, ready to just split this weird prima donna scene.

"You won't leave." Renee swiveled in her chair to face me. She hit me with her stare, an X-Ray, a lighthouse, a green spotlight laser, and my insides dropped 57 stories and splattered on the pavement below.

"What else would you be doing tonight?" she said. "Sitting in a bar feeling sorry for yourself? Sitting in front of a TV in your apartment wishing you had something to do? Acting like a drunken moron for disinterested ladies? Lying in bed, staring at your ceiling and wishing for work to start so you could take your mind off of how pointless your existence is here?"

I smirked at Renee, who didn't take her big green eyes off me. I wanted to laugh, but we both knew she was right.

"No," she continued. "You won't leave, and no Donald, Shaquille here is one of us. We're the most interesting thing to happen to him in a long time." She grabbed the football helmet and pulled it over her head.

"Bullshit," I muttered, without any feeling. I let go of the doorknob and sat on the brown backstage carpeting, waiting for the show to start, and everybody in the room knew I was defeated in the argument.

"Anyway," Renee huffed, ten minutes later, like what we were just talking about had nothing to do with the matter at hand. She stood up and handed each of us a sheet of paper. "I've made the set list."

I keep this set list in a box with the rest of my Enchanters memorabilia. I remember looking it up and down, written in Renee's inimitable cap-scrawl with circled dots above the I's.

ENCHANTERS SET LIST: MAY 25, 199-
VENUE: SCOTT WILSONSON'S LIVING ROOM
1. I LOVE A PARADE
2. A SCHOOL FOR FOOLS
3. NUGGET (I LOVES YOU)
4. SPRAWLBURG SPRINGS AU PRUTEMPS
5. THE GUITARIST=GRABASS CHAMP
6. YOU A EM/YOU B EM: F—- THE LINE OF SCRIMMAGE
7. MY RANCID CABIN
8. MC MANSION ON THE HILL
9. I LOVED YOU ON MLK JR. DAY

As I looked the list over, it occurred to me I had never heard any of these songs. Therefore, I had no idea how to play them. When I broached this minor problem with Renee, she laughed and shook her helmeted head. "Oh Shaq! Always complaining and worrying! Just follow along and you'll be fine." (No, I didn't notice she was calling me by my real name.)

"Only don't fuck up," Donald interjected, by way of constructive criticism.

"Why don't you pretend you've practiced with us for months, Little Buddy?" Mickey suggested.

Scott stuck his head in the door and yelled, "Showtime! Places, everyone!"

"Showtime? Places?" I looked for any acknowledgement that this was all one big joke, but all I saw was Mickey stretching next to the bed, exposing a rather large plumber's crack. He strapped on his bass and gave it a couple test punches across the open strings. Donald picked up his guitar and jogged in place, grunting like a defensive tackle, "I'm gonna fuck this audience, baby! Fuck 'em! Fuck 'em hard!"

Renee extended a hand and pulled me up off the floor. "You'll be fine! You *really* mustn't worry."

And before I had a chance to worry, Donald yelled, "GOOOOOH!" and we were running down the hall to play my first big concert with The Enchanters.

chapter two

The amps popped on and everybody semi-encircled us, a couple feet in front of Renee, who bowed her head with eyes closed, back turned to the audience as Mickey and Donald spent an eternity tuning. She ignored the actually funny "Blue! 17! Hut! Hut! Hike!" heckles because of the helmet she wore. Her arms were at her side. She marched nervously in place, moving only her tan panty-hosed knees and raising only her white tennied heels while her purple skirt swayed with the movement. She opened her eyes and smiled like a Romanian gymnast on the Olympic medal stand whose years of hard work have finally paid off as the orchestra plays "Oh, Romania" and the red, yellow and blue rises in front of her. I wanted to believe that look of confidence was all for me, like a corny "Go for it, Shaq!" but Renee was off wherever it was she found her inspiration.

Over Mickey and Donald's open-string poundings, Scott approached the mic and yelled, "Hey can you guys hear me?" He was answered with "Shut up, dick!" and Scott laughed and yelled even louder, "OK everybody! Here they are, live from my house,

Sprawlburg Springs's Littlest Dreamers: The Enchanters!"

To the enthusiastic claps of twelve pairs of hands, and a whole lotta standin' around waiting to be impressed, Mickey and Donald started playing. I sat there waiting for a drumbeat to come into my head and through my arms and legs, and it took root quickly. It grew from thought and spread to action in my limbs. Somehow, it worked.

Instantly, you could almost see the twelve light bulbs blinking over those kids' heads as we played and they shook and spun slowly, eyeballs and pupils expanded, toothy smiles, epileptic seizures without all that pesky blood and foam.

Mickey stayed in what would be his usual frozen position, back between his amp and my ride cymbal, and Renee and Donald fell around each other, orbiting and crashing, staggering dangerously close to the drums, veering away just in time, within inches of bumping the bass drum, within seconds of me smacking them with my sticks, because I'm never more violent than when my drums are touched while I'm playing them. The more Donald flailed around, the more his guitar cord disconnected from his amp, emitting deep electrical buzzes, leaving nothing but the rhythm section and Renee's singing:

"I love a parade
so much it kills me
but it will not kill me
and it will not slay me
it will be all right
it will be all right
all right
hey!"

And for everybody else at the party, resistance to movement was futile. It was all too strange for a rube like me, but I kept playing as people slowly lowered their inhibitions and started made up dances, mouthing the words to the songs like they knew them, dancing like Rockettes in some '40s musical, forming two wagon wheels, the inner wheel spinning clockwise and the outer spinning counterclockwise, backbends and kicking legs, arms reaching for the heavens. Then, the wagon wheel unfolded and a line formed and one at a time they each picked a partner and one held the other by the ankles and then there was a string of wheelbarrows plodding along to the music, moving like dogs on the trail of another dog's pee.

*I Love a Parade* ended maybe ten minutes later (time lost all meaning with those songs), and when it was silent again, nobody clapped. There was a long moment of silence where everybody, band included, looked stunned, like the first moment of a power failure before you realize what's happening. My hands and arms shook. Donald looked across to his brother, eyebrows furrowed in disbelief, and Mickey's tomato-head features squinted at the carpeting like he was stumped over a crossword puzzle. Renee didn't move; both hands wrapped around the microphone. Nobody moved in that moment, but once the audience knew, they stood from their wheelbarrow positions and, no, they didn't cheer and go "whoo." They just yelled "PLAY MORE NOW!!!" like the spoiled children they were.

The wait wasn't long. Donald yelled "NOW!" and *A School for Fools* started all at once, except for me because I had never heard the song before, but I figured it out quickly enough.

"a school for fools
we're living in the wind
you won't see us again
you mealy mouthy taints"

For me, it was relying on instinct, of making all the drums and cymbals sing at once, flailing my limbs until the drum set became the jungle rhythms of cannibals dancing around the rotisseried explorer tied up over the flame two minutes before carving time.

The overall sound was churning and torrential, more than just music: the sounds of gridlock on Cimarron Boulevard, the sounds of thousands of TVs, VCRs, computers and stereos never turned off, the heat from all those black parking lots on dog day afternoons, the taste of fast food, the smells of nature converted into cosmetic decoration for a roadway median. Our music was the whole steaming stucco turd that was sweet home Sprawlburg Springs, consumed and reformulated into something, well, *I* thought it was beautiful, even when it was ugly in the conventional (and unconventional) sense.

The dancing everybody was doing was so far removed from the dancing you see in typical dumb nightclubs where everything's a collective mating ritual practiced by sheepish unfortunates with no musical ability to speak of. There was real self-expression happening, however sloppily executed. Kids bounced off the walls like jai alai players, knocking over the family portraits. Blond Cathy kept attempting sloppy and wobbly pirouettes. Wide-eyed Jonathan leapt into the air like he was shooting a jump shot, then he'd raise his hands in the air in triumph. Alison with the long black hair and Balding Norman hopped around the room shadow boxing. Hirsute Sally punctuated her karate chops with the obligatory "Hi-yah!" Mark and Melissa pretended to have missionary position sex on the carpet, fully clothed.

Mickey never moved. He just stared at the floor and smiled to himself like it was all too funny. Donald, from time to time, would turn around and scream at me constructive musical directives like "Play faster, fucker!" or "Play slower, fucker!" He'd swing the neck of his guitar close to my cymbals until I smacked the neck with my right drumstick, shooting a copper echo out the amplifier. And Renee, in the middle of all her moves, she'd look at me when she thought I wasn't looking, and she smiled, and I'd smile back and plunge into nonsensical drum fills that miraculously worked each time. Her eyes darted out in sharp birdlike turns of her head, still singing like a karaokeer, Swiss Miss oom-pah-pah knee bends with arms outspread and spinning then falling to the floor and steamrolling into the mic stand and it would fall into the dancers, who immediately picked it back up again. Then, she'd laugh at herself and run back to yell the next line of the song, but sometimes, she'd just drop the mic and run into the dancers, falling and flailing around them as Scott or somebody else would grab the microphone and bellow made up nonsense like, "Shadoobay, dandy don wants a praline!" The new singer was inevitably tackled and dogpiled as we played on and on, and to the casual observer (even though there was no such thing at an Enchanter show), the silly dances and funny faces might appear like it was all just one big joke, but it only took the smallest effort to see there was so much more going on than a sham and a put-on. You either got it or you didn't, and if you were too myopic to not see Renee clearly having fun in a way so far above and beyond most people's conceptions of fun, well, I'm sorry, but you're ignorant.

There was never a break between songs. One song ended, and they'd start up the next, and I got better at knowing where and what to pound. Donald, after his guitar was disconnected yet again, threw it off his waist and joined Renee in instigating the audience even more (not that they needed it), leaving me and Mickey to supply the music as they barreled into people with cartwheels and handstands. Inspired, I fell back, stood up and kicked over the drum stool, jumping in the air with each cymbal crash, swinging arms, falling over, getting up, spinning. It was the sense of urgency, of real high drahmuh, the inexpressible awkwardness, frustrating there in that living room, in spite of the goofiness and the absurdity, that must have been what was driving us besides the inherent fun. And this must have been what inspired all those kids to start their own bands, to see us behaving like a bunch of retarded lunatics with musical instruments surely gave them permission and a kind of validation to the latent creativity in their own lives, long left dormant on the doorsteps of the Great American Public School.

Oh: In the midst of my masterful descriptions, have I forgotten to mention how *loud* we were? Well, we were. The amps bled shrill feedback every time the instruments weren't played. Renee howled over and over again:

"nugget: I loves you
lickin' pink till I can't think
nugget: I loves you
neon latch me on snatch"

At least that's what it sounded like to me. I had a set list by my left foot next to the high hat stand, but I didn't know where we were in it because we never seemed to stop, so I quit paying attention, and I think we were all surprised when we did stop. I mean, it sounded to me like the songs were loose enough to play them as long as we wanted, but they weren't. And Renee sang,

"integrated there on the short bus of love
sharing the very front green seat
holding hands, chatting bands
I loved you on MLK Jr. Day
and it was fun
such fun
yeah
yeah
all right now"

Only Renee knew when it was really over. She yelled over all that noise, "We're out of songs now! Goodbye!" and she dropped the microphone with an amplified plop and off she skipped away, and I watched her disappear into those dancers, linking arms with Jonathan long enough to do a couple skip-your-partner-do-si-dos, and then we couldn't see her anymore. Donald charged behind her, knocking people over with his guitar, carried in his hands like a machine gun. Mickey followed his brother through the gap he made, and then it was just me, trying to find a good place to stop, but stopping felt like leaping out of a turnip truck bumping down the freeway. My brain at that point only thought in drumbeats and nothing external to drumbeats.

When it did finally register that the other Enchanters had left for good and people were still dancing like they were, clinging to what was left of the concert, which was me still jumping around on those red sparkly drums, that's when it made sense to stop, because by that point I was too exhausted to continue. I was suddenly aware of how sweaty I was. My blue oxford shirt had turned purple with the wetness. My khaki pants turned brown. Sweat stung my eyes. My breathing was a rapid inhaling/exhaling gulp. My fingers were swollen with bruises from smacking my hands into the metal of the drum rims. My throat was dry. Every muscle in my body was sore. I felt great, better than I had ever felt.

Finally, I just stopped after one last drum fill and a couple cymbal crashes. I stumbled through all those dancers, who, in the new and strange silence, were falling to the floor around me as I staggered past, dropping like detonated buildings. Somehow I remembered to carry my snare drum and sticks to keep anybody from trying to get on my drums when I left, but I also knew that wouldn't be a problem. Those beautiful drums were untouchable to anybody but me, and the reasons—after what we had just finished doing—were obvious.

## chapter three

Yeah, I felt like King Drummer the Magnificent, walking back to our makeshift backstage. I was great and everybody knew it. My ego had its own gravitational pull. I walked into the room saying stupid shit like, "God, we were awesome!"

"What're you talking about? That was horrible!" Donald said, dropping his guitar into his case, shaking his head in disgust. The guitar landed with an acoustic clang. "We're terrible! We fucked up every song!" He stood there in the middle of the room and yelled, long arms outstretched and gesticulating every syllable all like, "I fucked up every song. Me."

"Oh, it was oh-*kay*, I guess," Renee said, sitting in front of the computer screen and reapplying red lipstick to the top lip, then green lipstick to the bottom, "We all made *tons* of mistakes, but at least we had fun. I had fun, anyway."

I tried telling them how great they were, how it was the best, craziest, most intense thing I had ever seen, much less been a part of, but nobody listened, and Donald just repeated over and over again, "God! We suck!" and Renee unscrewed her lipstick and swiveled around her office chair and tried reasoning with him: "It wasn't that bad. I mean, it wasn't good, but it was oh-*kay*, Donald." Mickey lay on his back in bed over green and white Sprawlburg Springs Hessians blankets with eyes closed, hands behind his head and catching his breath, the lump in the blanket above his face rising and falling with each gasp for air, the mattress now concaved.

I wasn't in the mood to be around such a bummer scene, so I set down the snare drum, tossed away the sticks and said, "Well, I'll see y'all later. I'm goin' back out there to have a good time."

"Hang on a second." Mickey threw off the blanket and his eyes opened. The bed bounced in the air and creaked happily when he stood. "I'll go with ya, Shaq."

"I'll be out in a minute," Renee said, not looking away from Donald.

"What's his problem now?" I asked as we walked down the hall and the sounds of excitable party chatter grew.

"You don't know?"

"No."

"We were bad, Little Buddy. Really bad." I started to contradict Mickey, but he interrupted me. "But it's OK. Nobody knew but us. Let's forget it and have more fun, 'kay?"

The living room had evolved into a drunken dance party where everybody was spinning and staggering around happily to the music Scott played, which was (of all things) *Caroline Says (Part One)* by Lou Reed. When I jumped into the dance circle, everybody was cheering like, "Hey it's the drummer!" Whatever "mystique" ideas we had before the show had long since vanished on both sides. The mood was so upbeat in there; it was like when the Home Team wins the championship after years of languishing in last place and I was the Scrappy Rookie who helped make it happen, and now, he's got the proverbial lampshade on his head belting out in his best Lou Reed talksing: "She tells me that I am a fool/but she is still my Germanic quee-ee-hee-hee-uh-hee-hee-heen!" dramatizing it with lots of Shakespearean arm flair.

In the corner, the TV showed mustachioed Burt Reynolds as the Bandit fleeing from jowly Jackie Gleason as Buford T. Justice. Now familiar bodies bounced around me—afro Mark did the mashed potato, pimply Melissa did the alligator, Balding Norman did the Peppermint Twist—and the dancing was the sloppiest I had ever seen as Scott played Gang of Four and kicked his red pants and shook his blond curls arhythmically to the beats, but this was also the most earnest dancing I had ever seen. This made it great in my book. You don't need too much coordination or rhythmic sense when you're dancing without a partner. All you really need to do is loosen up and shake, and it's OK.

Almost everybody there wanted to pat me on the back and say something like, "Way to go, champ," and talk about what they had just seen, and I didn't want to talk about it, because it was over, so I'd change the subject and say whatever popped into my head, crap like, "Yeah, well, if there were more bands like ours, this wouldn't be such a big deal" and "Where are the nuggets, dude?!" while fluttering around like a wasted social butterfly from the keg to the dancing to the backyard to pee and back again. Mickey towered over the dancers, at least a foot taller, shaking and swiveling with Cathy. This made me just a little jealous, but I didn't really care about anything right then. I only wondered when Renee would come out from backstage.

Everybody formed a nice roomy circle around me when *Emotional Rescue*, my very favorite Rolling Stones song, started playing. I don't know why it's my favorite, or even if it's really my favorite, but it always makes me laugh. For my money, there's nothing quite like the Stones playing disco and Mick Jagger trying to sing like the Bee Gees to get the yuk-yuks rolling, and I love busting out Mick Jagger dance moves on unsuspecting partygoers, to see the shocked amusement of laughing friends when I start strutting like a proud peacock, pouting my lips and scolding with my right index finger. He's my favorite musician to imitate, and I'm the best at it, anywhere.

Or so I thought. Through the cheering arms and laughing faces, she stepped into the circle, and I almost froze in mid-scold, but I had too much momentum to stop. I pranced around, fueled by the encouraging woo-hoos of my new friends, as I mouthed the lyrics "Is there nothing I can say?/nothing I can dooo?/To change your mind/I'm so in love whichoo..."

Although it didn't happen this way, I always see Renee's emergence from that circle in slo-mo, with no external sound except for *Emotional Rescue*. She's changed clothes, dressed down in black lo-cut Chuck Taylors, purple pants, and the same "I WANT PIZZA NOW" T-shirt. The back of her hands are on her hips, wrists bent, lips extended, pouty and parodic, and (still in slo-mo) she struts closer, head turning side to side like a big beautiful bird, crazy black coiled hair shaking all over the place, and it's the look of the karaokeer's embarrassed amusement at being cajoled onstage in the dimples and emerald eyes, and I knew, for once in my life, I would have some serious competition on the dance floor.

She circled around me in a rhythmic strutmarch, and I kept my body facing hers, fingers pointing, arms flailing, mouthing the words *I come to you/so silent in the night/so stealthy/so animal quiet [here I clawed the air like a tiger]*. I saw the laughter, but I could only hear the song. She moved around me like that for five laps, our eyes locked on each other. Then she stopped, right arm outstretched and pointing to the vaulted popcorn ceiling, two thin silver bracelets reflecting the lights, stunning my pupils and shooting purple splotches across my field of vision.

She moved at regular speed again, leaping and kicking her legs like some stoogey slapstick vaudevillian, still scolding and jolting, lips still pouty, but there was a trace of a smirk, and then a cocky nod and she strutted up to my face and whispered, "Beat that, Drummer."

I stayed right in Renee's face, still shaking and pointing. I knew I had the advantage because we were moving into the talking part of the song. The idea formed as it happened. In my best Mick Jagger *leer*-ical seduction, I purred into her ear, "yessss... you could be mine...tonite and ev'rynite...I will be your knight in

shining ahr-muh coming to your, emotional, rescue."

Renee, so determined to keep a straight face, heard me clearly, and she was a couple seconds ahead of what was to come in the song. The moment I said the word "*ahr-muh,*" she tilted back and tittered machine gun laughter that almost drowned out the speakers and it only increased when I kept on all like, "riding across the desert on a fine Air-ub *chah-juh.*"

She caught her breath long enough to grab my arm and raise it in the air and shout, "The winner!" Before I could respond, she dropped the arm and grabbed random partygoers, pulling them into the circle filled with other bumbling intoxicated dancers incompetently swiveling to the Charlie Watts disco beat. It was all too fun, and Renee pulled me in by the hips, smiling and staring right through me, and we stopped pretending we were Mick Jagger and just danced with festive ass and elbow dodge n' weave.

Over all those bobbing and weaving heads, Donald stood off to the side, leaning against the wall and brooding, slitted eyes scanning the room like everything was beneath him. His brother was on the opposite wall making out with blond Cathy, this hulk of a man pressed against a pair of long fishnetted legs. Renee tried yelling something in my ear, but I couldn't hear over all the party noise. She tried again, but all I could take in was the grapey smell of her breath, and the cigarette smoke clinging to her shirt. Rolling her eyes and grabbing my left arm, she led me through the crowd, through the dining room, the Florida room, out to the backyard.

The ringing in my ears was a steady eeeeeeeeeeeeeeee. The humidity hung in the air like a sauna full of the types of guys who get every meal at all-you-can-eat buffets. We sat in these pastel blue-and-white horizontal striped lawn chairs on the opposite side of the diving board, staring at the shallow end under a giant matching parasol connected to a round white table.

"Can you hear me now?!" Renee yelled, like I was a doddering grandpa who had lost his hearing aid.

"Yeah," I said, laughing and even-toned. "Just fine."

"Oh good," Renee smiled, voice lowered. "I thought we made you deaf."

"Not yet."

She hit me with that scrutinizing stare again and said, "That dancing," then she looked away to the gurgling pool waves, "was pretty hilar—" then she cut herself off. "Like, do you practice that at home or something?"

"Yeah," I admitted. "In my boxers."

"How sad," Renee laughed softly.

"No, it cheers me up better than anything."

She laughed again, crossing her long left leg toward me, almost kicking my left shin. "And I thought you were so angry and uptight. But you're a strange drummer, Shaquille Callahan. But that's OK." She reached across the edge of the table, tapping me on top of my left hand with her right and added, "I think it's funny."

That was when I first understood the expression "falling" in love, because when she tapped me like that, I was overcome with vertigo. It punched me in the ribcage, spread up to my temples and down to my knees, the feeling like I just realized I was shoved out of a plane 10,000 feet in the air with either a parachute or an anvil strapped to my back.

I was temporarily snapped out of it by a couple of party dudes falling into the Florida room spieling all like, "Fat blunt, dude!" "I'm sayin'! The fattest!" "No schwag, right dawg?" "For real! No man...fuckin' kind bud and shit..." "Right on. See that trim in there and shit?" "Fuckin'. I wanna get me some of that, right?"

I laughed to myself, and it wasn't entirely because of the party dudes.

"What are you laughing about?" she asked.

There was so much I wanted to say, words and thoughts I hadn't fully formulated yet, but all I could manage was an "I don't know...I guess it's all funny, like, I never thought a bad Mick Jagger imitation was all it took to get in your good graces."

She didn't respond. She just looked away, toward the pool, and then finally said, "I thought you'd be taller."

"I am tall." Well, relative to the other Enchanters, who averaged 6'5", I wasn't, just a mere 5'11", but that's not short.

"Not really," Renee said. "I think drummers should look like surfers. Like Dennis Wilson or something."

I felt cold gray nausea in my veins. Nervousness. Apprehension. Love. "Oh, well, sorry to disappoint you."

"It's OK," Renee said, as if I were really guilty of something. "When you stood up like that to hit the drums, why did you do that?"

"What do you mean?"

"I mean: Were you just showing off? You could have just as easily played the drums sitting down. Are you attention-starved?"

"No, um, I don't know." I said, unsure of how to explain myself. "It just happened."

"Well, Donald thinks you were just showing off." Now her voice was definitely in deliberate snob-tone mode. "He thinks you have a crush on me, but I think he's jealous because he's had a crush on me ever since he's known me. But I don't date people I play music with. It would violate my professional ethics."

"What?" A sinkhole formed in the pit of my stomach when she started in with not dating people in her band.

"This isn't some weekend hobby for me," she continued. She turned to look at me. What the hell went on in that head? I never could figure it out. The face revealed little except a wide-eyed curiosity. "You should get a good haircut so girls can see your eyes. You have nice eyes. Very blue."

"I know," I said, batting them a couple times.

"He knows…that's not a very nice way to take a compliment."

"Oh sorry. Thanks. I'm flattered."

"That's more like it, even though you didn't mean it. You should always mean what you say." She leaned in closer. "You always look like you're about to say something, but then you don't."

I started to say something, but I held back. "There!" Renee pointed and yelled. "What did you want to say just then?"

"I don't know. 'Gosh?' 'Wow?' 'Really?' Something like that."

"Well, you should say that stuff. I never think when I speak." Renee glowed like a senator who just made the speech of a lifetime.

So from there, we just opened up about everything, about our lives and what we wanted to do with them. She worked as a manager at the Great American Shampoo Shoppe in the Perimeter Square Circle Centre Mall, and like me, wanted something more, but wasn't entirely sure what that Something More was. Maybe a band. We talked about music, about bands, about anything to keep the conversation going. I forgot we had just played a concert, forgot we were at a party. Nothing else mattered but to be around Renee. That was it.

I was nervous as hell and drunk as hell but I didn't care, thoughts screaming, "Do it do it do it now!!!" I figured I was wasted enough to have a lame excuse if shot down, so I reached for her hand and leaned in for the Big First Kiss, blood flooded with vertigo, her hand squeezing mine, my sweaty palm an embarrassment, but our eyes were closing at the same time except for little peeks to see if the other's eyes were shut too and swirling tongues and puckery lipsmacks then panicky yells from the Florida room: "Open the screen door! Oh shit: Keep it open!"

Renee unlipped me and opened her eyes. I stopped, and reluctantly, very reluctantly, I turned around to see about all the hubbub.

It was Scott, Mark and Jonathan, lugging the keg three inches off the ground, hobbling quickly past us off the porch and through the shrubbery, followed by Cathy and Allison, who carried the red keg tub, still full of melting ice bags and cold water. When they got to the fence, Scott was like, "OK...on the count of three: One...Two....Three!" and they grunted and lifted until the keg was over their heads and they tossed it over the fence, landing in the neighbor's yard, with a clankety clank clank. This sent out an All Points Bulletin among every single barking dog in the Golfer's Wet Dream Subdivison, where this party was being held.

Alison and Cathy hid the tub behind some bushes. Everybody ran back and they stopped when I asked what the fuck was going on. Scott was like, "The cops are here, but it's cool, because we just threw the keg over the fence, so we're hopin' they'll leave soon, so just stay there all right?" and off they marched back into the house.

So we kissed some more, interrupted by several up-to-the-minute reports of "The cops haven't left yet! Stay there and hang out it's still cool!" and "The cops are sending everybody home but you guys can stay don't worry." At first, we stopped what we were doing to listen, but learned to disregard the *smoochus interruptuses*, letting Scott give his report as we floated along on the lawn chair, grabbing fistfuls of hair, tightening and loosening the grip, and in my head were the screams of 100,000 imaginary fans in some giganto stadium drowning out the very grief-stricken and enraged, "Oh Jesus NO! Why *HIM*?! What the fuck are y'all doing?! We gotta get outta here. Now!"

It was now Donald instead of Scott yelling, "Hey! Hey! Assholes! The cops are here and they're kicking everybody out! Let's go 'cause I'm leaving!"

Donald stormed off cursing to himself, and we stumbled hand-in-hand through the remnants of the party we had forgotten about like dazed moviegoers stepping out into the sunlight. Almost everybody had left. The party aftermath was a cumulonimbus cigarette smoke cloud while crushed beer cans crunched underfoot. "Hey, where's Mickey?" Renee yelled through the haze, answered back with an embittered "He left with some slutty gash!" from Donald's disembodied voice. "Let's go! We'll pick up the instruments tomorrow!"

We stepped outside, through red and blue sirens flashing from five (count 'em) five green and white Sprawlburg Springs PD sport utility vehicles. I guess this good time was a Code Red back at HQ.

"Move it!" one of the cops yelled as we passed two inches from him on the driveway. Five cops stood around waiting with gay porn 'staches and spiky hair like asshole porcupines.

Donald was twenty feet in front of us carrying his guitar case, about to open the back van door when one of the officers approached and said, "Hey! Come here!"

Donald stopped. The cop pointed behind him and said, "Did you have anything to do with that graffiti over there?"

We stopped a few feet away from them and looked to where the cop was pointing. On the gray garage door, under outdoor house lighting, somebody spray-painted, "The Enchanters make me wanna crap in cop cars."

"No sir," Donald answered, trying not to laugh, trying to be civil, but there was a definite uncontainable undertone of hostile bitterness in his voice.

"There's graffiti like that all over Golfer's Wet Dream. Would you keep your hands where I can see them?!" the pig yelled at me because I was scratching an itch on the bridge of my nose.

Donald said nothing. "Are you in The Enchanters?" the cop asked. "Yes, sir." Donald answered, even-toned, but with just enough sarcasm in the "sir" to make the cop straighten up and yell, "All right. The three of you. Put your hands against the van and spread your legs."

We stood there on the passenger side, my hands against the back window as the pig patted us down, searched our pockets, and found nothing. The other four cops joined us, one of them all like "So you're The Enchanters? We know all about you. They tell me you're all crazy, but you don't look that crazy to me, just look like a buncha little shits who like vandalizing property. You got spray paint cans in that van?"

"No sir," Donald said, very, very, even-toned.

"Ya mind if we search the van then?" the first pig asked.

Mind? Mind! Mind?! My hands clenched and pushed against the window, instinctually tightening into a fist, but I held back the urge to hit those fuckers, and I couldn't imagine what Donald was going through.

"Go ahead," Donald finally said, quieter and resigned.

They took Donald's keys and ransacked everything, but found nothing except for greasy old fast food bags, and a long lost cassette of Black Flag's *My War* under the driver's seat. They threw all the trash around and left it on the seats.

This took thirty minutes longer than it should have, and as we stood there assuming the position, I heard the quick footsteps of other partygoers trying to sneak by us without getting caught. Halfway through the van search, when it slowly dawned on the pigs that we had no spray paint, or drugs, or fireworks, or any other contraband, they took Donald aside and asked him how much he had to drink. "Nothing sir. Not a drop. I'm the designated driver for my friends here."

They had him turn around and walk a straight line. Then they had him touch his nose, then they shined a flashlight in his eyes and told him to follow the trail as they moved it around, then they had him say the alphabet backwards.

"Z, Y, X, W, V, U..." You could barely hear the nervous cracking humiliation in his voice under the attempted bravado.

On our side, one of the cops was trying to make nice with me and Renee, all friendly like, "How long you been playin'?"

"Just started."

"You guys know any Jimmy Buffett?"

"No."

"Well, that's my kind of music, not like what you kids like nowadays."

From the very depths of our beings, we managed to rustle

up two soft, polite and very insincere chuckles as the Nice Pig regaled us with how he saw the Allman Brothers one time back in the '70s. We just ignored it, arms falling asleep, preferring jail, prison, anything but this.

Finally finally finally, the Head Pig stepped out of the van, slammed the door, and said, "If it was up to me, I'd be hauling you to jail right now, but just this once, you're free to go, but we'll be watching you, Enchanters, so you better watch yourselves, got it?"

"Yes, sir," we mumbled, climbing into the van, tossing aside all the trash they were kind enough to leave on our seats. Donald started the van and drove off, miraculously sober after all the wine and cough syrup from earlier, Renee in the passenger seat and me in the far back bench. Through the windows we saw all the graffiti on garages, on cars, on street signs, slogans like "I luv The Enchanters more than my parents" and "If you don't like The Enchanters, you're a dumb dickless," down all those stupid streets with names like Gary Player Lane, Jack Nicklaus Fairway, and Avenida de Sevé Ballesteros.

The whole night tilt-a-whirled in my head and I wondered what exactly we had created, and what did it mean, and what about Renee, whose big green eyes reflected off the streetlights shaped like golf carts. She looked as stunned with everything good and bad that happened as I was.

**chapter four**

The ride home was this huge shouting match between Donald and Renee. I stayed safe in the back, wanting to ignore and not wanting to get in the middle of their arguing about me, so I stared at the billboards through dark purple curtains, billboards with smiling kids on swings pushed by ecstatic senior citizens with ever-faithful beagles wagging their drooling tongues. The slogans read, "SPRAWLBURG LANDINGS: IT'S NOT WHO YOU ARE BUT WHERE YOU LIVE," "AFFORDABLE LIVING FROM THE $750'S: SPRINGS MEADOW WOOD COVE POINTE TOWNHOMES," "SABAL SPRUCE OAK CHERRY WOOD APPLEBERRY VILLAS: IT'S SO GOOD TO BE HOME."

The blue, white-lettered sign announcing the entrance to the city limits came into view, a sign that should have read:

SPRAWLBURG SPRINGS WELCOME
**PLEASE DRIVE WITH EXTRAORDINARY CARE**

...but in a time-honored tradition, the newest generation of civic-minded prankster teenage geniuses changed it with blue spray paint so it always read:

SPRAWLBURG SPRINGS WELCOME
**PLEASE DRIVE        EXTRAORDINARY CAR**

The streetlights illuminated all the gray-acred parking lots and garishly hued strip malls. There's a warped kind of creativity in my hometown in how they painted every last one of its commercial buildings with the unused colors in the back row of the 64 Crayon Box, the ones that never needed the Built-In Sharpener, because kids always had tastes far too discriminating for them. Darkness always made everything even brighter, tackier.

All those endless strip malls with hokey Olde English spellings floated by: Shoppes of Sprawlburg Springs, Sprawlburg Springs Towne Square Circle, Ye Olde Salmon Coloured Strip Mall, Chesterbury Manour Town Village. Automatic sprinklers tommygunned across manicured medians, drooling onto the street and stinking like rotten eggs.

Beyond the parking lots, bright white signs above each business in every shopping center screamed their wares: Deep Dark Tan World, Poppyseed Bagel World, French Café Oui! Oui! World, Asbestos Removal World, Thin Crust Pizza World, Tattoo World, All-American Bigass Butterburger World, Canadian Meat Pie World, Liquor Time World, Compact Disc World, Tub n' Tile World, Cushy Mattress World, Gym Shoe Outlet World, Air Filter World, Frozen Fishstick World, Worldly Pancake World, Cockring World, Australian Map World, Good Time America Family Restaurant World, Bitchin' Car Stereo World, Giganto Right Wing Video Chain World, Mr. Baked Potato World, Riboflavin Vitamin World, Roast Beef Au Jus World, Yer Basic Chicago Style Pizza World, The Wisconsin Universe of Cheese Castle World, Planet Clitpierce World, and on and on, the top-down worlds imported from someplace else came and went until you reached the stinking edge of town, The Glenda Hood Memorial Landfill, a once-beautiful meadow where teenagers used to park and neck that's now, literally, a festering hole of shit.

"You could have said something to the police instead of making me handle it," Donald said way up front in the darkness. "But no, you were too busy with the drummer!"

"Just shut up," Renee said. "There was nothing we could have said. Just be glad we're not in jail."

"Aw bullshit! You're such a hypocrite."

"Don't curse, Donald."

"'Don't curse, Donald,'" Donald mimicked in a really annoying baby girl voice, "'Don't curse, Donald. My name's Renee Eisner, and I can't date anybody in my band because I'm gonna be a big star. Look at me, hee hee hee.' So what were you doing with the drummer out there by the pool, Little Miss Professional Ethics?"

"Why are you being such a jerk? It's my band and I can do what I want." Then Renee turned and yelled in my direction, "With who I want."

This led to an argument about "whose" band it was, with lots of "It's my band!" "No! It's my band!" back-and-forths culminating in Donald announcing, "Fine! It's your band 'cause I quit!" Then Donald turned and yelled in my direction, "I can't follow along with your drummer anyway."

"Good! I'll start a new band, and the drummer's name is Shaquille."

"I don't care what his name is. You both left me talking to the cops, and you, Renee, are a fickle hypocrite. So fuck off. Both of you."

Renee unbuckled her seatbelt and swiveled off the seat. "Where are you going?" Donald asked, sounding pissed off yet helpless all at once.

"Just drive us home Donald. Please." Renee said, walking bent over, hair scraping the purple roof of the van, walking toward the back, Donald mumbling the whole time about "professional ethics...what a batch of shit...goddamn liars...all women...fuckin' liars..."

Renee sat next to me and laid her head just below my chin, hands running through my hair. We were coming up on Lake of the Balsawoods, the apartment complex where I lived. "You can turn here," I said.

"Why don't you just get the fuck out right now?" Donald yelled, pulling off to the side of the road, stopping the van with an abrupt jolt.

"Just please take him home," Renee yelled back. "It's been a long night. We'll talk tomorrow. Please."

"Jesus Christ..." Donald muttered, turning right into Lake of the Balsawoods. "So you both know this band is over, right?"

"Yes Donald. We'll talk tomorrow."

"Turn left here," I said.

"No. I mean it. It's over. I don't play with hypocrites, and drummers with bad form."

"Turn right here."

"We'll talk tomorrow."

"I'm serious."

"So am I. Tomorrow?"

"Turn left here, then a quick right, then that left over there."

"Goddamn...how can you live in this ugly maze?" A crescent moon reflected off the retention pond centering the haphazardly plopped three-story purple apartment units, the retention pond that put the "lake" in Lake of the Balsawoods.

We arrived in front of the apartment. Renee followed me out of the van. "Goddamn, now you're gonna fuck this guy?" Donald said.

"Thank you for the ride, and we'll settle this tomorrow," Renee said, cold and distant, slamming the side van door shut. "Goodnight Donald."

She took my hand and we walked to the stairs leading to my apartment. The van idled behind us, and then we heard a series of staccato honks. We turned around, and Donald was just staring straight ahead, both hands on the steering wheel, but he'd rear back with his right fist and yell "FUCK!" then punch the middle of the wheel where the horn blew. He punched it again, yelling "FUCK!" Again: "FUCK FUCK FUCK!" just a series of punches, angular face squinting straight ahead in pure frustration, not looking at us, and not wanting to, and then he looked up and screamed "FUCK!" once more, then he pulled away, the van decrescendoing through the Lake of the Balsawoods parking lots.

I started to say, "God, what an assh—" but Renee's mouth tackled mine before I could get the final word out. My drumsticks fell out of my hand and splat-tat-tatted onto the pavement as the force of Renee puckering herself against me almost knocked me off my feet, against the wall by the bottom of the stairs, smacking my head hard against the concrete.

"Are you OK?" Renee whispered, laughing a little in my ear while running her hand along the growing lump on the back of my noggin.

What lump? What noggin? "Oh Renee...let's go upstairs," I whispered like the melodramatic dashing seafaring muscle-tittied protagonist of a romance novel.

Renee laughed at me, shook her head and said, "Settle down, Johnny Emo. Don't be such a tard. Just relax. Have fun with it." We made out some more, you know, like smoochie-smoochie-swirlie-q's punctuated with lip-puckers at the end? Mouth to neck to eyes to face? It was like the painful parting kisses of high school sophomores before the Driver's Ed tardy bell rings, and to make it even more sophomoric, I was getting one of those enormo-boners, the kind of enormo-boners birds of prey flying overhead mistake for safe perches, so I was all too happy when Renee leaned in and whispered "Let's go," and off we went.

We stumbled into my cluttered apartment like blind twins conjoined at the mouth, still drunk, tripping over things. Except for a streetlight beam through the backblinds illuminating a small patch of shaggy brown carpeting, visibility was zero.

"Let me turn on a light," I said between kisses.

"Don't worry about it," Renee answered between kisses. "Just put some music on."

I fumbled around the living room for the "On" button to the stereo, glasses and mugs and cans spilling and falling onto the carpet. I thought I hit the "play" button, so I fell to the floor and Renee landed on top of me, her hair falling from her face like looking up in darkness at the Casselberry trees and there's all that Spanish moss hanging off the branches. "Are you all right?" she asked again, and I answered with more kisses and the clothes were slowly coming off, B cup breasts in my hands, and we're grinding there until she pulled away long enough to whisper again, "Music."

Nothing was playing, so I hit random buttons until I heard the beginning of what I wanted to hear. *Funhouse*, by The Stooges. Now, *Funhouse*, to those of us fortunate enough to have heard it, is clearly well beyond mere "make-out music." *Funhouse*" is screaming ecstatic lowdown-n-dirty Fuck Music, the crazy embodiment of the absolute best of James Brown, Albert Ayler, the Stones, Jim Morrison, and homegrown Midwestern mutancy reshaped into what still could very well be the most frenetic record ever made. There's a wild high energy in all those repetitive grooves, layers of uninhibited desire, passion and intensity, inarguably one of White America's greatest contributions to our culture. If Iggy Pop screaming "I feel all right!" over and over again does nothing for you, well, I'm sorry, but you're not worth the trouble.

Iggy screamed and the Stooges screamed and I screamed and Renee screamed and the neighbors didn't do shit. Everything was unexpected surprise, and in my head were still the cheering of thousands of fans, hands through the chest hair, gasp, moan, yell, as "Funhouse" demanded, "Stick it deep inside, I'll stick it deep inside, cause I'm loose!"

then "Loooooooooorrrrrrrrrrd!"

then "Whooooooooooooooooo!"

and then two relatively shorter "Hoo! Hoo!" the sweat soaking her white freckled skin, shaking areolas the size of 45 RPM record holes. We were bouncing the whole Lake of the Balsawoods apartment complex, boinging like a trampoline there in my living room, yelling with the sex and the music, just screaming "AHHHHHHHH! AHHHHHHHHH!" and then laughing about it, but it was fun laughter, vulnerable laughter, nothing mocking, with "I feel all right!" howling to syncopation and honking sax squeals, sex when your eyes roll to the back of your sockets and your brain explodes and your bodies collapse into each other from perfect exhaustion as the free-jazz freakout of *LA Blues* rings *Funhouse* to a glorious skronky close.

When it was over, I just fell, slowly pulling out and falling onto her chest sideways just below her breasts. I could have slept on the floor like that, but we had just enough energy to get up and walk to my room and tumble into my bed as the outside changed from black to purple.

# chapter five

"What's that smell on your hands?" Renee asked the following afternoon. We were still in bed. The spooning had me pinned like a wrestler, a professional wrestler, stuck in a position where only my right eye could see and my left eye was buried in the pillow. It was Sunday, and I wasn't used to the idea of Renee from The Enchanters with Shaquille, the new drummer for The Enchanters.

"The sweat? The beer? The smoke?"

"No...it's like a fishy smell."

"Oh. That." I yawned. "It's squid."

"Squid?"

"It's my job. I cut squid at Cleveland Steamerz. You know that."

"Your job."

"Yup."

"Oh. How sad."

"Why is that sad?"

"You're so good on the drums, and you don't even know it, and you have to work as a squid cutter."

"Yeah," I sighed. The sun and the heat made my room stuffy, but I didn't care.

Renee imitated my "Yeah" sigh then added, "No: I mean it. You can do better."

"Well of course I can. We all can. What do you do then?" I untangled myself and sat up.

"I told you: I work in the Great American Shampoo Shoppe. In the Perimeter Square Circle Centre Mall."

"Why?"

"Cause I love shampoo," Renee said with pure sexy sarcasm. "All the different varieties, the colors, the scents. Strawberry, chamomile, jojoba."

I laughed and cooed, "Ah, jojoba," craning my neck and planting a wet one on her cheek.

Renee laughed. "Well, it's good to do work you're passionate about, but really, I just need the money. The Enchanters aren't paying the bills. Yet."

"Will they, I mean, we, ever?"

"Of course," Renee immediately replied. She looked a little tired, a little gray in the skin, with rumpled clothes. I didn't care. "We're a pop group."

I laughed. "We're a lot of things, but we're definitely not that."

"No, we are, because like, our songs have things everybody can relate to. I don't mean pop like in the traditional sense of it, but in the universal, the stuff everybody knows about but doesn't talk about everyday, like, in *Nugget (I Loves You)*, there's the line, "Lickin' pink 'til I can't think," and that's when you're getting oral sex and you look down at the giver and you're so happy it's happening you can't think straight. We've all been there, right?" Then she laughed and said, "I know *you* have."

I laughed and gave her another kiss on the cheek. "But I don't see how that makes us a pop group."

"We are, and I know we could never make a living here, but we're moving to New York City. To Brooklyn."

"Why there?"

"It's the land of opportunity," Renee stated matter-of-factly, and I was too comfortable to disagree there in my dumpy garret with my squidy hands. The afternoon sun squeezed orange and blue through the cracks in the blinds in my cracked white bedroom, rusted bed perpendicular to the window, beat-down silver boombox on the chipped faux mahogany dresser against the opposite wall, the rest of the room empty except for random clumps of thrift store clothes dotting the large floor like giant withered carnations. The ceiling fan spun like a loose roulette wheel under the burnt popcorn ceiling, fan blades slowing down every few revolutions then speeding up again to fast, the fan motor dying in a buzzing wail.

We stayed like that for a long time, just talking in the sweet-nothings of the beginning of the relationship.

"I really like you." (Kiss kiss.)

"I really like you too," Renee said. "And I don't know why."

"What do you mean?"

"I mean, I just met you, and I never wanted to date anybody in my band, and that's why I never hooked up with Donald."

"So he's jealous then, huh?" I said, inwardly gloating.

"Yeah—I mean, I *wanted* to, but I didn't want to mess up

the band. It would have been weird, but you're just the drummer so it doesn't matter."

I sat up in bed, hand over my eyes, blocking the glare. Her eyes stayed closed, smiling. "Why do you keep saying that I'm just the drummer?" I asked, frowning.

"Well," Renee yawned, eyes still closed, "you don't write the songs. You're just the guy that keeps the beat."

"A band's only as good as its drummer. Joe Strummer said that, and he's right." Renee laughed.

"Why is that funny?" I demanded, now sitting up and sulking.

"Well..." Renee sat up, stretched, yawned, rubbed her eyes and fell back to bed. "You haven't been in this band more than three days, you've managed to seduce the lead singer, and you're saying you're the reason our fans love us?" She looked at me and smirked. "And you're complaining?"

"Yes I am. And yes, I am." I said, answering both questions, lying, annoyed by Renee and trying to return the favor. I just wanted some respect. "But what fans? Who loves us?"

"Oh, don't start this again," Renee moaned, pulling the blankets up to her face.

"Well, I'm just sayin'. The Enchanters are great because of me." Then I added, in a rich fat kid's snob tone of my own, "I'm the greatest drummer in the world."

Renee sat up and shifted her legs out of the bed. There was no touch between us for the first time in several hours. "Maybe this isn't such a good idea."

"What?" I was thrown off-guard, unpinned.

"Me. You."

"What're you talking about?"

"Hey, what time is it anyway?"

"Um...it's almost 4."

"PM?!"

"Yeah."

"Oh no no NO NO!" Renee was suddenly wide awake. She leapt off the bed, smacking herself in the head like she forgot something important. "Get up! We have practice and we're late!"

"Practice?" I laughed, still in bed. "We just played a show last night."

"Shut up! Where are your sticks?"

"I don't know."

"Never mind. Just get dressed and hurry up. And don't think that we're dating, 'cause we're not."

I grabbed clothes as I found them, sort of like an Easter egg hunt—a black bra here, a blue pair of boxers there, jeans in the corner, a red T-shirt with the handwritten words "STEELY DAN," a pair of mismatched black socks (one golden-toed, the other holey), tied up my black Chuck Taylor hi-tops, Renee yelling "Hurry!" the whole time, and off we ran out the door to my car, too confused and in too much of a rush to feel heartbreak.

My drumsticks were where I dropped them the night before, by the curb in front of the apartment. I picked them up and we fell into the car. Instead of heartbreak, I just felt annoyed, like the only thing bothering me about Renee was how self-important she could act, and I wanted to call attention to it by making fun of her. "I'm sorry. I didn't know we had practice. But I don't need practice! I'm the best drummer around! Without me, you guys would be nothing!"

"Shut up and drive!" Renee yelled as I started my car, a dishwater blue Ford Tempo. "And it's not practice, it's rehearsal. We're artists, not athletes." The stereo turned on automatically and sang, "Do you think that/you can make it/with Frankenstein?"

"And turn off that racket!" Renee yelled.

I laughed at Renee's use of the word "racket." "It's the New York Dolls! How can you call that—"

"I know what it is," she interrupted. "Just turn it off. I need silence before rehearsals. And concerts. You know that."

I turned it off. The traffic faded around me as I weaved around what looked like thousands of identical SUV drivers who equated active and patriotic participation in the democracy with sticking the biggest American flag on their back windows.

"You drive like a blind snail," Renee informed me, arms crossed, staring out her window at the passing stucco scenery.

I laughed. None of what she said bothered me anymore. I was too tired to care. "Aw, come on, Renee, don't be mad at me. I'm just sayin' that nobody drums like me. I'm the rockinest sockinest muthafucka to ever pick up a pair of sticks. I'm the fucking king, baby!"

"Watch your mouth, and turn left here." Renee now looked ahead, tap-tap-tapping on the dashboard with the nail of her index finger, looking nervous, mumbling "we're late we're late we're late oh no oh no."

"Why ya gotta harsh my mellow?" I smiled. "I'll say whatever the fuck I want." Inside, I was starting to feel miserable, but I didn't want Renee to know it.

"You're like a sailor, do you know that?" She looked at me for a reaction, and I just laughed. "I don't think I can date a sailormouth. I mean really," she added, grabbing me by the chin and shaking, "Do you *eat* with that mouth?"

"Yarrgh and shiver me timbers," I answered, smiling.

Renee didn't smile. She was all like, "I said you were a sailormouth, not a piratemouth. There's a difference you know."

"Oh, you mean like the one between "lame-ass party" and "venue?"

"This is all your fault we're late!" Renee yelled while I parked in front of the Enchanter House. "If you hadn't gotten me drunk and seduced me, this never would have happened."

"I didn't get you drunk, you fucking prima donna. You were already drunk when I picked you up. And I can't help it if you fell for me. I was just trying to dance like Mick Jagger."

"Yes you did seduce me, sailormouth! Oh why did I let myself get mixed up with a guy like you? Everybody knows drummers are the biggest flakes in bands!"

"Actually, everybody knows a band is only as good as their drummer," I oh-so-wittily retorted. "Why don't I just drop you off here and you can find another drummer, who will naturally be nowhere near as good as me and maybe he won't let you follow him out of the van into his apartment."

"No! Wait!" Renee mock-pleaded, hands folded in sarcastic prayer. "Please don't go. Please oh please oh please!" Her green eyes bugged out sort of crazy like, with just enough of a mischievous glint to be sexy and not at all threatening. "You're really not a dime a dozen, Shaquille. No, more like a dime a gross, drummerboy sailormouth!"

I gave her the ol' "thumbs up" and a charming smile and put the car in reverse. I watched Renee walk inside the house, and I made to leave.

But instead I sat there just staring out the windshield, thinking about it all. That song *Venus* by Television reverberated in my skull with Tom Verlaine's goaty warble, "but then something/

something/it said 'you'd better not.'" I had nothing better to do, and as crazy as she was, she wasn't boring.

These people. The Enchanters. Annoying. Pretentious. Insane. Why should I get mixed up with people like these? I'm a squid cutter.

I could cast my fate with these clowns, or I could be safe and go home, back to this dumb life I was leading. I was tired and hungover. Everything felt distant, as if observed from third person, but beyond the Television lyric, there were other thoughts bumping around, thoughts much more fundamental and clear.

Drumbeats: bouncing, fluid, angular, chaotic. They were there, and I knew they would not be leaving. I looked into the house and saw a hand holding the blinds open, then quickly shutting them and pulling away a split second after I looked up. The white vertical blinds swaying from the force like wind chimes.

So I said "Fuck it," shut the door, and went inside the house.

"Get outta here!" was the last thing I heard before BAM! I was punched in the left side of my head. I fell back against the threshold. It was too dark to see anything. I backed out into the daylight, my whole head aching with sharp pain.

Through my longitudinal dizziness, Donald stood there, too damn tall and too damn strong.

"Get outta here!" he repeated, shoving me backwards into the yard and knocking me off my feet. I stood up when he approached. "We don't need you. You're just another Yoko Ono bandwrecker, only you're a guy, and you play drums, and you're not that annoying, and you don't shut up enough like her, but, uh," and Donald paused here, surely because he realized I don't really have much in common with Yoko Ono. "Other than that, you're just like her!"

I stood there and laughed in spite of myself. Donald was five feet away. "I'm not trying to be funny, jerkoff!"

He charged and tackled me, knocked me back with more swinging. We tumbled and rolled in the ant-infested grass. I got one good shot to his left eye, and he got me good in the mouth, before Renee screamed, "Get off him, Donald!" Mickey stepped in and separated us, pulling Donald away, my head and lips swollen. I was still dizzy. Flat on my back, feeling the occasional ant bite but too stunned to move, I watched a grasshopper arc over me.

I followed its trajectory and that was the last thing I remember besides Renee yelling, "You killed the best drummer we had, and he was my new boyfriend too..."

*...like endless black turnip trucks were running over my skull, each one raining turnips out the back, splashing through the mud puddle into my face, each one identical, and I watched the trucks fade over the gray horizon. I was a speed bump, a steady rhythm of one front tire over my head, then the darkness of the turnip truck's underside, then the back tire, then gray light again...*

When I woke up on their red couch, Renee held a white towel of ice over my mouth, the wet coldness dribbling off my chin onto my chest through my shirt, speaking in exaggerated matron tones, "Oh, you poor, poor dear..."

Mickey was watching *Father McShorty*, that hit TV drama about a midget priest and his challenges in an inner-city leper colony. My mouth felt like it was injected with Novocain. Numb, with the slight taste of blood. Donald stood over me, hands on hips, but his left eye was swollen shut.

"Oh goddamn, Shaq," he pleaded. "I thought I killed you. I'm really, really sorry man." For once, he didn't look bitter or sarcastic or negative. He actually looked concerned, and did he actually use my real name? "Let me get you a beer, Shaq. Oh shit, I'm sorry, but I'm glad you're alive!"

He gave me a can of Buck Urine Lite. Mickey joined them as they stood over me. I sat up and managed to pour the beer down my throat past my swollen lips. My temples throbbed.

"How're you feelin'?" Mickey asked. I nodded. "Oh good!" Mickey said.

Renee pinched Donald's arm and whispered, "Go on, keep apologizing!" and Donald said, "I did already!" and Renee whispered, "Keep going!" "Fine!" Donald said, and continued.

"Aw dude...I'm sorry. It's just that Renee was crying and y'all were late for practice and I thought you were quitting anyway, and you got Renee drunk and all." Renee punched him hard in the arm. "Ow! Fuck! Sorry. I was just kidding around, but really, Shaq. I mean it. I'm sorry."

Through the fading dizziness, yeah, it did look like Donald actually did mean it.

"So do you wanna practice now?" Mickey asked. I sat up, removing the towel from my swollen chin. My head ached. I was covered in bruises. I was covered in ant bites. Beneath the physical pain was the vague ache of last night's hangover. "I feel great!" I smiled, numb lips outspread. "Let's go!"

Everybody's eyes widened. Everybody smiled. Donald ran down the hall, followed by Mickey. They plugged in their amps and started playing, but Renee stayed with me on the couch. We tried kissing, but I yelled "Ow!" the moment her lips pressed against my fat lips, so we just sat there holding hands, with Mickey and Donald playing *Nugget (I Loves You)* in the background.

"You're crazy," Renee said, placing her hand on the side of my face. "I mean it, like, really crazy."

I laughed and shrugged. "Well, so are you."

"And that's why you worship me."

"Worship?"

"Yeah, admit it. You think I'm great."

"You're great," I admitted. "Crazy, but great." Since I couldn't kiss her, I gave her a big bear hug.

"I'm glad Donald didn't kill you, Shaquille."

"Yeah. Me too."

"Let's go practice. Drummer. Shaquille."

Hand in hand, we walked down the hall. For once, something in my life made perfect sense, even if it didn't make any sense at all.

# part two: theatre is the life of you

"Things are better for me now 'cause I
found that I love music
So I learned to play the drums and got
myself a band, and now
We're startin' to make it
And if you can make it at somethin' you
love - wow, you got it all!"

**The Barbarians**

# chapter one

Bruised on the outside, and apathetic on the inside, I returned to work from the rock party weekend with The Enchanters, with Renee, thoroughly disinterested in facing the squid again. I was twenty minutes late, caught in sluggish Monday morning Cimarron Boulevard traffic. When I finally made it to Cleveland Steamerz Good Time Bar and Grille World, I snuck in through the back-door employee entrance, the white, black-lettered sign reading "THRU THESE DOORS WALK THE WORLD'S GREATEST EMPLOYEES." I was dehydrated and a little dizzy, with a headache like beavers chewing on my optic nerves. My unwashed work clothes—black regulation slacks and teal floral-printed button-down short-sleeved shirt—stunk like rotten seafood. My thoughts were a blur of the last three days as I moved through and around the stainless steel kitchen's line cook pot clangs, the prep cook's machete thwacks on the cutting boards, Hobart the Dishtank's whooshes, the abandoned squid-cutting station in the far corner next to the walk-in cooler, wherein the stoner line cooks and coked-out servers took turns tiptoeing inside with furtive little giggles, then hopped out, coughing and sniffling like a TB ward.

Hungover like I was, it was all I could do to keep from throwing up as I moved into the gaudy dining room. The walls were painted in green and blue seafaring shades with fishnets stretched out everywhere holding taxidermied swordfish, starfish, lobsters, coral reefs, crabs, and squid, hovering above kitschy painted signs with bluegray corncob smoking men in sailor caps winking above the caption, "Mmm Mmm Oyster Co., Baltimore, Maryland, USA." The men's room speakers played that '70s song *Captain of Her Heart*, and that was all she wrote. I ran into the stall, bleched out all the green pancake batter poison from my body, and suddenly felt a whole lot better.

I bent over the white sink, washing my face and rinsing out the acidic remnants of the vomit from the roof of my mouth and tongue. Puffy lips. Head rattling with random stabs of pain. The mirror was not kind. Red veins squiggled across my eyes. Unwashed brown hair hung in clumps. Black stubble poked through the gray skin hanging off my face. I dunked my head into the sink. Over the rushing water I heard the exuberant bellow of my loud-talking boss, Mr. Ronald Cozumel.

"Good morning, Mister Shaquille! How are things in ShaquilleWorld?"

"My world is fine, Ron," I said to the newly locked stall and the sound of echoing urination behind me. To confirm this assessment of my world, I exploded into a fit of violent coughing.

"Well, all right! Fantastic!" the stall yelled. "It smells like somebody had a rough night in here!"

"I'm sayin'" I said, punching the automatic hand dryer and rubbing my hands under the hot air.

"Do you think you can see me in my office a little bit later?" Ron asked, voice unmodulated and still easily heard over the noise.

"Um, OK," I said, walking out the bathroom. Through the dining room, I wondered what kind of trouble I had gotten myself into, and if it even mattered anyway. For good luck, I balled my right fist and punched the gold and green sign above the kitchen entrance that read, "CLEVELAND STEAM LIKE A CHAMPION TODAY." The smells of patchouli and fried fish, of garlic and detergent, hung in the air.

I worked with neo-hippies, burnouts, mallsluts and assorted other douchies of varying flora and fauna. Sequestered in my corner, my Cleveland Steamerz Good Time Bar and Grille World Shipmates always provided me with lots of silent bemusement, but now, sleep-deprived and giddy in post-vomit bliss, with kinetic drumbeats shooting around my head like a drum set tossed down a flight of stairs, the whole scene was fucking hee-larious! Removing the plastic cartilage inside each squid, segmenting the squid with my trusty large and sharp knife, and segregating the squid ringlets from the inky tentacle parts into two silver bowls until I had enough to fill the Ziploc bags and plop them into the walk-in cooler was never more fun.

"Praise the Lord! Hallelujah! Another glorious day of prep cooking, brothers and sisters!" Dan the Aspiring Improv Actor stood in the middle of the kitchen and preached like a southern televangelist possessed by the Holy Spirit, shaking the belly of his Belushi build with arms outstretched. He was always "on," seeing the kitchen as the perfect opportunity to perfect his lackluster free association skills. Somehow, he sometimes landed bit parts in the only theater in town. That day, I was the only one not laughing with him, but at him. Further hijinks ensued when members of the kitchen crew lined up to be touched by Dan as he yelled, "Be healed!"

"Let's hear some Jimmy Buffett, hoss!" yelled Brantley the Confident Rube, who cut cherry tomatoes to Dan's left. Instantly, the kitchen's ceiling speakers played a Jimmy Buffett song that went something like "well I'm a lecherous alkie beach bum...sand and surf in your camel toe...peach daiquiris on ice...yeah oh boy" or some shit, I don't fucking care. "Yee haw! My man Buffett is tits, shaka brah!" Brantley had blond hair spiked like a cop's with two gold chains around his neck. His low-rider truck had a sticker on the back window that made him a proud member of the Bad Boy Club. He was a cocky little hick with no idea that he wasn't half as cool as he thought he was.

This too was funny to me. Fortunately, I had my own tape player at my work station, and the Buffett was the natural cue to play the Minutemen. Always the Minutemen.

"What happened to you?" Bohemian Mary asked me while stumbling out of the walk-in cooler, rubbing her arms and wiping her nose. Bohemian Mary had short hair dyed bleach blond, a tattoo of barbed wire around her upper right arm, and she liked the alternative rock station. This made her the non-conformist of the kitchen. I told her about the fight and the band.

"You're in a band?" Mary narrowed her eyes, like she was getting a better look at me, an inspection. I said, "Yeah?"

"What type of music do you play?"

"I don't know." I answered while cutting off the tasteless tip of the squid. I always hated this question. No matter what answer you give, it never feels quite right. "It's the Enchanters, and—"

"Oh, I've heard of them." Bohemian Mary said, walking away immediately. To me, that was just as hilarious as everything else anymore.

"Hey Rahhhhn!" yelled Lardass Alicia, everybody's favorite boorish corpulent loudmouth pseudo-authority on everything, actual authority on nothing, with a voice that was the most grating Midwestern nasal tone you'd never want to her. "We need mur cil-AHHHN-tro and I could go fur a candy burr break, heh? Cil-AHHHAN-tro's ur biggest selling condiment dare." That voice alone made me wish she would get run over by a shortbus.

"Wouldn't that actually be ketchup?" asked Bobby the Dishwasher, who was back there somewhere through all the steam and piles of pots, pans, and dishes. He was ignored, as usual. Bobby was the only kid back there I actually liked, because when he opened his mouth, it was often the smartest thing anybody said all day.

"You're packing on the pounds," said Snorting Tiffany, the rail-thin, coke-slutty, frowny-lipped hen server to Tuff Chad, the macho surfer line cook whose slightly leathered skin and bulging paunch made him look just a little past his prime. He worked next to Dan the Aspiring Improv Actor, and Snorting Tiffany rubbed both of their guts.

"I got a Cinderella belly," Tuff Chad informed the kitchen. "At midnight, it all turns to dick." This wasn't funny the first time we heard it, and after the one millionth time, it still wasn't. But that was just me. Everybody else laughed.

"(It'll be busy today (well, busier than it already is (not that I mind that (I need the money (but who doesn't right? (OK, Autumn, you can shut up now (OK, I will.)))))))" said Dizzy Autumn, a scatterbrained horse-faced dingbat who, especially when tweaked-out, spoke entirely in parentheses.

My God, you couldn't have asked for such a wide array of genus subspecies *jagofficus sprawlburgspringsicus*. Sir Lord Kevin, the fastidious and overdramatic kitchen manager, who thought his job was a ticket to the finest restaurants in Paree, stood over shoulder after shoulder, latest issue of "Bon Appetit" stuffed into his stained white apron, inevitably looking over my shoulder long enough to micromanage, "Keep those squid rings as bite-sized as you can make them, Shaquille. Bite-sized."

Stinking Dandelion, the Queen of the Neo-Hips, fell out of the walk-in cooler, smelling like weeds, and weed, and I don't wanna know what else, white-girl dreadlocks dangling from her pink kitchen crew ball cap, pleading with a blank cassette in her hand, "Let me put this Dead tape on! It's the show from Denver in 1976!"

"Later! I wanna hear Buffett first! Buffett, hoss!" yelled Brantley the Confident Rube.

I couldn't get over how ridiculous it was. After a long weekend of drumming and being around Renee, my eyes were refocused. While cutting the squid, Renee encircled my fellow employee-watching. A particularly clear image would come into my mind and my blood fluctuated between hot and cold everywhere. The image never held, but it was always of her stepping in to dance with me, black kinky hair bouncing all over the place, flawless pale skin tinged with yellow, the full lips and mousey nose, the big loud laugh and big green eyes...and what was I doing here, working with these jerks, when I could be home with Renee?

But my feelings about my co-workers weren't entirely negative. They were good at what they did, and I envied their focus on the immediate task at hand as my mind wandered all over God's Green Earth, especially when the hustle and bustle of the kitchen really took hold. The flames roared out the line cooks' sauté pans as the prep cooks lugged their food pans of the freshly made sauces and cut veggies to their stations. Bobby ran from one end of the dish machine to the other, in dirty and out clean. After awhile, the kitchen took on the stress of an emergency room. At least that's what the voices sounded like, yelling in urgent tones, "86 the marinara! 86 the marinara pronto!" "Behind you hot plate coming through!" "Can somebody run this Assload of Wings Platter to Table 5 I'm like sooooo in the weeds right now!"

They could do their jobs and still talk about the things that interested them. Bobby the Dishwasher ran the clean plates, silverware, and glasses to the bussers, who wiped everything off with white towels while talking about the Sprawlburg Springs Hessians and their chances of playoff glory this year: "They're gonna go all the way, dawg!" "I got Hessian fever!" "Totally!" "Boo-yah!" "That's what I'm talkin' about, baby!" "Show me the money!"

And the waitresses, while taking orders and running around getting drinks for all the customers, still found time to laugh about "Acquaintances," that horrible sitcom about five painfully self-absorbed unemployed artist types living in lofts in Central Park West. "Oh my God, when Preston accidentally used the big bottle of Tabasco sauce instead of tomato juice for their Bloody Marys, and they all drank it at the same time and got violent diarrhea all at once?! Oh my God, that was soooo funny!" "That show? Is? Genius." "It is. It really is."

Well, it wasn't unfunny to me at least. My job was very easy, and that was the way I liked it. I was pretty much left alone to rock out to the Minutemen, and the days passed in blurs of squid after squid after squid, cleaned out and cut into bite-sized ringlets, caught in the South China Sea and shipped on boats and freezer trucks to face their fates, to be stuffed into the mouths of our obese sports-watching clientele in their too-small T-shirts with their guts hanging over their orange and blue soccer shorts so they couldn't see their sandaled feet below them. Not even Ron Cozumel gave me any orders, and Ron Cozumel gave everybody orders.

Ron Cozumel. I enjoyed watching him buzz around the kitchen with the stature and speed of a basketball point guard, barking square-jawed orders upon his arrival to each new work station, pointing at whatever didn't tickle his fancy while saying "Shitcan this!" "Shitcan that!" "Clean out those trays, they're disgusting!" Then he'd hold something in the air for everybody to see that he thought was good: "Look at this parsley garnish! Now *that*, is fabulous!"

"We need more anchovies in this Caesar!" "Run this plate to table seven and please hurry!" He jumped in when he was needed, squat and muscular with perpetually sun-burnt skin and close-cropped blond hair in his Hawaiian shirt and Bermuda short manager's uniform, never unfocused and never unsmiling, heating up the Assload of Wings when the line cooks were in the weeds, squashing the plum tomatoes when the prep cooks fell behind, running food to the tables when the servers were swamped with orders, even helping poor Bobby the Dishwasher back in the steaming dishtank when it got to be too much, and believe me, it's rare for a manager to help a lowly dishwasher.

The sweat soaked his gray bushy mustache, formed rings around the pits of his shirts, and the food stains accumulated all over his apron. When the rush was over, he'd clean himself up and approach all the tables all like, "How was everything? Oh, that's fabulous, fabulous!" Ron Cozumel loved the word "fabulous." I should have hated him, but I just couldn't. He was decent.

The rush of diners came and went in less than two hours, and with my squid all cut for the day, I took a fifteen-minute break in the aptly-named Break Room, a not very relaxing small square dirty white room which held a small TV with a cracked screen only transmitting through bright green and white, a soda machine, and various Department of Labor posters taped to the walls. There was a brown folding table and some brown chairs on the opposite wall of the entrance. I sat there with my back to the table, spaced out on the kitchen chaos, trying to kill some time before closing up my station for the day. I thought about calling Renee, but I didn't see the point.

Dan the Aspiring Improv Actor peeked into the doorway, improvising a cowboy, but then he switched inexplicably to a Mexican voice: "Darn tootin' Shaquille, you better move your rump to the bossman's oficina. Sí, he wants to see you now, mang." I was confused by this, but who am I, are we, to fathom the actor's mind?

I cut through the decreasingly hectic kitchen and knocked on Ron's office door. He looked away from the numbers he was crunching into a calculator and ballyhooed, "Shaquille Callahan! The squid-cutting master! Have a seat, and I'll be right with ya, champ!"

I sat down, wondering how I should react to being called a "squid-cutting master." Ron's office was faux wood-paneled walls like a Michigan hunter's basement, covered with certificates of merit and motivational successories and a large bar graph with two bars, the first reading, "THIS MUCH" and the second reading, "THAT MUCH." Behind me was the window looking out at the kitchen. Looking through it made all that activity like watching an exhibit in a zoo.

My knees pushed into Ron's metal desk. The desk was covered in papers, office supplies, and a computer's monitor screen scrolling the caption:

### "SQUID=$$$=SATISFACTION=$$$"

The fluorescent lights gave everything an ugly old urine glow. Ron looked up from the adding machine and said, "Shaq? How about you and me step into the bar over there and get ourselves some wine? Just us men. How does that sound?"

"Sounds great, Ron!" I said, standing up to leave.

We sat in the empty mid-afternoon faux-thatched roof bar as Ron shouted over the noise of the fifteen TV screens playing random sporting events—curling, log rolling, a Stanley Cup Championship from 1972—to nobody, splitting a bottle of Merlot. Drinking anything in my condition was pure obligation on my part.

He spieled away and gesticulated. "Now, Shaquille." He cheers'd me with a clink of our glasses. "How long have you been a Cleveland Steamer? Six months?" He held the wine glass in front of him with his thumb and index finger, trying to look as French as the other Enchanters did with their wine, and about as successful.

(And while Ron talked, I smiled and nodded, tapping a kick drum beat on the brass rail at my feet, boom boom boom, slowly tuning out whatever he was talking about as the drumbeats spread from my right foot to my left, now kicking out the imaginary high-hat pedal, tss tss tss tss, right finger smacking around the crash cymbal along the top of the wine glass, kish kish kish, left fingers leaping around the 2s and the 4s of the beat. Pssht. Pssht. Pssht. Feeling it in my nervous system, swiveling my ass around the bar/drum stool, trying to look engaged even though I had no idea what Ron was getting at here 'cause I was trying to make my limbs match the thoughts in my head, and in words it's like the language of bees or bad beatniks: DOON DOON DISH DIGGITA BOP POP POP BAM BOOM KISH KISH KISH DIGGITA BAM DIDDLE LOP-POP-POP-BAM DOUCHE KOODA KISH! DOONK KOODA KISH DUH DOONK then open the high

"Do you have any questions about how we do things here? Good...well, Big Guy, here's the deal: I want you to succeed with us here at Cleveland Steamerz Goodtime Bar and Grille World, and the next step for you is line cooking. You do much cooking? No? That's OK, because that's how I got my start and I didn't know anything about cooking either. I can tell you're a smart guy and you can clearly do more than what you're doing now, and I want you to keep on with us. See, I'll make you privy to some top-secret information coming down from headquarters. You won't tell anybody, will you? Otherwise, I'll have to kill you. No, I'm kidding. Just trying to have some fun wichya, Shaquille. But here's the deal: We're introducing a new line called the 'Shitton of Meat Sandwiches.' It goes into place next week, and what I want you to do is this: When one of our customers orders a Shitton of Meat Sandwich, you leap off the squid cutting post, wash your hands real real good, hat and leave it alone there KLISH KLISH KLISH KLISH DINT DINT DOONT DOONT DOUCHE DEE BOOM PISH BI-DOOM PISH, stand up and play there, "Sounds good, sir," I said, unsure of what I was agreeing to, wrapped up in wondering if the fill should be DU-BIDDA BOOM PISHT or DU-BIDDA BOOM PISHT KISH CRASHHHH with my right hand reaching across to crash the ride.)

and then hop to the line and make up the sandwiches. And based on how you do that, we'll see if we can't get you a raise and give you even more responsibility cooking some other entrees for us. How does that sound? Great! We'll be giving you more hours too. So...let's finish this wine, and before you leave today, if you could just give the parking lot a good sweep, I'd appreciate it. Congratulations, Shaquille!"

We clinked our glasses once more, downed the wine, and off I went. Broom and bucket in hand, I swept up all the cigarette butts and beer bottles from the night before stuck along the curbs, brooding about what was to happen next. The wind blew warm in my face. Cimarron Boulevard roared in front of me, sputtering gridlocked exhaust from cars holding one person and one person only.

I stood under a Casselberry tree in one of the center medians of the parking lot, pretending to look busy, but just lost in thought while watching the traffic, the way it backed up with idling cars, then disappeared, then repeated itself in an endless cycle. I wanted profound thoughts out there, some answer to everything, but the hangover just left me numb. All I could think about was the worry that I was getting sucked into something I didn't want to do with my life. Did God put me on this earth to cut His squid into ringlets for overweight sports fans?

I clocked out and walked out the "THRU THESE DOORS WALK THE WORLD'S GREATEST EMPLOYEES" door, trying to forget about the day, back through Cimmaron Boulevard and all her innumerable worlds and past billboards advertising fascist talk radio hosts.

I called Renee and she came over after I showered for like an hour and scrubbed off half a bar of soap onto my hands and arms in a futile attempt to remove the squid stank. Of course, it didn't work, so I considered using the cologne I got from the Secret

Santa exchange at the restaurant last Christmas, but that never works—everybody knows that—and you just end up smelling like *eau de perfumed* squid instead of just squid.

It was the early days of our whirlwind romance, where everything's sugar and you haven't done anything too retarded to piss off the other person yet. Renee's silhouette in the front door peephole, like springs exploding from a Sasquatch hourglass, was enough to make me forget about the bullshit of the day.

She tackled me right when I opened the door, and I fell back onto the cold yellow/brown linoleum of the foyer, falling BOOM on my side and I pulled her down and we smooched and steamrolled into the living room, eyes closed as the clothes came off one article at a time, then we opened our eyes long enough to smile and say,

"Hi."

"Hi."

Then it was right back to the smooching and steamrolling. *Funhouse* screamed out the stereo again. We screamed, and Iggy screamed, and everything was how it should be, how it was over the weekend, only sober.

Afterwards, Renee's first romantic afterglow words to me were, "You still stink."

"I smell fine," I said, stretched out sideways next to her as she lay on her back. All I could smell was the dirt and vacuum smoke of the carpet mixed with our sweat. "I smell like a man," I announced, flexing my biceps.

"You smell like fish, Shaq." She smiled as she said it, so it wasn't a big deal, really.

I told her about my job promotion.

Renee jumped up and said, "You turned it down, right?"

"I haven't answered yet," I said, feeling like an ant staring up at a naked giant.

"Well why would you take it?" the giant asked.

"Money. Why else?"

"Well, don't," Renee said, moving to the couch and pulling on red panties followed by green corduroy pants. "It's not worth your time; that's time you could spend practicing."

We could have argued, but I said "all right" just to end it.

"Shaq. I'm serious." She fixed me with that green stare again, insistent, pleading.

"I said all right. I will."

"Good."

Something about this annoyed me. Renee put on a pink T-shirt that said "'NOTHER BLOOMIN ONION, GUVNOR?" in black puffy iron-on lettering. "Are you telling me this because of me, or the band?"

"Both!" Fully clothed, she rolled back to where I hadn't moved, still naked on the carpet. She steamrolled me and pinned my shoulders before saying "Jeezum Crow, Shaq! You're better than this, and the band is more important, right?"

I nodded uh-huh, feeling my third drumstick harden once again, and I took off her shirt, and I knew we would have to play *Funhouse* again, and I knew my heart wouldn't be with Cleveland Steamerz Good Time Bar and Grille World, and I was casting my lot with these goofs, because I too was a goof—an Enchanting goof.

## chapter two

When we weren't working, and when me and Renee weren't going out on "dates," The Enchanters practiced. All the time. Constantly. Really a lot.

We had this ritual where we stood in a circle, with a bottle of wine in one hand, and a bottle of cough syrup in the other. First, you'd take your wine-drinking arm and link it with the wine-drinking arm of the person across from you, wrap it around the arm, then guzzle straight from the bottle. You'd count one, two, three, four Mississippi and then yell "NOW!" This was answered by everybody else yelling "NOW!!!" Then, you took your cough syrup-drinking arm and linked it with the cough syrup-drinking arm of the person across from you, then you'd down a quick shot from that bottle and yell "NOW" which was answered by three more shrieks of "NOW!" After two or three rounds of this linking and drinking, we'd run to our instruments and start playing.

I'd never seen three people more committed to what they were doing. We would start around 6:30 as everybody returned from their dumb jobs, and then we'd go nonstop until it got to be too late and all the soundproofing inside was no match for all the silence outside and the ultimatum was stop or go to jail. Strings broke, hands bruised, hands bled. It was like we were in a contest to see who could go the craziest during each song. Mickey, Donald, and Renee writhed around on the floor as their instruments shook and screamed feedback while I jumped up and down bashing the drums and cymbals. It was heaven.

Mickey always started the songs. It surprised me how he was the one who wrote the music, or at least the bass line foundations. It would be a three- to four-note repetitive rumble, and the rest of us built upon it from there, playing around and squeaking, tweaking and skreeking until it sounded right. Mickey just went on and on with it and stared at us until we got something going, and then Renee howled whatever came into her head over the music: jumping, spinning and swiveling the whole time.

The practices were played like shows in front of thousands of people, and the shows were played like practices where it was just us. There was no difference. We were always fully in the moment, and the songs never got old because we played them differently each time, always caught up on that thin line between creation and falling on your face. Me and that red sparkly drum set exploded and reformed continually, my head swimming in the wine and syrup torpor. Donald leapt around and smashed the guitar into his head and smiled, and Mickey stared at the floor in dextrapamorphanic ecstasy. It was the best.

With Renee, I wondered where all that energy came from. She never got tired the way most people do. We would have played all night if the neighbors and cops were tolerant. Everything spun nonstop around her—she jumped and fell and smiled under her leather football helmet, making up new lyrics and laughing into the microphone while we went apeshit on our instruments. Renee was the center of this maelstrom, two hands of long fingers wrapped around the mic, sinewy long arms extended, wearing a white T-shirt with the handwritten words "I SING FOR THE ENCHANTERS. LET'S GO MAKE OUT OR SOMETHIN'." There was always one strand of curlicue hair falling across her face from the helmet off her forehead, between the eyes and down past the mouth to the softly shaped chin, and it swung from side to side as she bounced like an aerobicist in her white gym shoes. Of course it was sexy—moot point—but more than that, there was so much heart and mind going on with her when she performed. It was all so great, and it just made sense to assume that the rest of the world would catch up, especially after the Master Controllers of American Culture got wind of it and told the idiots it was OK to like us, because that's all most people want is to be told from far far above: What's Hot and What's Not, because God forbid they actually think for themselves.

When practices ended, we stunk like a high-school locker room after a week of football tryouts. Our skin glazed with sweat and our hair went greasy wet. For fun, at the end, we'd pretend we couldn't play our instruments just to see what came out of it. This inevitably ended with us falling to the ground and just punching our instruments until there was nowhere left to go but to turn off the amps and run into the living room, catch our breath, finish off the wine, and watch TV.

We typically ended our rehearsals in time to watch *American Concentration Camp*, the hit "reality" TV show of that summer where fifteen hand-picked contestants were placed in a historically accurate simulation of the Buchenwald concentration camp for six months. The last one to "survive" won $1 million and a kiss on the cheek from the celebrity of their choice.

After my first practice with The Enchanters, I leaned against Renee's shoulder as we sat there in their big blue beanbag, eyes closed. Donald muted the TV and played *Marquee Moon* by Television on the stereo. It was dark except for the jolting flickers of the TV as we started falling asleep.

"Renee?" Mickey asked. He was stretched out on the red couch behind us.

"Yes, Mickey?"

"Talk about the loft space again, Renee. Please?"

"Oh, Mickey, please," Renee yawned. "I'm sleepy."

"Please Renee? Please?"

Renee sighed in mock-annoyance and sat up a little bit. I slid off her shoulder and faceplanted into the softness of the beanbag. "Awright, Mickey, awright. Most bands, they haven't anyone to take care of them."

"Nobody to take care of them," Mickey repeated.

"They just play a show here, a show there, and they never make any money and nobody notices them because they're just like all the other groups."

"But we're different, Renee. We're not like that."

"That's right! Bands like ours? We're different. We have each other. I have you, Mickey."

"And I have you, Renee." Now, Mickey was standing and smiling. "Tell about the drink pouring, Renee!"

"Say, you know this pretty good, hmm Mickey?"

"Tell about it, Renee! Tell about I get to pour the drinks and—"

"Hang on, Mickey. Let me get to that! See, we have each other, so we will save our money. Together."

"That's right. And as soon as we scrape up the money, we'll move to New York City."

"Brooklyn."

"That's right: Brooklyn. We'll get a loft space there."

"And nobody can tell us what to do, right Renee?"

"That's right, Mickey. No one can tell us what to do, and we can have parties and rehearse whenever we want, and cops or neighbors can't bother us because it will be our loft space!"

"Ours!"

"And when we want to invite people over, we'll invite them over. And if they want to stay, why, we'll let them stay, because we'll have a guest bedroom!"

"Don't forget the drink pourin'!" Mickey said, clapping his hands.

"And in the corner of the loft, we'll build a bar, and we'll stock it with anything we want to drink."

"And I'll pour the drinks!"

"That's right, Mickey. You'll pour the drinks, and we'll play shows all the time and lots of fun people will come see us, and we'll live off the fat of our music."

"The fat of our music," Mickey repeated.

"And that's that." Renee put her hands in my hair and played with the brown curls in the back. I smiled in my half-sleep, as naive as everybody else, dreaming of Brooklyn, where beautiful music sings from every rooftop, where the poets proclaim from every street corner, and the painters paint masterpieces on every brick wall.

Where The Enchanters would be loved, where our art could flourish and blossom like all those posies growing everywhere you look in Brooklyn. Although I wasn't ready to give up on Sprawlburg Springs and her left-brained, right-wing ways, Brooklyn sounded like a place where we belonged. Where everybody would understand us, and it wouldn't be like smashing your head into a turnip truck.

## chapter three

That Brooklyn talk happened on the first night I spent at the Enchanter House, in Renee's bedroom. It was a Tuesday and all of us had the day off. When I woke up the next morning, I went into the kitchen for a glass of water. Mickey and Donald were seated across from each other at the table, eating bowls of Chocolate Frosted Sugar Plum Faeries cereal. They didn't look up and acknowledge my entrance, but then Donald said to Mickey between spoonful chomps:

"Honey, whatcha thinkin'?"

"Oh Renee, just how soft you are."

"Aw Shaquille, you're so sweet."

"Nuh-uh, you are."

"Nuh-uh, you are."

"Aww."

"Aww."

I turned around from the sink and looked at them, but they stopped. I turned back around to fill up my glass, and they started again, Donald like:

"Baby: When I'm with you, I can really be myself."

"Aww, baby, I gotta hang up the phone now."

"Aw. Don't go."

"I'm sorry," Mickey whined. "Sugar wookie num-nums. But on the count of three, we'll hang up at the same time."

"OK...1...2...3..."

"You didn't hang up!"

"I know! You didn't either!"

"I know! Aw, Shaquille: I wuvvs wooo soooo much," Mickey said, punctuated at the end with smoochie smooches.

"Aw, Wenay, hold me in your arms. Let me hear your heartbeat."

They snickered like rednecks as I walked past them and said, "Very funny, Alexander Brothers," just like a corny high school administrator, and they snickered even more.

Renee sleepwalked into the kitchen, rubbing her eyes and yawning in an orange robe with stuffed alligator slippers. "What's so funny?"

"Oh, nothing," I said. "We were just—"

"Oh OK," Renee interrupted, moving around me to get herself a glass of water. "Well, let's get ready then, Shaquille. I have someplace I want to take you before we get breakfast."

"Oh. OK." I said, walking out of the kitchen to Mickey and Donald's obligatory whip noises and cat meows. I gave them a dirty look, but they just laughed.

As it turned out, the "someplace" Renee wanted to take me was the Glenda Hood Memorial Landfill all the way across town. Like I said before, the Glenda Hood Memorial Landfill was just a big black smelly hole you couldn't park closer than twenty feet to because a fifteen-foot high fence surrounded it, topped off with barbed wire. You wouldn't want to park that close anyway because the smell was what you'd figure and there wasn't much to look at except a void with a bunch of vultures circling around it. For a long time, we sat there in the big purple van in silence as Side Two of *Sticky Fingers* played.

Finally, I had to ask. "So. Why'd you wanna bring me *here?*"

"Have you ever been here before?" Renee asked, looking straight ahead in the passenger seat.

"I've just driven past it. I never felt any desire to hang around."

"Look at it."

"Yeah?" If we were in a comic strip drawing, the stench of the landfill would be shown in squiggly vertical lines.

"Do you remember when this was a field?" she demanded, arms outstretched and hands extended and spread to take in the remembered panorama. "There were tons of Casselberry trees here, and a big meadow. You could sit and relax and nobody cared. I used to go on picnics here with my parents when I was a kid, and it wasn't that long ago. I mean, I don't want to sound like Woodsy Owl here, but this used to be a nice place, and look at it now. It's a big hole, filled with trash and vermin and wasted things."

"You actually grew up here?" Most people didn't.

"Yeah." She reclined in her chair and propped torn black

Chuck Taylors up on the faded purple dashboard. She told me about her parents, looking straight ahead through the windshield like the meadow and the Casselberry trees were still in full bloom.

"No, really, Shaquille. It used to be so nice here. We'd picnic every weekend. This used to be called the Bob Morris Memorial Garden Park. And my mom? She'd pack these fabulous lunches. Fresh strawberries from our garden, homemade jam for our PB & J sandwiches, homemade French pastries, everything homemade because she was, after all, the home ec teacher over at Coupland High—you know, "Home of the Braying Jackasses?" —before she went crazy?"

"Crazy?"

"I'll get to that in a minute. My dad would catch butterflies for me, and place them in my hands, and I'd let them flutter and flap against my fingers before I let them fly away just out of arm's reach. And I'd run through the field after them; this field used to be so green and bumpy, and mom would always play the same joke on me.

"I'd be chasing butterflies up and down these little hills, and I'd hear my mom yell, 'Renee?! Would you please come here please and thank you?' She said it just like that—like the matriarch in a Cheever short story."

"Whuh?"

"Never mind. She'd call me, and I'd run back to them as fast as I could, and mom and dad would be drinking red wine out of Dixie cups on the picnic blanket. Mom was so beautiful then, in these long floral dresses and long blond hair, and she'd bellow like, 'Renee darling, could you please be a dear and pull my finger for me.'

"My dad would always huff, 'Now Renee,'" (She imitated her sad in a very haughty professional tone.) "'You know you mustn't do this.' But I'd reach over with my little hand." She acted it out, her adult hand reaching for an imaginary finger. "And pull, and my beautiful mother would bust out the loudest, longest fart you've ever heard. It was hilarious, and I'd have to run away again, and I'd always fall down the little slopes of the meadow like that one girl in *Little House on the Prairie*. My dad would always try not to laugh. He'd light his pipe, but there was always a smile he couldn't quite hide from beneath the beard."

She reached into her purse and took out a picture. "This is them," she said, handing it to me.

The picture was Kodachromatic and faded. Her Mom looked like Elizabeth Montgomery from *Bewitched*, with flowing hair falling to her shoulders, with emerald eyes exactly like Renee's. Her brown and yellow sleeveless floral dress looked like kitchen wallpaper circa 1978. Her Dad wore glasses with rectangular lenses with a mustache, beard and pipe that made him look like the curator of the Sprawlburg Springs Museum of Art before it went under due to lack of funds and interest. And guess what? He was.

"These are my parents, and we're right here," Renee said, pointing through the windshield to the void of the Glenda Hood Memorial Landfill, where a couple of rats gnawed on a bunch of dead cardinals out there on the hole's edge just twenty feet away.

"And that's me." I held the faded picture in my hand and saw little Renee standing between them, with the same crazy hair and dimpled smile, holding a dandelion up to the camera. She wore overalls with a sewed on red sign that read, "HERE COMES TROUBLE" in black lettering.

"It's my favorite picture," she said. "It was taken maybe a year or two before things went bad."

"What happened?"

She looked away from the landfill and off to the side, speaking hesitantly, softly. "My Mom, she just started acting really weird. My parents started fighting all the time, with slammed doors and yelling or the just-as-bad silence and cold shoulders. Mom started acting goofy. Out in public? Instead of asking me to pull her finger? She'd ask bag boys at grocery stores to do it, and if they refused, she'd get upset and demand to speak to the manager. And if they did pull her finger? It was humiliating, especially when you're at that age when you already don't want to be seen with your parents in public."

"We'd go to restaurants and she'd throw food at people then blame it on me, denying her involvement. She'd point in my face and yell, 'Renee! How *dare* you! How many times have I told you *not* to throw food at these nice people!'

"She started documenting—and please don't laugh at this, Shaquille!" Renee said, laughing. "Because, it really isn't funny."

Renee laughed even harder, harder than I'd ever seen her laugh. I just watched her laugh this way, her head back and tittering like when we were dancing. It was all too beautiful, the way the laughter made her kick the dashboard and lose her breath and fall back in her seat.

"OK," she said. "I confess: It is funny, but if you ever tell anybody, I'll kill you."

"What the hell is it?" I demanded, wanting to join in the laughter.

"All right," she said between erupting chuckles. "Promise you won't tell?"

"Yeah! Tell it already!"

"All right, well my mom? She had an oddball sense of humor I think I may have gotten a touch of?"

"Really? Think so?" I smiled.

"Yeah, but she had a tape recorder, and she...she thought it was funny to document all her bodily noises. Like, she kept different cassette tapes—one for burps, one for urinations, for farts, for poops and for queafs."

Now, here, in my defense, I was trying real, real hard to be the supportive boyfriend. But godDAMN if I couldn't help but laugh like crazy, and Renee went back to her own manic HAWHAWHAWs.

"But no, Shaquille." Renee continued between gasps of laughter. "What made it really funny was how she'd preface each bodily noise by saying the time and date. Like, if she farted, she'd first speak into the mic in a very serious voice, "April 23rd, 1989, 3:27PM: ffffffffffffffffffffRRRRRRRRRRRAAAPPP!"

"She was trying to get me to make tapes too, but I was kind of creeped out by it, even though it was my mom. It was so strange. Funny, but strange. But it gets better. When the divorce proceedings were going on, somehow my Dad got a copy of those tapes? And they played it in the courtroom. I mean: Can you imagine?"

I could indeed imagine, and I couldn't stop laughing. I pictured the courtroom in black and white, like "To Kill a Mockingbird" or something, and Gregory Peck announcing, "I present to the jury Exhibit A." And with great flourish, Prosecutor Peck sticks his right index finger high into the air and lowers it onto the cassette player, followed by Renee's mom saying,

"January 12th, 1989," followed by the sound of her queafing, the jury's laughter as hysterical as mine.

"So obviously, dad won custody of me, and because the story made the news and stuff, all the kids in school made fun of me about it for years before I did the sensible thing and dropped out and got my GED. Mom moved far away, in Chicago somewhere. I get letters. Sometimes. I don't think she's crazy so much as she is misunderstood. And dad? The museum closed three years after that, and by that point I was on my own most of the time anyway. He was just depressed a lot. Now he moves from town to town, working in convenience stores, restaurants, anybody who will hire him. The last letter I got from him was a year and a half ago. He was in Chattanooga then. I don't know where he is now.

"And that was around the time they turned our park into this," Renee said, pointing again at the giant black hole in front of us.

She looked over at me, and I was trying not to laugh. "See?" she said, punching me in the arm. "I told you it wasn't funny."

Then we both exploded into laughter, like the kind of giggles you get when you've been up all night and you're so tired, everything in the world is too ridiculous not to laugh. There was no better way to react to it.

"Well, let's go get breakfast now," Renee sighed. "The smell here is simply un*bear*able."I put the van in reverse as Side Two of *Sticky Fingers* approached the end, and *Moonlight Mile* played, and when Mick Jagger sang, "I'm only living to be lying by your side," my insides burned warm with love far and above everything, even the Enchanters, and this feeling heightened with each ha-ha as we made each other laugh the whole ride by giving dates and fart noises like, "October 15th, 1987: FRrrrrAAAP!"

Now, when I hear *Moonlight Mile*, I don't know whether to laugh or cry or bury my head in my pillow and punch something, anything. It evokes too much of all that happened and all that was lost.

chapter four

Our dates were little more than a pretense to act as obnoxious as possible without getting arrested.

Sometimes, I'd meet Renee for lunch at the Perimeter Square Circle Centre Mall Food Court. I'd stand outside the Great American Shampoo Shoppe she managed, watching her sell expensive imported bottles of shampoo to frumpy and materialistic middle-aged white women. She'd plop little creamy dollops of shampoo on her wrist while holding it out for customers to smell while doing her sales spiel in her affected snob tone: "Now this is a lavender and rosehips fusion meshed with undiluted mountain spring water, perfect for those humid days when hair can be *so* unmanageable."

The customer, invariably attired in pink sweatshirts with embroidered teddy bears, would bend at the waist, purse swinging from her elbow, sniffling, then smiling, then saying, "Oh yes, that's nice. Wrap that one too."

"Fabulous." Renee grinned like a bible salesman who successfully sold a gross of King Jameses at an agnostics convention. Then she'd look up at me, smirk, and roll her eyes just long enough to let me in on the joke of the job, as if I didn't know. Watching her work, it was hard to believe this was the same woman who howled lines like, "Lickin' pink til I can't think."

The other girls working there were teenagers, and they always gave me the once-over, like a 50-point quality inspection I felt like I always failed. I don't think they trusted me with Renee; they looked up to her so much. As the self-created Enchanter Fashions evolved, they kept pace. They would have worn football helmets if they had been part of the employee dress code, but first The Enchanters buttons were worn on their blouses, then The Enchanters armbands, then the other accoutrements, each getting more and more ridiculous as the summer humidified the outside world and we stayed safe inside the ac'd indoors.

"Mind the store, ladies," Renee would say after clocking out, and one of the girls would say, "Bye Renee. Be careful," whatever that meant.

Off we'd go, up the escalator, Renee speaking over the din of the fountains, of commerce, of the poorly played organs from Whizbang Whirlyfun Piano World.

"Oh, Shaquille," Renee moaned, head on my shoulder. "This job is so dreadful. I don't think I can take much more. When *will* our pop group be discovered, hmmm?"

The Food Court of the Perimeter Square Circle Centre Mall

was purple-topped plastic tables and periwinkle plastic chairs shaped like flamingos packed within inches of each other. They seemed to go on to a kind of pastel infinity, encircled by second-tier fast food restaurants like Gong Happiness China World, El Huevo Loco Costa Rican World, Malibu Beach Surf n' Turf World, Iowa Hot Buttered Corncob World, Yee-Haw Wyoming Big Black Angus Rump Roast World, Mountain Oyster King World, Nuthin' But Cranberry Sauce World, Loud Willie's BBQ and Blues World and the Hard Rock Cafe. Eating there gave you a strange feeling of claustrophobia from all the shoppers and their shopping bags so close and loud, and carsickness from the stale mall air and the weak white skylights, to say nothing of the big screen TVs everywhere blaring bargains to all the benches outside along the mall's perimeter filled with old people looking like they were just waiting to die, and they were getting impatient.

We'd find a table—me with a bowl of cranberry sauce, Renee with a ranch-flavored super-sized corncob. After a few bites, that's when the fun began.

"Well, look," Renee would say loud enough for everyone within ten feet of our table to hear. "I can't help it that you're impotent!"

Renee always got a mischievous stare in her eyes, then an evil smirk across her lips, and then I'd be taken aback for maybe a second before playing along.

When I noticed people looking in our direction, trying to be subtle and failing, I'd say to Renee and all eavesdroppers, "Yes you can help! No man can love a woman with a smelly box!"

We'd make these exchanges in the thickest hick Sprawlburg Springs accent we could muster, like the hybrid of Southern twang and So. Cal. valley girl. The people around us shifted uncomfortably in their periwinkle chairs, holding their brand name merch bags closer to their lardy forms.

The real challenge was not laughing when Renee would counter all like, "I can't help it if my box smells. The doctor says it's *glanjeelur*, and that's no excuse to not never make sweet love to me like you used to done did."

I'd have to look down at my bowl of cranberry sauce to keep from laughing upon hearing the word *glanjeelur*. But I couldn't laugh, because then I'd lose the game. All I could do was fight back with, "Now baby: I love you like flies on shit, but your box needs a deep, deep cleaning. I can't help it if I can't express our love when that smell hits my nose."

Renee would then look around at all the shoppers and say, "Some boyfriend! Just because I can't help it if I have a smelly box. If the doctors say its *glanjeelur*, what am I supposed to do? Some boyfriend!"

This is when the crocodile tears gushed out of her eyes like the worst kind of tragedy, punctuated with pathetic blubbering sobs. I'd pretend to console her, skidding my chair next to hers and putting my arm around her all like, "It's OK, baby. Please don't cry. I'm sorry I said you got a smelly box."

"I can't help it," Renee sniffled.

"I know, I know. The doctors said it's glanjeelur." It was damn near impossible, not laughing at that mispronounced word. "But please dry your eyes, my sweet puddin' pop sugar booty." Renee would finally emit a laugh, but it was a laugh that sounded like a cry so none of our enraptured audience knew.

I'd grab a napkin and wipe the tear streaks from her face and say, "Aww sweets, I promise I'll love you, and I don't care if you got the smelliest box in the county, I promise to always love you."

Renee would look up from her food, wet green eyes and croc tears, pleading, "Can we express our love...now?" She'd reach across the purple table and take my hand.

I'd stand up and look deep into her eyes and say, "Yeah baby." I'd pull her up off the chair. "Let's go have some sex."

We left our food and ran out of there hand-in-hand, and everybody around us just stared at us like we were aliens. Idiot aliens. But once, and this was the best, these three women I recognized from the Men's Wear Department from one of the big department stores they had there stood and applauded in their navy blue casual suits, laughing out popular catch phrases like "You go girl." One of them opined, "Mmmmm hmmm. Girl, that boy better give that woman the lovin' she needs." We'd ride the escalator back down to her store, and then we'd let out all the repressed laughter held in over our lunches. Even now, whenever I hear the word "glandular," I laugh out loud. We did this act in grocery store lines, bank lines, the DMV, anytime we were bored and needed self-amusement.

Renee, more than anybody, showed me the possibilities of

fun in almost any situation. Like, we'd go to the early bird special at Happy Time America Food and Drink World—ostensibly to visit Donald at work—but really it was just another place to goof off.

First we'd sit at the bar and answer trivia questions against all the mental midget regulars. The questions popped up on the TVs and we knew each one way before anybody even came close. As soon as we were bored with trouncing the drunks, and as soon as we had our own buzz going, we'd get a booth seat and laugh at poor Donald, who dressed like all the servers there, like Uncle Sam in a candy-cane sport coat and pants with a red, white and blue top hat, shuttling between all the cranky senior citizens. Our town was full of retirees who labored for decades under the delusion that they would always get their way no matter what once they retired, because they earned it, right? Wrong, and their bitterness showed in every waking hour of their winter years, and their driving was more dangerous than the worst drunkard's, and their crankiness made everything that much worse there. Nothing Donald did was ever good enough for them.

We were inventing new fashion statements. None of the old rebellions worked anymore at freaking squares, so one of our early inventions was to walk around with globs of green hand lotion stuck under our nostrils made to look like snot. There was something almost romantic about applying each other's green hand lotion below our nostrils just before entering Happy Time America Food and Drink World.

"How do I look, Shaquille?" Renee said, looking through a compact mirror. "Is it natural?"

"Perfect." (Kiss. Kiss.)

Upon entering the restaurant, we'd go up to Donald and ask, "Excuse me, sir, but is there something on my face?" while touching our hands to the outside of our mouths. It got a smile out of Donald, and then the inevitable, "Jesus, you guys are idiots," before he went off to deal with more miserable old folks.

Other times, we'd do the opposite of the impotent gag and we'd full-on make out across our table, but only if Donald wasn't serving us. The server would approach us, and we'd start smooching, going so far as to lick each other's faces while the server waited with order book in hand. They usually just laughed it off, making corny jokes like "Get a room!" until finally saying, "Are you done yet?" Then we'd stop, look at the uncomfortable server, then say "No," and then we'd make out some more until they'd say, "I'll be back in a few minutes," walking away.

But the most fun for me, and the thing that got Renee laughing the most was when I'd do the infamous Hanging Brain. If you don't know, that's when you take your nuts out of your unzipped fly and squeeze them so they stick out not unlike a brain, then you zip up your fly high enough for the brain to hang outside your pants. Trust me: It's never not funny.

I'd come out of the Men's Room and approach Renee at our booth and do a bad server imitation: "Hi! My name's Shaquille and I'll be taking care of ya tonight! Do you have any questions about the specials?" and Renee would look at me, then she'd look down, and the moment she saw my nut sack hung like that outside my pants, she'd laugh like the kid at the lunchroom table whose chocolate milk would shoot out his nose after hearing a funny joke.

But other times, I'd do the Hanging Brain, and Renee turned to somebody at a nearby table all like, "Excuse me, Miss, but you look like you know a thing or two about fashion. Do these pants make my boyfriend look fat?" And I'd model my pants and my exposed scrotum, and the distinguished older woman would be all like, "Oh, well let me see. No, they look OH MY GOD!!!" Then Donald, standing off in the corner trying not to laugh, would run over and say, "Look: You guys gotta leave now! You're acting like total retards, and the manager's about to call the cops."

And we'd run out through all those ferns and brass, past those zombie customers, the great silent majority of uncreative, uninspired ninnies, out the door and back in the van, Renee kicking me in the seat of my pants, yelling, "Zip that up, please Shaquille! That's so disgusting!"

"But it's a medical condition! The doctor says my nut sack needs adequate ventilation!"

We drove off in the van, laughing until it hurt. I still think the Hanging Brain is one of the stupidest, funniest gags in the whole world.

Sometimes, we'd throw dance parties in one of our rooms, shaking and singing along to T-Rex or Cheap Trick. But, inevitably, we'd return to our roots: *Emotional Rescue*. It got to the point where we started having Jagoffs, or, Mick Jagger Dance Imitation Contests, with Mickey and Donald as judges, surely indulging us

because they were just as bored as we were.

It worked like this: Mickey started the song on the living room stereo, then he'd sit next to Donald on the sofa as one of us emerged from the hallway and pouted our lips and strutted out scolding, shaking, strutting, and then, in our best Mick-as-Andy-Gibb voice, sang.

Renee had more of the body for all those elastic moves, but I had more rhythm, natch. Mickey and Donald insisted on wearing sunglasses because, according to Mickey, "It makes us look more Hollywood." They took their roles as judges quite seriously. They learned to laugh less and less as we continued with these contests at least once a week, evolving into sophisticated surveyors of our abilities.

"I liked Renee's voice this week," Mickey said, seated behind the coffee table next to his brother. "But her strut was more like a waddle. Like a dumb turkey instead of a cocky rooster."

"And Shaq still can't get the British spoken voice," Donald said. "He still sounds like a sinister German. But his dance moves are pretty right on, especially the strong beginning." They kept yellow legal pads in their laps as they scribbled comments they never allowed us to view.

"Yes," Mickey continued. "But Shaquille can't keep that beginning going throughout."

"Decisions, decisions," Donald sighed.

"You know what? Shaq wins it this week." Mickey said, clapping his beefy hand once, like one who has made a final decision.

"Really?" Donald said. "I think Renee wins it."

"Bullshit."

"I don't know man, I just think—"

"That's right: you don't know," Mickey said. "Look bro: I think you forgot about the pouty lips. Shaq was on it, and Renee, she just looked mad, like Billy Idol or something."

"Yeah you're right. Shaq wins," Donald said without any hesitation, like he knew I was the winner all along.

"What!" Renee screamed. "You changed your mind, you sell out!" She charged Donald, leaping over the sofa and throwing him to the ground, and Donald, clearly relishing the power of being a judge, just giggled like a ticklish child, saying, "Better luck next week. Loser!" Then, Renee chased after me, and I ran out the front yard, gloating and prancing and dodging her slapping, punching hands as I turned into Mick circa Altamont: "Brothers and sisters, everybody needs to like cool out! Who's fighting and what for?" This received thunderous applause from Mickey and Donald.

"I'm fighting because you cheated!" Renee yelled, tackling me, dragging me down into the yard, steamrolling me and, well, I guess it was all just a prelude to sex, like most dates that aren't the first couple two or three, right?

But it wasn't always fun and games. We argued quite a bit, and like the dumb pranks, we did it out of boredom more than anything else, the kind of arguments forgotten about two minutes after they're finished, but there was one fight we had that was just horrible, a fight that actually hurt and left me wanting to quit the band and break up with Renee, all of it instigated by my cooking.

I've lost more girlfriends over my cooking than anything else. Like Charlie Brown kicking the football, I always think I'll get it right, this time, and it wasn't like my heart was in the wrong place, because I've always meant well behind the oven, and I'm just trying to be romantic, and with Renee, it was no different.

I lit candles and cleaned my apartment, right down to the crusty green toilet. I was to cook pasta and pre-made French bread that only required a quick stay in the broiler and that was that, and the sauce for the pasta was canned, so all I had to do was heat it up in a sauce pan.

None of it turned out. The pasta was undercooked and crunchy, and while I drained it in the colander, I forgot about the sauce, which burnt, which made me completely forget about the French bread, which charred black and set off the smoke alarm.

Renee ran into the kitchen as I was up on one of the chairs shutting off the alarm. She took one look at the coal lump that was once French bread, the rather unwieldy strands of spaghetti in the colander, and the bubbling, smoking remnants of the sauce glued to the sauce pan, looked up at me and said, "Wow, Shaquille. You sure are stupid sometimes."

"Yeah," I smiled back, thinking she was just kidding.

"No, I mean it," she continued, not smiling as much. "You can't even cook a simple pasta dish with canned sauce. How retarded is that?"

"I don't know," I said after shutting down the skrreeeeeee

of the smoke alarm and stepping off the chair. "I can't cook. I tried."

"But it's so easy! How can you not know how to make pasta? You just boil water and throw it in and wait a few minutes until it's tender but firm. You know: al dente?"

"No. I don't know." I hated that helpless feeling. It tapped some dark, rarely visited corner of my psyche, flashbacks of school, of teachers giving me shit for daydreaming, for getting lost in my own, more interesting, thoughts.

"And sauce!" Renee continued, not in the least bit amused. "You just heat it up!"

"I know. Sorry. You can shut up now! If you wanted to make me feel stupid, you've done it. Happy?"

"And French bread! You just broil it! What's the *matter* with you?"

"Fuck off!" I screamed, not really knowing why, but I felt like a raw nerve was tapped, prodded and poked with a taser gun she held and wouldn't stop using.

"I'm just saying, Shaq. Sometimes I feel like I'm supposed to be your mom."

"Seriously. Fuck off!" Like a kid again, like a dumb kid who can't do the simple things everybody else could do.

"You forget things all the time! You have the short-term memory of a goldf—"

I threw my glass at her, filled with the wine Renee brought to the "romantic" dinner, all over her nice blue blouse, which she wore especially for this occasion. The stain spread across her chest like blood from a bulletwound.

Renee screamed then threw her glass at me. I ducked, and it shattered against the side of the fridge, then she jumped on my back and we just spun around. I couldn't get her off of me until I backed into the wall, dangerously close to the window leading to the parking lot below. The sauce pan fell off the stove and Renee burned her hand.

"OWWWWWW GOD!" She scooped up the sauce and shoved it in my hair, and I leapt up and grabbed a handful of crinkly spaghetti from the blue colander in the sink and whipped it in her face and screamed, "Get the fuck outta here!"

I pushed her away and ran into my room, locking the door face down on the bed and screaming "GodDAMMIT!" over and over again into the pillow, wanting to cry but not crying, just buried in the pillow and pissed off that I fucked up yet again over something so easy and stupid, and how everything I try always falls short of my expectations.

Renee didn't leave. She punched the door, over and over.

"Shaq! Let me in you jerk." I ignored her, still buried in the pillow and my own lousy pity party—but she was strong and she kept smashing the door, louder and louder. With one last violent shove, the door broke off one of its weak hinges, slamming the doorknob through the drywall.

"Shaquille! What's the matter with you?! Turn around!"

"Just get the fuck outta here ya fuckin' snob!" I yelled through the pillow.

"Look. I'm sorry. I didn't think you'd get that mad," she said with a giggle.

I ignored her, mad at myself for sucking at something so easy.

"Aw, c'mon Shaq! I didn't think you'd flip out like that."

I turned around and started in with, "You were—"

And that's when I saw her. She had sauce all over her hands and face, spaghetti strands dangling from her kinky dark hair, wine stain darkening her blouse in the exact shape of Antarctica, beige hand towel wrapped around her burnt right palm. She looked so ridiculous, I just had to laugh. We both laughed, and the clothes and the food flew off and we screamed and made up over the din of "Funhouse."

When we finished, we laid in bed, covered in the remnants of the disastrous dinner, pasta stuck on our naked bodies.

"I'm sorry," Renee said.

"Me too." I said. And that was the end of it.

Our courtship got us thrown out of every place we went: movie theaters, supermarkets, restaurants, banks, parties, even Latent Republican Hipster Music Club World, the only live music venue in town. We'd go to shows there, sometimes with Mickey and Donald if they weren't too broke or intoxicated to come with, and you could smell the fear in all those catatonic indie rock types packed in to see the latest musical abomination, like when that horrible band Frenchie Pie came to town.

God, they were awful. Bland 1990s self-absorbed go-nowhere noodlings, where everything's so self-conscious and arty, so "pretty picture," so cold and prefabricated. Like everything else about our town, we'd wonder if we were the only ones who saw it, because if you stripped away the hoo-haw, there was nothing but pretentious bullshit hipster types were too dumb to suss out.

Renee threw her wine glass at the diminutive guitarist's feet. It shattered louder than the music they played. "This band's *terrible.*"

"Yepper." I threw my wine, then a couple other drinks from a nearby table. They arced beautifully and splashed into the eunuchy lead singer's pensive face. Nobody in the audience had the guts to stand up to us, because we were The Enchanters, and we had an unearned reputation as total psychopaths.

After sitting through half of their boring set just wanting to go to sleep, I daintily cursed at the band.

"You lousy limpdick asshole fucks!" I screamed, picking up food from tables and hurling chicken wings, shrimp, lemon wedges, potato wedges, everything landing on stage or on the performers, who didn't respond to our attacks, trying to remain above the fray while looking around wishing somebody, anybody, would deal with us. This reaction to us just made sense after drinking two bottles of wine each.

"You guys stink! Go back to Chicago!" Renee screamed. I made to throw a chili dog at the showoffy overly syncopated drummer, arm arched back like Joe Montana, but was sacked and grabbed, and my throwing arm was forced behind my back. Some goon bouncer with chocolate pudding ring facial hair threw me out, promptly followed by Renee, who landed next to me on the sidewalk, and inside, we could hear, for the first time, a gut reaction: applause.

"It's about time you showed some humanity, you fools!" Renee yelled inside, standing up and extending a hand to pull me up.

"I was only dancing," I slurred as I rose to my feet. "Why would they kick us out?"

"Oh, don't worry about them," Renee said as we walked to where we parked the van. "But my neck is sore." She looked up to the sky like a soldier waiting for the freedom bird that's gonna take him back to his hometown. "Hint. Hint."

I laughed and rubbed her neck as we walked down Apple Avenue, past all the lame dance clubs and theme bars blaring their synthetic house noise out onto the street, through and past armies of black-silk-shirt–wearing, gel-headed club dudes and their scantily clad silvery sparkled women. We had put on a good show back there, and I was proud.

Most of the time, though, it wasn't all that crazy. It was craziness interspersed with periods of boredom relieved through lying in bed on our days off until practice, listening to T-Rex at full blast, which, for my money, is pretty good afterglow music, but T-Rex is pretty good anytime music.

Other times, we'd spend afternoons in bed googly-eyed on cough syrup, just staring at each other or at the pretty visual images on the insides of our eyelids. It was a boring town, for sure.

Then there were afternoons we'd waste hanging out in front of the counter of Li'l Scamp Gimme Now Convenience Store, where Mickey worked. He'd hook us up with free 72 oz. sodas and show us the midget porn they sold in the magazine rack behind us. "Look at this one, dude," Mickey would say, before flashing us (with zero warning) a spread-beaver pictorial of a lesbian midget orgy on a pool table. This never failed to make me laugh, and Renee would be like, "Does this turn guys on?" and I'd blurt "No!" feeling embarrassed but feeling a little sad more than anything, because in this great free market, there exists a supply and demand curve for midget pornography, and is this what the Founding Fathers had in mind, you know, midgets with strap-ons and pool cues up and in their orifices? But we could never bum around there for too long because the customer traffic was nonstop and Mickey would be too nice to kick us out, but our presence clearly flustered him as the consumers bought their gas and smokes and beef jerky.

But many times, I'd pound the drums while Renee read book after book. I needed to practice alone and get my chops how I wanted them, and she'd drag the big blue beanbag into the practice room and plop it on the floor and read while I drummed. She said the beats helped her concentrate, if you can believe that. My guess is that it really just kept her awake, because books always just made me sleepy. She was on a big Russian novel kick that summer: Bulgakov, Sokolov, all those Lovs of the past and present, in addition to plays, history, sociology, psychology, music—anything she could get her hands on.

I played along to mix tapes she made for me, Volumes One

through Ten of what she titled *Shaquille's Drumming Tutorial*. The songs were never boring, and often difficult, provided by bands like Captain Beefheart and His Magic Band, the Germs, Mission of Burma, Black Randy and the Metrosquad, Flipper, Public Image Limited, Minutemen, Television, Richard Hell, X, Testors, Dead Boys, Electric Eels, Pere Ubu, the Fall, Buzzcocks, and on and on, all these bands I didn't know as much as I should have, bands I would grow to love as much as the few bands I actually liked at the time. I played above my abilities all the time when Renee was in there reading, because I was drumming for somebody whose opinion actually mattered to me. We were trying to make something happen. Something good. I wanted it to work. All of it.

## chapter five

Over the years, I've managed to hold onto this small white box marked "ENCHANTER CRAP" in black permanent marker over its label, which reads, in a threatening Mario Puzoesque font, "MOM'S TOMATO PASTE: REMEMBER YOUR MOM'S TOMATO PASTE? IT'S LIKE THAT." The box is bruised black along the edges, torn and frayed after years of moving from garret to hovel to dump to shithole, year after year, its sides held together with layer upon layer of packing tape wrapped around its perimeter. Every little object inside has its own story. I open it up every year or two just to remind myself of a past I could easily forget.

To anybody else but me, the "CRAP" in this box doesn't look like much. Like this broken half of a 90-minute cassette, the shredded tape unspooled and dangling from the sharp jagged edges of the split plastic casing, the whole thing sticky to the touch and stained red with syrup, the white label sticker at the top marked with Renee's cap-scrawl: "ENCHANTERS 4-TRACK RE-," abruptly cut off with a tear.

We had attempted to record our songs on several occasions, but nothing ever met anybody's high demands of perfection. There was always something wrong with the recordings, and they were inevitably destroyed.

Frizzy-haired Scott bugged us repeatedly to let him record us with his 4-track.

"Please please PLEASE PLEASE MAN!" he yelled daily through the phone. "I promise it'll sound good, fuckin', please please!"

"I'm sorry, Scott, but we're not ready, and besides, we can't allow anybody not in the band to our practice space. It's our sanctum sanctorum." Renee said.

This went on for much too long, and when we finally relented, Scott showed up, all like, "This is where you live, huh? Where you practice? Where it all happens?" He gawked at every little thing in his red pants, shook his curly hair now in an old leather football helmet (the fashion was catching on, believe it or not), set up the mics and squatted in the middle of the room, setting the levels with headphones stuck over the raised helmet flaps. He shook his head in time as we leapt around him, and the songs, to my ears, came out flawless each time, but whenever we played the tapes back, somebody would always find something wrong. In recording terms, The Enchanters made Steely Dan look like Thelonious Monk.

After four hours of trying, we finally got what we thought was a perfect version of all fifteen minutes of *Nugget (I Loves You)*."Scott played it through the speakers in the living room.

"This sounds fantastic," I said, smiling at everybody. Scott returned the smile, but nobody else did.

"Yeah," Mickey said, reluctantly, tomato face wincing with the effort of thought, like this was something he was admitting in spite of himself. "It does. We should keep this."

"Wait," Donald said, lanky body leaning into the speakers at a 45-degree angle, head cocked like a dog, eyes squinting like he was just waiting to hear a mistake. "Hear that? There's a slight ritard toward the end."

"No there isn't," Renee said, staring at the bouncing red sound levels on the 4-track. "There is no ritard anywhere in the song."

"Yeah there is!" Donald said, standing up, shaking his head from side to side and pacing. "Listen!"

"That's not a ritard," I said, not even knowing what that meant, but just trying to make sure we could, just once, have a song documented and kept, at least for posterity's sake.

"Yeah Donald, that song's not retarded, you are." Mickey said.

"No, you're the retard of the group," Donald said to his brother. "If you can't hear the ritard, you're all retards. Seriously."

Then it turned into a shouting match between the four of us, arguing about who was the biggest retard in the band, punctuated with *Shaddaps* and *Fuckyous* and *Ohyeah?s* and *yeahs* before Renee inevitably announced,

"Stop it, everyone. This take simply will not work." She marched off to her room and left us to sort it out.

"Well fuck it then," Donald said, reaching over Scott, pulling out the tape from the 4-track and bending it until it cracked in two, all of us screaming "NOOOOO!" and running at him, but it was too late. To further ensure that the ritard-laden tape would be unplayable forever, Donald soaked it in a splash of cough syrup.

"You...douche!" Mickey yelled, grabbing Donald by the neck and shaking him.

"Shut it, bro!" Donald yelled, shoving Mickey into the couch and knocking him over.

"Cut the shit!" I yelled, trying to break it up, but they were both too strong and cast me aside, and in the middle of all the rolling and punching, somehow Scott's 4-track was covered in spilled cough syrup, rendering it unplayable. Donald promised Scott he'd replace it, but I don't think he ever did. For our troubles, we were left with nothing but a broken tape, a broken 4-track recorder, bruises and damaged furniture.

When I went inside Renee's room, she was in bed reading a book.

"Shaquille," she said as I climbed in next to her and laid my head on her chest. "No more recording, OK?"

"No argument here." I fell asleep like that, bruised and exhausted. We never again tried recording, and we have no recorded proof of The Enchanters, anywhere, and this broken tape I've kept is the closest thing to it.

Also in this old box, I've managed to hang on to a faded old off-white cocktail napkin, covered in drippy black almost illegible chickenscratch passionately scribbled from Donald's hand one night at Faux Irish Bar World.

I hung out at the Enchanter House pretty much all the time once the band got going, and not just when we were practicing or when I was hanging out with Renee. My apartment was too uneventful. Even the dullest day at the Enchanter House was better than the most exciting day at my own place, and as the summer went on, I needed the constant stimulation of being around Renee, Mickey and Donald. There was an excitement there, of playing off each other's ideas, no matter how inane.

Sometimes, it would just be Donald standing there pacing when I came back from work at the Enchanter House.

"Hey, what's up, douche? What're you doin'?" he'd ask me the moment I walked in.

"No practice?" I asked, marching straight to the bathroom to try and fail to clean myself up.

"Renee has to take inventory of all the shampoos. Mickey's off gallivanting with his floozy." Donald said. He was shirtless and sweating, wearing navy blue pants cut off to above the knees. The Enchanter House held the heat well, that was for sure.

"Well then," I shrugged, talking over the running water, "I have no plans then."

"All right, well, hurry up." Donald growled. "We're goin' to Faux Irish Bar World. I'll drive."

Faux Irish Bar World was the only bar in town that didn't have 55 screaming big-screen TVs everywhere you looked. This fact was its only saving grace, because it was actually possible to hold a conversation in there. Other than that, it looked like any other bar, except for ubiquitous Ol' MacFancylad Stout merchandise, Irish Family Coat of Arms posters, reprinted paintings of tipsy leprechauns dancing jigs around mugs of beer and a remarkable overindulgence of green in the overall color scheme.

"Goddamn, I hate U2," Donald sneered. We sat there drinking our first pints of Ol' MacFancylad Stout, leaning over the dark red bar. "Hey bartender!" he yelled to the jaded pasty-faced bartendress at the opposite end from us. "I'm Irish, and I hate this band! They're self-important and dull!"

"Pompous!" I yelled.

"Right. What he said," Donald continued, poking me in the arm with his free hand. "We hate them, and since we're the only ones here, can we hear something from my homeland that doesn't blow goats?"

"And not Sinead O' Connor, or the Cranberries, or the Undertones, or the Boomtown Rats, or even the drinking singalongs!" I yelled. "Not even Van Morrison. Not tonight."

"The U2 stays," the baretendress informed us in the thickest, most phoniest Irish unbrogue I've ever heard in my life.

"All right," Donald said, shaking his head from side to side. "It's your tip." This got little more than a disgusted smirk from our friend behind the bar. "Pathetic," he grumbled to me. "These U2 idiots get all the glory, and here we are. I'd like to piss all over Bono's face."

"Yeah," I said, unsure of how to respond.

"What do you mean, 'yeah'?" Donald said, staring right down at me.

"I mean, I guess I don't care all that much," I said, refusing to meet his glare. "I mean: It's just music."

"Just music?!" Donald yelled, pounding on the bar with his fist. "This is your fucking life, buddy, and your life is way more important than 'I guess I don't care all that much.' Fuck that."

Donald was so disgusted by my answer, he stood up and stepped back. "All right: fine," he said. "Where will you be in ten years?"

"Ten years?" I said. "I don't know. I won't be here though."

"Where will you be?" Donald asked, condescension oozing from his voice.

"Um..." I took a big gulp from my pint glass and said the first city that popped into my head. "Chicago."

Donald laughed and looked up at the ceiling. "Chicago? Are you fucking kidding me? You'll freeze your ass off there! Then they'll mug your ass off and strip it down for parts! Chicago! Jesus Christ, what a douche!"

"Well, it gets cold in Brooklyn too," I said. "And people have been known to get mugged there too."

"Yeah but that's different," Donald said, waving a dismissive hand. "They won't fuck with me, and I don't care about cold. But you're just a little guy!" He gave me a noogie.

I threw his fist off my head. "Why are you such a dickhead?" I asked.

"Never mind that. I'm trying to help you here. Ten years from now: Will you still be playing music?"

"I don't know. I doubt it."

"Bullshit!" Donald yelled. The bartendress twitched when his fist punched the bar once again. "You're an Enchanter! You'll be in this band for the rest of your life! That's how it works!"

We drank two more pints as Donald unveiled The Enchanters'

Ten-Year Plan. He wrote it out for me on napkins as he recited it, each idea getting more and more delusional with each sip: "So we move to Brooklyn by the end of this year, right? Next year, we get the loft going—no, no, fuck that—we get that going within six months after moving. We make things happen: we get bands we like, we invite fun people, people interested in the same things, and just like here, we create our own scene, only we incorporate ourselves into what's already there. As this is going on, we reinvent ourselves as real fuckin' New Yorkers, like, nobody'll ever know we're really from Sprawlburg Springs. And with that going, we put out our first record. That'll happen a year after we move. See what I'm writing here?" And here, Donald pointed at the blotchy black mess on the napkin that read: "First year: First record." I nodded.

Then, the steps followed in semi-logical sequence, scribbled out on wherever there was room on the napkin: "east coast tour, west coast tour, America, Canada, Europe, another record, a second album, a seven inch record put out by some sixteen-year-old in the middle of nowhere ("That way, we keep our hard-earned street cred," Donald slurred.), a three month break to pursue solo projects, a third album (double), Australia tour, New Zealand, Japan, Africa ("I want to be the first band to tour all over Africa. They need us," Donald said, in all seriousness.), a live record, Greatest Hits (Volume One)."

"And that's just our first ten years!" Donald said, sliding the napkin into my hands. "Here. Keep it. And don't forget it."

I looked at it and smirked. "You honestly believe this is gonna happen?"

Donald leapt off his barstool and started screaming, "YES I FUCKING THINK THIS IS GONNA HAPPEN! WE'RE A BAND, AND I'M NOT ABOUT TO STAY IN THIS SHITHOLE OF A TOWN FOR THE REST OF MY LIFE!"

I was enjoying this. Donald was always fun to egg on. "What do you care?" I said. "It's just music."

"SHUT THE FUCK UP! IF YOU WANNA STAY HERE AND BE A JERK, I DON'T CARE! BUT IF YOU WANNA KNOW WHERE YOU'RE GONNA BE IN TEN YEARS, YOU BETTER STICK WITH US! YOU'RE A DRUMMER, YA DUMB DICK! AND DON'T FORGET THAT!"

The bar was silent. Donald stared at me, catching his breath.

Then, like nothing happened, he sat down and said, "Bartender. Two more please."

"I think you've had enough, laddie." the bartendress said, not leaving her seat at the other end of the bar.

Donald stood up and announced, "Yeah. I have had enough. Let's go, Shaq. This place is gay."

We stumbled out into the bright sunlight of early evening. "Hey look, I'm not trynta' make ya mad, Shaquille," Donald said. "I just don't wanna go to work anymore. I wish we could leave now."

"Yeah. Me, too," I said, climbing into the van.

"Or maybe I just need a girlfriend."

"That could be it, too," I said, trying to make heads or tails of the scribble-scrabble written down on the napkin.

"Shut up," Donald said. "You can drive now. I'm too fucked up."

But he wasn't always a dick. Or, more accurately, he could be nice in spite of himself. Like the time we were sitting in his room listening to music. In this box, I've kept a yellowed cassette that still plays even though it's so old the black song listings have all faded away.

On one of the rare occasions when I was at my own home, taking a nap after work and before practice, Donald called.

"What are you doing?" he asked.

"Taking a nap."

"Well come over and we'll listen to music. Bring some records over. Get wine." The phone hung up.

I drove over with a couple bottles of not vintage red wine. We drank straight from the bottle and I sat on Donald's floor while he stood by the record player and flipped sides constantly. Only, he didn't want to hear any of my records, so we just listened to his.

Donald's room was practically empty except for a concave bed, an ancient wood-paneled stereo system with a functioning 8-track player, and a white bookcase stacked to the ceiling with records. There wasn't much room for anything else. The vertically stacked spines provided the only color in the room besides a dim butter-colored light reflecting the cream walls. The window was covered in tin foil and dirty white curtains.

He played *Sad Song* by Lou Reed. In silence, I listened to both the music and Donald. "Listen to this line," he said, and then

he sang along: "I'm gonna stop wasting my time/somebody else would have broken both of her arms."

"I've heard this before," I said.

"No! Listen! I mean, really, really listen!"

So I did. The wine enhanced the feeling of transcendence over suffering, or, to use Donald's term: "Self-affirmation in the face of shitheads." The lines were very simple, said all that needed to be said: "staring at her picture book/I thought she was Mary Queen of Scots/she seemed very regal to me/just shows how wrong you can be."

I laid flat on my back and closed my eyes. Yes indeed, it was a sad song all right, but like the very best of the blues, hearing it made me happy. I felt like I was set free. Optimistic. Like there was a lesson learned, and I'm a better person for it.

I sat up and took a big slug from the wine bottle. "Now do you see what I mean?" Donald asked.

I paused for a second, trying to think of something profound to say, but all that came out was a humble, "Yeah."

"It's my favorite record," he said, placing the record back in its sleeve and cover.

I was so in awe of it, I didn't say anything. Donald stared at me, towering over me on the floor.

"I really loved her, Shaq. I just want you to know that."

I started to say something, but Donald interrupted me by plopping the tape in my hand. "Here. Take it," he said.

"What?" I said, not reaching out to take it.

"It's yours. I want you to have it."

"But it's your favorite record."

"Yeah, but I'm sick of it. Just take it before I change my mind."

I said "OK. Thanks," and grabbed it. To this day, it's one of my favorite albums, and when I'm down in the dumps, I always put this tape on and I feel better, even though it inevitably reminds me of Sprawlburg Springs and The Enchanters and all that happened and all that's now over, good and bad.

But with Mickey, it was different. We didn't go on adventures and act obnoxious. No, all we really did was watch TV. On those days off from being a clerk at Li'l Scamp Gimme Now Convenience Mart, he'd sleep in until around 1 or 2 in the afternoon, which would be around the time I'd get off of work, and I'd stop by and let myself in and he'd be there in his boxers and a white T-shirt plopped on the big blue beanbag watching old sitcoms like *Hogan's Heroes* and *Saved by the Bell.*

"Hey, Little Buddy," he'd say upon my arrival. "Have a seat." Then, as if I couldn't tell, he'd point at the flickering screen in front of him and say, "I'm watching television. It's so hot today."

These were oppressively muggy days outside, when even if there was something going on, you wouldn't want to do it because the weather just sapped you of the energy to do anything except sit there and watch whatever was put in front of you.

During commercial breaks, this was how I got to know Mickey better. For once, he wasn't wasted on anything, and he revealed more about himself to me than just the Loveable Idiot Gentle Giant persona.

"I like it when Colonel Klink says 'Schultz.'" Mickey said.

"Yeah. Me too." I agreed, stretched out on the couch, waiting for naptime to hit me.

"You know, all like, "Schultz! You dumbkopf!'" Mickey yelled, in a fair attempt at Colonel Klink when angry.

"Hogan!" I yelled, also trying to imitate the comical colonel. "Those Nazis sure were a slapstick bunch, eh?"

"This laughing's making me hungry," Mickey said, standing and stretching during a commercial for Albert's Discount Mufflers, in which this loud old white salesman in a cowboy hat, green cardigan sweater, and black and white checkered pants yelled like Red Foxx, "Now I know muffluhs ain't pretty! They ugly! But what's uglier is when you ain't got 'em, and when you want a good deal on muffluhs, you come on down to ALBERT'S DISCOUNT MUFFLUHS!"

"Yeah, this commercial's making me hungry too," I said, and then I did my best imitation: "COME ON DOWN TO ALBERT'S DISCOUNT MUFFLUHS!"

"Say, that's pretty good, Little Buddy," Mickey said, walking toward the kitchen. "Hey, I'm gonna make a pizza sandwich. You want one?"

"Pizza sandwich? What the hell's that?"

"You've never had one?" Mickey said, eyes widened across his tomato face in pure incredulity.

"No," I said defensively.

"Well come in here and I'll show you."

Mickey took two frozen pizzas out of the freezer and proceeded to lecture me on the intricacies of making a pizza sandwich. "OK, so you get two frozen pizzas like these, and make sure they're the exact same size. You can use whatever toppings you want, but I prefer sausage and mushroom, so you might want to do that the first time you make it. Next, preheat the oven to 425, and don't put the pizzas in until the oven is good and hot. Do you follow me so far?"

He was so serious as he talked, so earnest, I couldn't laugh, so I nodded and said, "425, got it."

"Good. On most ovens, that takes about five minutes, and while you're doing that, you can remove the pizzas from their plastic casings. Like this." Mickey grabbed a knife and cut a slit down the middle of both pizzas' plastic and removed them, placing them side-by-side on a brown cutting board.

Every 30 seconds until the five minutes were up, Mickey opened the oven door and held his hands inside long enough to feel the oven warmth, determining if it was hot enough yet or not. Finally, with the last hand placement, he announced, "OK, it's ready. You take these two pizzas," and so he grabbed both pizzas by their edges, fingers holding them underneath, "And you place them on both oven racks, right in the center, and slide them in carefully so none of the toppings fall off, are you with me?" I nodded. "Good," Mickey continued. He slid them in and closed the oven door. "Now we wait until they're done, and it's a good idea to have the oven light on so you can see how they're cooking."

I peeked inside. Yup. Two pizzas in the oven.

"You look confused," Mickey said, stepping back from his culinary masterwork. I was about to answer, but he cut me off and was like, "Here: I'll write out the recipe for you."

So as we waited for our pizza sandwich to finish, Mickey scribbled out the recipe on a loose leaf sheet of paper, now stained with old tomato sauce and crumpled from being stuffed way at the bottom of my "ENCHANTER CRAP" box:

PIZZA SANDWICH
1. BUY TWO 12" PIZZAS
2. KEEP THEM FROZEN UNTIL YOU'RE READY TO EAT THEM (IMPORTANT)
3. REMOVE PIZZAS FROM FREEZER

4. TAKE THEM OUT OF THE BOXES
5. CUT A SLIT DOWN THE MIDDLE OF THE PLASTIC CASINGS AND REMOVE THE PIZZAS.
6. PREHEAT OVEN TO 425
7. WAIT FIVE MINUTES OR SO (IMPORTANT)
8. PUT YOUR PIZZAS IN THE MIDDLE OF THE OVEN RACKS: ONE ON ONE RACK THE OTHER ON THE OTHER RACK.
9. WAIT FIFTEEN MINUTES, BUT KEEP THE OVEN LIGHT ON SO YOU CAN PEEK INSIDE BECAUSE IT MIGHT GET DONE EARLIER OR LATER THAN THAT.
10. WHEN THE CHEESE HAS MELTED, REMOVE THE PIZZAS FROM THE OVEN ONE AT A TIME, BUT DO IT CAREFULLY SO YOU DON'T DROP THE PIZZAS.
11. PLACE THE FIRST PIZZA ON YOUR CUTTING BOARD.
12. (IMPORTANT) PLACE THE SECOND PIZZA ON TOP OF THE FIRST PIZZA WITH THE CRUST ON THE BOTTOM
13. WAIT UNTIL THEY CONGEAL (2 MINUTES)
14. GET A GOOD LONG KNIFE, LONG ENOUGH TO CUT ACROSS THE LENGTH OF THE PIZZAS AND CUT INTO SLICES
15. EAT AND ENJOY!

"This is the best pizza I've ever had!" I announced between bites through the four layers of pizza. "How'd you come up with it!"

"I don't know," Mickey said, also between bites of the pizza sandwich. "I just like pizza. And sandwiches. I thought they would be good together."

We took the pizza sandwich into the living room to watch more television, and as we ate, I started talking like, "You know, you could start a business making pizza sandwiches. You could patent it and sell it to the big pizza chains. You could be a millionaire. This is so good!"

"I just want it to be a secret for right now. It'll be something I can fall back on when the band has to retire because I'm too old to play. Like a hobby, right?"

"Right." While talking like this, and eating like this, I felt my body and brain turn sluggish. My eyelids couldn't stay up while watching Colonel Klink's latest fascist buffoonery. I looked over at Mickey, and he was nodding off too.

"This...pizza...sandwich..." I moaned, too tired to speak. "It's making me....sleepy."

"Me...too." Mickey yawned.

"Must...resist...but...can't..." I said, feeling the effects of sleepiness consume my fight to stay awake. The pizza sandwich weighed too heavy on us.

Two hours later, Mickey's girlfriend Blond Cathy came over. "Are you guys wasted on cough syrup? Again?" she said, peeking through the screen door, standing there all blond and young and beautiful and what the fuck was she doing with Mickey? With any of us?

She let herself in, saw the 3/4ths eaten pizza sandwich on the coffee table and lamented. "Oh, Mickey! I told you not to eat those! You know you can't rehearse after you eat those! And you gave some to Shaquille? Oh God, Mickey!"

Mickey grunted, half, if not all, asleep. Through my own narcolepsy, I could just barely make out Cathy, running into the kitchen and making coffee. My eyes closed but I could hear the percolation and smell the brewing coffee, our one hope for survival to get us through this practice unsluggish and alert.

She poured two cups of coffee and came back into the living room. "Here. Drink these," she said.

We each had three cups, and just as we were starting to feel relatively perky, with the added benefit of the caffeine being that it purged the pizza sandwiches from our bloated systems, Renee and Donald returned from work, ready to rehearse.

Renee took one look at us, heavy lidded and stretched out there in the living room and asked, "Pizza sandwich?"

"Of course," Blond Cathy said, with her hand on Mickey's forehead.

"I knew it!" Renee yelled. "I told him not to eat those anymore! Thank goodness you were here to save them. Nice work."

"Thank you." Cathy said, red cheeks blushing from Renee's compliment.

"You're welcome," Renee said, icy and professional. "Now please leave, please. We have a rehearsal."

Cathy, used to this treatment, remained unfazed, gave Mickey one last kiss on the cheek and a "Please don't do that anymore, promise?" and walked out the door. She was a good kid, and we never ate another pizza sandwich again, although I kept the recipe.

The only thing new in this box is a shiny red left boxing glove, used only once. This is a relic from the only known case of vandalism The Enchanters engaged in, despite how, after each party the band played and as our notoriety grew, the Sprawlburg Springs *Reaganite* reported waves of vandalism in each subdivision every morning after. It was pretty easy to implicate us in these acts, seeing how, besides the damaged property, there was always graffiti spray-painted on garage doors, car doors, front doors, driveways, and roofs, all proclaiming our greatness in absurdist slogans like: "Enchanter? I don't even know her! Haw haw!" or "Lawdy Mama I Gots Enchantermania Up My Fagabeefy Taint!" or "Potatoes. Badgers. Enchanters." It was admittedly stupid, and we never found out who did it, but Mickey and Donald would sweat it especially hard because, like many of our fans, they were into vandalism in their tweens, and they had the permanent record to prove it.

Me and Mickey and Donald went to go pick up our equipment the afternoon after a party we played at some house in Park Meadow Glen Crossing Estate, because the cops had arrived much earlier than anticipated, so we had to sneak out one at a time without our instruments amidst the escaping throng.

Driving under an orange creamsicle sky through the gently winding neighborhood, Donald and Mickey reminisced about random acts of destruction they engaged in like a couple of old codgers reminiscing the big band days.

"Right here: This house. This was where we slashed the tires of that yellow IROC-Z, remember Mickey?" The radio was set to the oldies station, playing a program called *Back Seat Memories* in which the DJ crooned the slogan: "The songs that were playin' in the front seat while you were playin' in the back seat."

"Yeah, and fuckin'," Mickey said, "we blew up all the mailboxes down that street with fireworks."

"Remember the golf course?"

Mickey laughed. "Yeah. Racing and crashing golf carts down the fairways and shit?"

"Yup. And over here was where we set those cars on fire. And down that street was where we spied on Michelle Candaleria when she was in the shower stall."

"Oh yeah!" Mickey yelled. "I remember her. She was

beautiful!"

"I still think she had the hairiest box I've ever seen," Donald said. "Except for Renee of course."

"Hey!" I yelled.

"Aw, I'm just kiddin', Shaq. Just joshin' ya, but down there? Remember Mickey? That kid Josh whatever-his-name-was had that quarter pipe in his front yard and we'd all ride it before it got dark and we went out and fucked shit up, and that was when we met Renee, right?"

"What was she like then?" I asked.

Donald hrumphed and answered, "Skater betty."

"Totally." Mickey chimed in. "But she always had a book with her and she didn't really seem all that interested in any tricks we were doing. Like, she'd yawn a lot and stare at the sky."

"Yeah, she didn't really say much," Donald continued as the radio played the golden oldie *Down in the Boondocks*. "But we all had huge crushes on her so we didn't care."

Inevitably, the wayward Alexander Brothers were caught by the police for the attempted robbery of a Baby Jesus from the manger of a front yard nativity scene. They had on their possession two cans of spray paint, and their pockets were stuffed with highly-explosive fireworks. Their incarceration was three months in juvey hall, spending a lot of time cleaning out the deliberately unflushed toilets in sheriff's bathrooms. "Two months of cop piss and cop shit," Donald recalled. "That taught me more about the world than four years of high school."

Despite their histories, the only time I know they did anything like that was when they got it into their heads to make a boxing ring in the backyard. I had returned from another increasingly strange and newly stressful day at work brought on by a long practice the night before and my new responsibilities at the job, and went straight to the Enchanter House.

Renee wasn't home yet, but Mickey and Donald were in the living room, inches away from each other's faces, pointing and yelling.

"I don't care if you're bigger than me, motherfucker!" Donald shrieked, spit flying into his brother's face. "I can still beat the shit out of you any time I want 'cause I'm your older brother and I'm smarter than you!"

"Donald." Mickey said, completely calm. "I'd fucking kill you and you know it."

Donald turned to me and said, "Oh good. He's here. Let's go, Shaquille. You're driving the van."

"Where are we going?"

"To the fucking House Depository World, dumbass! Where else? We're making a boxing ring in the backyard so I can kick this motherfucker's ass once and for all!"

First, they had to cash their just-received paychecks so they could spend a ridiculous percentage of said paychecks in the orange-gray House Depository warehouse on wood, drills, screws, planks and posts for the four corners.

We got all this into the van, and Donald was like, "OK, we gotta get the boxing gloves now." So I drove them to Sporting Factory Outlet Supply World, and they spent even more money they didn't really have on perfectly new red boxing gloves, and as I drove them back, Mickey quite innocently asked, "Don't we need ropes?"

There was a befuddled silence, then Donald answered, "You're right, Mick. Ropes. Well, we don't have any, and we need what's left of the money we have for wine, so I don't know." Donald was in the passenger seat, brooding over what to do. "OK, I got it," he announced. "Let's just steal a bunch of garden hoses."

It was getting dark enough to do it, so we drove around random rich neighborhoods like Live Oak Sweet Pine Estate Manours and Mill Farm Meadow Wood Manour Estates, rolling slowly past the McMansions until somebody would say, "There's one!"

I'd stop just past the house, and both of them would run out of the car, Donald furtively unscrewing the hose from its spigot, Mickey rolling it up in his hands until it was coiled green around his arms, then they'd run to the car, giggling like the tweenage vandals they once were. I'd speed off until we thought we were safe, all of us laughing from the adrenaline rush and the sheer idiocy of the endeavor until we could hardly breathe, and then I'd slow down again on a new street in a different subdivision, the three of us searching and scanning, Donald with his head out the window, his right hand over his eyes to block out the setting sun's glare.

The whole thing was so retarded; I'm amazed we didn't get caught, especially since we were in this bright purple van that was conspicuous as hell among all those SUVs and minivans. We found another hose; they stole another hose in the same way; we found another; we stole another in the same way.

"OK, that's enough," Mickey said, reaching out across the passenger seat to pat me on the back. "Thanks for helping me beat up my brother, Little Buddy."

"No. We need one more." Donald said.

"No, we're good." Mickey answered, and I agreed with him.

"No. Just one more. Right there." Donald pointed from the back seat at a giant green hose spread out across a thick emerald lawn undulating in front of a giant colonial style mansion that looked not unlike The White House's kid brother.

"Are you sure about this?" I asked. I was getting a little tired, even though I couldn't stop laughing. I also wanted to get back to Renee.

"Yes!" Donald announced. "Just this one, and we're ready to go." He opened his door and was already running out before I came to a complete stop.

"Fuckin'...fine! Wait up, bro!" Mickey yelled, at least waiting until I stopped before running out to coil the enormous hose.

I waited in the van, finally aware that there was no music playing, so I put on an old Buzzcocks tape and looked straight ahead at the darkening road lined with cocoplum trees and 19th century looking street lamps.

Over the Buzzcocks' unrequited love laments, I heard somebody yell "Hey! What the hell're you doin'!?" By the spigot, a shirtless old man with a big sunburnt belly and gold chains around his neck holding a glass of iced tea ran up to Donald, about to grab him.

"Um, nothing!" Donald answered, lunging at and then shoving the poor old man. He fell into his shrubbery in a kind of Nestea Plunge, arms outspread across the leaves and back, iced tea spilling all over him as he collapsed into the snap of broken branches.

"Go! Go! Go!" Donald yelled, sprinting away down and then up the slight inclines of the yard to the van.

Mickey saw this and kept running with the hose. The old man bounced up and ran roly-poly style after them, remarkably fast, yelling, "You sons of bitches! Gimme back my goddamn hose!"

Donald leapt into the van, through the passenger seat window Luke Duke style, yelling "Go!" over and over again as Mickey approached, garden hose trailing behind him uncoiled like an impractical tail on an unfortunate animal.

The old man ran, bouncing his flabby chest down the final small hill, twenty-five feet and ten seconds away from the van, and we still weren't moving. Mickey jumped inside, leaving the side door open so he could pull the hose inside, which was within diving distance of the old man.

"Fuck the hose!" Donald yelled. "Shaq, just get the fuck out of here." I sped off, laughing out of fear, and Mickey held on to the hose as it rattled down the road. The old man kept running, and now we were all laughing. We drove like this until we were well out of sight of our pursuer, and then stopped the van long enough for Mickey to reel in the rest of that very long hose. He threw it next to the other supplies.

"Now I'm really gonna punch your stupid face up and down!" Mickey yelled. "Making us get more hoses than we needed! We could've gone to jail thanks to you!"

"Shut up, bro!" Donald yelled. "You should've just let the hose go then and it wouldn't have mattered! I can't wait to punch you!"

Finally, we made it home. For the next three hours, Mickey and Donald worked nonstop in the backyard, sweating and nailing and drilling and setting up the boxing ring. I sat out there and watched them work.

"Pass me that drill, Mickey."

"Here," Mickey said, handing him the drill. "Gimme those nails and hold this board steady."

Renee came home and asked what they were doing. When I told her, she said, "For two people who want to beat each other up, they sure are working together remarkably well."

I laughed and said, "Well. They're brothers."

Renee shrugged and I followed her inside.

Six hours later, at midnight, it was finished. They called us out to watch the fight, both showing signs of hours of labor and hours of wine drinking. Their eyelids sagged and they leaned on their homemade poles—brown wooden posts stuck into the yard—on opposite sides of each other. The green hoses used for ropes hung taut around the edges of the plywood flooring.

"OK," Donald said, short of breath, a little slurred and sleepy sounding. "Let's do this. Shaq: You're the ref."

"The ref, got it," I said, climbing in between the hoses. None of this was strange to me. Mickey and Donald were in the backyard getting ready to box. Of course!

I walked into the middle of the ring on planks that felt a little wobbly underfoot, waving the two boxers to the center. Mickey shadowboxed over and Donald pointed and taunted, "You're a big ugly bear and I'm too pretty to scare!" in some horrible Muhammad Ali imitation.

Trying to summon any memory of what a boxing referee was supposed to say, I spoke in my fastest, most officious tone: "All right: I want a clean fight here. No kidney punches. No hits below the belt. When you hear that bell, it's the end of the round and youse go back to your corners. OK, now slap the gloves." They slapped; Donald tried shoving his a little harder into Mickey's, but Mickey was too strong and didn't move an inch. "When you hear the bell, gentlemen, start boxing. Good luck."

I stepped out of their way, but before I yelled "DING!" Donald swung at Mickey right at his left temple. The glove smacked his head in a sound that went "DOUCHE!" Mickey was unfazed. He reared back his left arm and smashed Donald in the forehead.

And that was that. Donald's long arms fell to his side, he took two baby steps backwards, and his legs collapsed from under him. I watched this from the edge of the ring, shirtless Donald wearing camouflage pants cut short just above the knees and a pair of red boxing gloves, falling flat on his back.

I jumped to the middle to see if Donald was still conscious. His head moved from side to side and his eyes were open, and he kept mumbling "My bruthuh. My own bruthuh...betrayed...me..." so I started and finished the ten count, and declared "The winner, by knockout: Mickey Alexander!"

Renee politely applauded by the screen door as Mickey threw his arms in the air and spun around in a victory dance.

"Very good. Now can we go inside?" Renee asked. I did as I was told. Mickey shortly followed after a rousing rendition of *We Are the Champions*, as he danced around his fallen brother, who was left outside to sleep off the wine and his glass forehead in the ring.

After all that work, the boxing ring was never used again,

quickly warped by rain and squirrel shit.

We started wearing football helmets with the facemasks removed to our concerts—but not only the concerts, any time we left the house—among other self-invented fashion statements. Regrettably, my helmet isn't in this box. I hurled it out the car window when I left Sprawlburg Springs for good. I found mine at a thrift store, some hand-me-down from a Pop Warner team who stole their look from the Chicago Bears. I blacked out the orange "C" of the helmet and dumped bright splotches of model paint—red, green, yellow and white—until it looked like my insides exploding into something chaotic and beautiful, which was how I saw and heard The Enchanters. Practicing with the helmet on also added a whole new dimension to how I heard our music, the way it echoed, ricocheted, and reverberated through the helmet's ear holes and around the hard plastic insides.

Renee kept her old leather helmet, because it belonged to her grandfather. It was from the '20s, back when he was a quarterback for the Morristown Vulcanizers. Mickey's was old, white, and dented. He painted the whole thing maroon and added a simple arrow pointing upward with black duct tape on both sides. Donald's was a chipped Nebraska Cornhuskers helmet, and he left it alone except he added "OWHERE" to the red "N" on both sides.

We walked and drove around town like this, and a few brave souls would yell things like "LOOK AT THE RETARDS!!!" at us, but most people were scared of the size and builds of Mickey and Donald, so mostly we were just stared at with lots of quiet pointing and laughing. We expected that. We wanted to stand out, tired of the same old boring retrograde nonconformity.

Yeah, it was ridiculous, and it only got worse, or better, depending on how you looked at it. We wore six-pack rings around our necks and wrists. We superglued shellacked Cheetos all over our black sport coats, and dumped whole bags worth of cheeto residue until the coats were stained fluorescent orange. We wrote absurdist slogans all over our shirts, things like "Hey how's your tennis?" and "Hit it when it's brown." We bought more green hand lotion and stuck it under our nostrils to resemble snot.

I lost the helmet, but I did keep two squeezed-out white tubes of orange face paint we found discounted at a costume shop. The four of us were at the mall, just walking around doing nothing, when we saw the picture display of a portly kid dressed like a pumpkin for Halloween with orange pants, an orange and black bulbous pumpkin, orange arms, topped off with bright orange face paint. Since it was the middle of summer and nowhere near Halloween, there was a handwritten sign that read: "ALL FACEPAINT 50% OFF!"

Mickey pointed at the kid in the display and said, "What if our skin looked like that?"

Nobody said anything. We just walked into the store and bought a dozen tubes of orange face paint and raced immediately home.

"How do I look?" Donald asked, stepping out of the Enchanter House bathroom with his face now a hideous shade of bright orange.

We laughed. Renee said, "You look beautiful! Like you have the worst sunburn in the world!"

When we all wore them, we looked scary as hell, especially when we played out. Scary, but amazing. Our faces glowed. Pretty soon, our fans copied this look and it was easy to spot Enchanter fans. Real easy.

It was really something, going through the day's routines with fluorescent orange skin, green lotion dangling out of the nostrils, a homemade facemask-less football helmet, six-pack rings around the necks and wrists, especially when it spread to our friends/fans. It wasn't uncommon for me, for all of us who were part of The Enchanter scene, to get things thrown at us as we walked or drove around. Coming home from work one day, a bunch of construction workers threw a milkshake at my car. Fast food of all shapes and sizes were hurled in our directions, always from moving cars and not pedestrians, because nobody would dare fuck with Mickey and Donald to their faces. Half-eaten bacon cheeseburgers, limp French fries topped off with ketchup, hash browns, yeast rolls, hush puppies. Lots of "Hey faggots!" and "Looks like the circus came to town!" or "Hey Devo!" I never understood that, like, how, in the redneck mind, by dressing in our own style, it either made us gay, circus performers, or fans of Devo.

I remember grocery shopping like this, pushing the cars up and down the aisles while the other shoppers just *stared*, with no shame or remorse about it. You'd get lots of "Looks like Halloween's a little early this year, huh?" Little kids either followed me around or else they ran away screaming. At the checkout counter, jowly clerks with way too much eye makeup would ask between smacks of chewing gum, "And who are you supposed to be?"

"I'm an Enchanter!" I'd say proudly. "I'm trying to rescue this town."

"Ohhhh-kay," the check out lady would sigh, unamused, ringing up my order. I got used to that kind of treatment immediately, and in some ways, it actually felt good, because it was still possible to do the whole proverbial "freak out the squares" thing in these jaded times. I felt young and wholly original. It made me think we were creating something even more unique than just the unique music, and I can definitely add that it made the straight job really strange.

My red and black nametag reads: "WELCOME TO CLEVELAND STEAMERZ GOODTIME BAR AND GRILLE WORLD, MY NAME'S SHAQUILLE! NO NO, KIND CUSTOMER, IT'S NO BOTHER AT ALL TO ASSIST YOU IN YOUR PURSUIT OF A FUN TIME!" Somehow, I didn't throw it out and it ended up in my ENCHANTER CRAP box.

When I walked into work with my new look, I was greeted with the kinds of laughs usually reserved for *Showtime at the Apollo* comedians. There were a whole lot of "What the fucks?" and "Wow, that's an, uh, interesting, look you got there, Shaquille."

"Thank you! Thank you all" I announced, smiling and waving like someone who just won a major award.

These workdays were long, and through vicious wine hangovers, exhaustion, dehydration, and ringing ears, I tried learning how to make Shitton of Meat Sandwiches. "Sandwich order up!" one of the line cooks would yell. "Let's go, Gene Simmons!" somebody would always yell because of my orange skin, yuk yuk yuk. I'd immediately leave the squid in mid-cut and race across the kitchen as Ron Cozumel yelled, "OK, Shaquille. Here we go: It's your time to shine."

And shine I did not. Sometimes, I got it right; other times, I'd forget to put on necessities like the cheese, and, on more than one occasion, the Shitton of Meat. I made messes, smearing drips and dollops of sauces and condiments until it looked like an amateur painter's canvas. I sliced my right index finger opening a can of tomato sauce and was sent home. The presentation of the sandwiches on the plates was almost always a mess, like something slopped together in two seconds. I sucked—there were no two ways about it—but my job performance at Cleveland Steamerz Good Time Bar and Grille World moved in an inverse relation to my drumming performances with The Enchanters.

But on that first day, when I first walked into work dressed like an Enchanter, Ron Cozumel asked to speak with me back in the urine yellow haze of his office with all those motivational slogans and the "THIS MUCH" and "THAT MUCH" graphs tacked onto the wood paneling. Ron just stroked his black goatstache and stared at me.

"So Shaquille," he finally said. "Why are you dressed like... like...." And here, he paused to come up with something good, but he couldn't come up with anything. "Like how you are there, Brother Man?"

"I don't know," I said. "Because I like it?"

Ron just stared at me, waiting for some confirmation that I was really just joking and I'd rip off the mask at any moment and go back to being the regular Shaquille he knew and loved.

"You can't dress like this at work," he said.

"Why not?"

"Because that face paint'll break off and get in the food."

"No it won't," I said. "It stays on until you wash it off. No flakes. No drips. No errors. That's what the tube says, and nothing's happened yet." I laughed to myself. "Don't worry. I won't poison our customers."

Ron tilted his chair back, looked up at the paneled ceiling, and sighed. "You know what, Shaquille?" he said, still looking up and away.

I cocked an eyebrow, expecting to be fired.

"I don't care," Ron said. He bent forward from his desk, and peered into my bright orange face. "No," he continued. "I don't. Just don't go anyplace else outside of this kitchen where you could scare any customers, and it'll be fine."

I nodded, and made to stand up and return to work, but Ron stopped me with a "But wait. You know why I'm not caring about this clear violation of our dress code?"

"No."

He reclined back in his chair again, completely relaxed, and smiled. "Because you're gonna get enough hassle from everybody else around here without making it any worse. You know that, right?"

At the time, I thought he meant the workplace, but I'd soon enough know what he meant. "I guess so..." I shrugged, thinking, *How bad could it get?*

How bad? Ha ha ha.

part three: **fourth rule is: eat Kosher salami**

*"A squid eating dough in a polyethylene bag is fast and bulbous, got me?"*

**Captain Beefheart**

# chapter one

Broken drumsticks and shredded fliers line the bottom of my "ENCHANTER CRAP" box, appropriately damaged souvenirs from all the house parties we played throughout that sweaty summer. The only club that might have booked The Enchanters, Latent Republican Hipster Music Club World, wanted nothing to do with us due to our annoying habit of getting thrown out for acting out our hatreds for the shitty bands they booked, but there was a loose network of houses that had us as word spread and more people understood.

In less than three months, we had a rapidly growing fan base of mutant high schoolers, collegiate party dudes getting their ya-yas out before their inevitable inheritance of suburbia, and random older eccentric music fans—all of whom would first see us dressed in whatever they considered "fashionable" and/or "rebellious" at the time, which was, invariably, too-baggy jeans with exposed boxers and too-tight T-shirts, with giant chain wallets dangling from their sides down below their knees, and the next time we'd see them, they'd be dressed like us.

There were some brave kids out there willing to host us and face the increasing harassment from the police, the only constant variable in these chaotic concerts. Just walking around wearing the same things we did wasn't an easy thing. Of course, now, everybody colors their skin bright orange with green lotion under their nostrils, but then, it was like you came from another planet, and it was just the pretense needed to be considered suspicious. But, more importantly, it also helped us identify each other as something separate from all the other youth cultures dry humping the past like so many rabid Boston Terriers. For a short while, it was worth it.

If you've ever seen bands or played in bands at house parties, then you know they're usually very cramped, very sweaty, the sound is terrible, everyone is wasted and lacking their workaday self-restraint, the house inevitably gets damaged by some calamity (accidental or not), strings detune and break, mic cords break, amplifiers blow, drumsticks snap, drumheads are punctured, and yet, in spite of all that, they're twenty-five times more fun than a club show, for 1/25th of the cost. Not having some slimeball club owner who's strictly in it for the money, and not having to deal with arrogant soundmen, helps matters considerably for all concerned.

The focus was entirely on having fun, and from this, the best was seeing all these great bands start up, like Noon Wine, Chloroform, the Smoking Corvairs, and so on, like something genuinely organic was coming out of our town as opposed to the usual unendurable garbage decreed by some rich idiot with more money and market research than taste.

Not to say there was ever a "Sprawlburg Springs Sound," but it was starting to happen, and it was happening fast. I would peek through the bedroom doors of our "backstages" and watch people like Alison and Norman. They never said much if you saw them out and about, but behind microphones and in front of amplifiers, they'd run around naked as their band Rubber Gone Bouncy Bounce played, one covered in peanut butter, the other covered in grape jelly, rolling around on each other and yelling gibberish into microphones. It was exciting, for once. Now, we were a lot of things, but we certainly weren't bored, because we'd had quite enough of that.

Occasionally, we played high school parties like Scott's, when the parents were out of town, but most parties (venues, sorry) were held in what passed for the university district, which was one neighborhood for Commuter State College, a neighborhood of small cinderblock homes from the 1950s with small front yards half covered in grass and half-covered in fire-ant hills. You had to be discreet with the passing out of fliers, without being so discreet nobody knew about it. There was an underground network throughout the high schools and the Commuter State campus, tiny fliers passed out in class, in the halls, to anybody who looked interesting, to cute girls, to anybody who might want to know about something cool to do. You didn't want the cops knowing about it any sooner than they eventually would, and you didn't want a bunch of frat brahs there wasting space and draining the Buck Urine Lite keg, so there were never addresses on the fliers, just names like "The Fine Rich Man's House," "Young Republican House," "Random House," "The Even Whiter House," "Broken House," "Monkey House," "Steven Spielberg's House," "The Little Cottage," names for the same houses that changed with each party, so the only way to figure it out was based on word-of-mouth. The names of the houses became more and more absurd and ironic as time passed, names like: "The House Where Everybody Sits Around and Watches TV Like All the Other Houses Here," "The Cops Can't Find Our House," and, my personal favorite, "The Uptight Yuppie Assholes Who Always Call the Cops to Complain About the Noise and How Their Neighbors Are Having Fun, Thus Diverting the Police from Stopping the Real Crime in This Town House."

We'd show up at these places just before eight (the parties started earlier than usual in the vain hopes of ending the music before the city's sound ordinances came into effect) and park the rattling and wheezing purple shag van in front of the house—never in the driveway because we always needed to make a quick escape. The houses always had cracked hardwood floor living rooms with minimum thrift store furnishings, chipped plaster walls painted red and covered with movie posters of '60s biker films and such, and a ramshackle back porch where the host is propped upside down on the already-tapped keg, sucking out its contents as spent whippet canisters roll around the creaking warped wood.

Upon seeing us, the host and his friends would stop what they were doing to stare at us like they couldn't believe it was really us in our football helmets and orange skin, and then the host would finally say something like, "Well, if it isn't the notorious Enchanters." He or she would smile and shake our hands and show us where to set up and where our backstage area was with our mandatory four bottles of wine. We'd be safe backstage as the Enchanter Contingent arrived, and not only were they becoming noticeable by their dress, but we could hear them in the other room, confidently goofy now instead of adolescently awkward, always yelling crap at the top of their lungs like, "Hey! Let's order a pizza!" followed by a large shout of "YEAHHH!" followed by a Rodney Dangerfield homage like "Hey everybody! We're gonna get laid!" "YEAHHH!"

Backstage, this made us laugh almost as hard as the talk from the collegiates, whose talk never went much deeper than, "Fuckin'...this is so killer, fuckin'...I hear this band is way fuckin' demented and shit...Yeah man...fuckin'...uh...yeah.'

The music from the opening bands (we were never an opening

band) rumbled through the walls and we'd smile to ourselves about it. There was local music, and it was actually tolerable. Somehow, people found these parties/concerts at these houses/venues. The fliers were never more than functional, artless black permanent marker scribble announcing who was playing, the date, and the newest made-up name of the house, which the flier giver would tell you if he or she thought you seemed potentially receptive to it, or if you saw it stapled to a phone pole, you'd have to figure it out on your own.

Our makeshift Green Rooms were hilarious to me because there were always party dudes opening the door without knocking, looking to get high, thinking they could use the room to smoke out, shoot up, snort lines, suck whippets, whatever. Donald especially hated these people. He would throw the nearest handy thing at their heads, and that would be enough. Those guys (and they were always guys) were useless, and not that we abstained from intoxicants, but it was always a means to a creative end for us where, for them, it was just the end itself. They did just as much to make Sprawlburg Springs the dull and stupid place it was as anybody else.

We never said much "backstage." Mickey took naps, Donald paced the floor, Renee made the set list, and me, I didn't know what to do with myself. Hysteria was impending, and this was the dull down time of waiting. Mostly, I'd sit Indian style in the corner with my back against the wall practicing drum fills on my legs, pounding out single-stroke drum rolls with my sticks until bruises formed. Finally, after a dramatic enough gap between bands, the host of the party would peek in the room and ask, "Ready?" and Donald would grab his guitar and yell "Go!!!" and we'd shove through the audience, get to our instruments, and to the sound of disoriented feedback, we'd play something, already starting a song while Renee yelled into the mic, "We're The Enchanters, from Sprawlburg Springs," and off we went, taking the audience along with us, wherever we were going.

From the get-go, everything and everyone turned to sweat, the sweat that only mid-summer Sprawlburg Springs humidity can give you, the sweat that made all of us—no matter what tribe we stomped ground with—koo koo kooky. We knew we had twenty minutes to play our set before the arrival of the police, which meant twenty minutes to pack in as much fun and get out as many frustrations as possible. When those twenty minutes were up, we were left with little besides sweat-soaked clothes reeking of cigarettes, ringing ears, big smiles, slippery floors wet with sweat and beer, random bruised and bleeding wounds, and the total confusion of wondering how we would get out of the house without being hassled by Sprawlburg Springs's Finest, but it was all worth it.

Like Ginsberg said: "Smart went crazy," but not only that, dumb went crazy too. All that mattered was that twenty-minute set. Our "fan club" of the kids we played for at the first concert I played for The Enchanters were always there to get things moving in the increasingly-large crowds in those dilapidated living rooms.

I could hear them "backstage," but to really see our contingent and how much they had changed in just two months was really something. The twelve of them always stood in the front in a row, each dressed in football helmets and all the other stupid fashions, no longer sheepish and awkward adolescents, but clearly a group who didn't give a shit what anybody thought about them. They didn't care, and it would be nihilistic if they had taken themselves all that seriously, but none of them did. It was all goofing. It was the playful energy of 12 teenagers tweaking nipples, grabbing nuts, slapping asses, pushing and shoving, and lots and lots of heckling, which was always a sign of love and appreciation at all those parties we played. When you heard somebody yell, "You guys are a buncha weirdo faggots! Go back to Sprawlburg Springs!" you knew the concert would be all right.

In the midst of all the sweat and falling around, Donald often dropped his guitar and jumped into the audience, leaving the amp squealing shrill white noise. I stood up over my drums for the entire set, jumping above them, crashing the cymbals, then falling to the ground only to get back up again, repeating the whole process. I'd join Donald out in the pack of onlookers, charging with a crash cymbal on its stand and riding it like a toy horse while bashing away at it, leaving Mickey and Renee to hold it all together. During the times when I just played the songs, there would always be the skisssssh slide of a playfully tossed beer can across a cymbal, and I'd glare out into the dark living room to find out who did it and it would always be one of our friends smiling wickedly and waving before the force of the crowd knocked him against the wall. And speaking of walls, there was this one dude who started showing up at the shows whose shtick was to drop his jeans around his ankles and *fuck* the wall while we played, pelvic bangs in rhythm with my drumbeats, hirsute ass bouncing from the vibrations, and nobody noticed nor cared, as oblivious as they were to getting whatever poison was inside of them out.

It wasn't unusual for me, Donald and Renee to be tackled and mobbed by the partygoers until it was only Mickey thumping his bass. My clothes were almost always torn up after the shows. I'd get tackled behind the drums, dogpiled under uncountable sweaty bodies, barely capable of breathing, face-down in a filthy hardwood floor, and a quick thought flashed in my mind: "What does all this mean?" and besides the simple "Fun" answer, there was the tremendous feeling of liberation. We were winning, and it wasn't political—that's always the last thing to change—no, it was energy. Something bigger was opening before us in our minds (assuming we didn't suffocate ourselves at these parties), the very possibilities of what life could give us. It was no longer just school or work, then home to the TV. We had reclaimed our lives, and while we didn't have the numbers, much less the guns, we at least had each other, and we at least had these shows.

Nudity was rampant. Total strangers made out with each other, fucked on the floor. Behind the drums, I could see the naked bodies off in the corners, rolling and contorting in spastic humps. We made skinheads cry. That was the best, because I don't know how it was where you're from, but in my neck of the woods, skinheads were bullies and musclethugs and nothing more. They were rich kids from hyperdysfunctional families, dryhumping a British working class subculture, dumbed down to fit their own KKK backgrounds. Skinheads, the kinds of geniuses who think thoughts like "Boy, Adolf Hitler really had the right idea!" The kinds of brave souls who got their kicks ganging up on one kid in groups of ten or more and kicking his head into the curb.

They showed up at a party, about fifteen of them, all jackbooted and red suspenders in their black bomber jackets that read "Sprawlburg Springs Skins" in white cursive lettering on their backs, yelling "white power" and "oi!" at everybody in the room, stealing beers, knocking furniture and kids around. Pimply Melissa ran into the room we were holed up in backstage, and before Donald could yell "Get the fuck out!", she was all like, "Those skinheads just took Scott outside! They're gonna kill him!"

Donald immediately stood up, grabbed Mickey's bass, and yelled "Grab something!" to Mickey and I. I grabbed the top half of my crash cymbal stand, a three foot silver rod that fit like a Billy club in my right hand. Mickey just ran after us. There was no time to feel anything but the adrenaline of righting a big wrong.

In the front yard, under a moth-infested amber streetlight, the skinheads circled around Scott, who was on the ground curled up with his arms covering his frizzy head, blubbering for mercy. Three of them were kicking him in the chest and back as the others walked around shouting encouragements. Partygoers just stood around nervously watching through the front windows.

Mickey and I followed Donald down the three steps from the front porch, Donald with the bass hoisted over his head like a sword. He swung it on the back of one of the skin's heads. I'll never forget the sound the bass made, a wooden thwack with just the slightest low ring of the strings. The skinhead fell forward and collapsed onto all fours. Donald kept swinging, and I had to sidestep to avoid the backend of the bashings, running to the other side of the rapidly disintegrating circle, no thoughts except swinging my cymbal stand until these thugs left Scott alone. While the sounds of my cymbal stand hitting skulls wasn't as, uh, melodic, as the bass Donald was wielding, it was just as satisfying nonetheless.

But we were outnumbered 15-3, and I'm not much of a fighter. Despite disabling about half of their numbers, the skinhead's counterattack would have been overpowering if other partygoers hadn't finally joined in. I was punched in the stomach and tackled, causing me to drop my cymbal stand, with three skinheads ready to punch and kick me until my drumming, if not my living, days were over. Mickey was way too big for these skinheads, most of whom were just dumbass kids who didn't know any better, and he could take them out two at a time, and then you had all the fat, scrawny, lanky, geeky male members of The Enchanter contingent, these freaky kids, jumping in like they were soldiers in hand-to-hand combat with the enemy, and I almost wanted to laugh except I could barely breathe from one-too-many kicks to the stomach, and it all happened so fast, the next thing I know Mickey's pulling me up, all like, "Are you OK Little Buddy?" and I nodded, feeling just a little bit lightheaded, but not enough to faint as I watched the few skinheads not incapacitated limp or run away down the street, all of them leaving except for one kid, sprawled out there on the front yard, curled into the fetal position.

"GET UP, YOU FUCKING NAZI MOTHERFUCK!" Donald screamed over him as the rest of us had backed up now that we thought the fight was over.

The skinhead kid laid there in a pool of his own blood pouring out both his nostrils and lips. Donald kicked him in the ribs and yelled, "GET UP, ADOLPH! WHERE'S YOUR WHITE POWER NOW YOU FUCKING COCKSMACK!" He spat in his face. The kid was crying, blubbering something about "stop...please..."

I walked over to Donald. "Leave him alone. It's over." I said, trying to stand between this kid, because, when I looked at him, I could tell, that's all he was, just a dumb kid looking for something to belong to, no matter how wrong it was, which made him not too far off from the rest of us, but far enough to deserve our contempt, but not this.

"WHAT, YOU'RE NOT GONNA GET UP AND FIGHT NOW THAT YOU CAN'T BEAT PEOPLE UP 15 TO 1 YOU GODDAMN WORTHLESS PIECE OF FUCKING BULLSHIT!?!" Donald yelled, spanking him in the ass with the bass. He didn't even look at me when I told him to stop. His face was all red, eyes bugged out, tall beanpole body bent over the kid at the waist and focused on nothing else like some kind of rabid attack dog.

The kid was really crying now, whimpering through his swollen and blackened face. Renee had come out to us now, watching from the front porch, also in tears. "Donald," she said, "Please stop this. They've left, and we have a show to do." She reached out with her left hand and squeezed his right shoulder.

Donald stepped back, catching his breath, still looking like he had more fight in him, more punches and kicks he wanted to throw, but instead, he kneeled down and got right in front of the kid's face and said between gasps for air, "You're gonna tell, all your faggot friends who left you here to die, that if they EVER think to start any shit with us or our friends, it's gonna be ten times worse, and you'll never read *Mein Kampf* again, do you understand me, you Nazi shitstain?" To emphasize his point,

Donald spat in his face, then walked back into the party, which wasn't really a party anymore, but a bunch of random people standing there in shock.

Renee followed him inside the house, yelling after him, "You didn't have to take it that far, Donald!" I stood there over the kid, and Scott joined me. His left eye was bruised shut, and he kept a white hand towel filled with ice across that half of his head. Me, the wind was still knocked out, but I was slowly getting it back, even though it hurt to inhale.

"How do you feel?" I asked Scott.

"I'll be all right," he said. "Thanks for coming out here and jumping in."

I nodded. It all happened so fast, like everything with The Enchanters. I couldn't process anything more about it. A couple party dudes came up to the kid and picked him up, one on each end, all like, "We gotta get this kid outta here and to the hospital so the cops don't come." They carried him half a block down to a green pickup truck, where they dropped him in the back, got in the front, and drove away.

Scott and I walked back to the house. Mickey was sitting there on the front porch steps, fat red face curled downward, sad.

"We coulda killed that kid," he said. "We really hurt those guys."

"Fuck 'em," I said, feeling the pains in my chest from those kicks. "That kid's gonna live, and besides, they started it, and he was in there with the other fourteen of 'em wanting to kill Scott here." I sat down next to Mickey and patted him on the back. "They started it, remember? We're just trying to play music and have fun, and we had to defend ourselves. From thugs. Remember?"

"Yeah, I know," Mickey said. "It still doesn't seem right though."

But I didn't give a shit. The skinheads in our town sucked ass, and they deserved any beat downs they got. And I'm not a violent person. At all. But those guys...it was worth it to see them run away and cry. The concert went on as scheduled, and it wasn't our best due to frazzled and exhausted nerves and a nearly cleared-out living room from people not all that eager to use party as a verb after the fight, but we got through it. Sometimes, all you could do with these concerts was to somehow survive it, all the unpredictable and myriad insanities thrown at us, most amusing, some not so, but, like I said, never boring.

But despite rare moments like these, lots of times it was cool, and the cops wouldn't show up, and we could just hang out with people afterwards and goof off and make friends. It was at these moments when I really got to know the twelve kids who made up the Enchanter Contingent. Once the shows were over and we knew we could stay, it was like a great tension within and without was released and there was nothing else beyond having a good time.

These house parties inevitably evolved into dance parties where the living room lights were turned down low and in the middle of the action, it wasn't uncommon for Donald to stand in the middle of the room with his pants and boxers around his ankles, looking up at the sky and yelling, "Why can't I get laid?!?" at the top of his lungs. Or I'd be in the corner of the room chatting away with Afro Mark and Hirsute Sally about names for bands that never went beyond the talking stage of the concept, no matter how much we believed we'd be starting them as soon as we got around to it, Mark all like: "I'm tryin' to get this other band goin' called Bobby and the Commercial Breaks, where we do like punk rock covers of TV commercial jingles and shit...that would be pretty funny, don't ya think?" he'd ask me, poking me in the chest with his finger then poking me in the forehead with his big-ass afro.

Before I could respond one way or the other, Sally jumped in, "No, Mark, that's stupid, but what was your other idea for a band? Remember?"

"Thick Jizzy?" Mark asked, as beer shot out of my mouth from my laughter.

"No..." Sally said.

"Pubeway Army?" Mark asked, as more beer shot out of my mouth.

"No, it was The Grannies, remember?" Mark shook his head, "Uh, no..." Sally continued, "You were talking about it at the last party, like starting a band where we dressed up like old ladies and sang songs about bingo and shuffleboard and Osteoporosis, remember now?"

We just stared at her, not laughing. "Fine!" Sally yelled, pulling at the whiskers of her short blond hair. "That's way better than Thick Jizzy, and you don't even remember or like it! God, you guys suck." With that, Hirsute Sally stormed off, and you could look across the room, and Jonathan would be on the opposite corner, playing a guitar that only he could hear over the noise of the dance music—which was invariably '60s soul—staring at Renee who would be shaking and spinning in the center of the room, smiling, then yelling pleasantries to all passersby. After dances with Renee, Jonathan would tap me on the shoulder and ask "Are you and Renee still dating?" to which I'd shake my head in fake sadness and say "Sorry, dude..." Jonathan huffed and puffed, then said more to himself than to me, "Ya know...it's OK. She's too good for me anyway." Alison with the long black hair and Balding Norman would always be slow dancing right next to Andy and Tommy, who would also slow dance no matter if it was Otis Redding or Slayer on the stereo. Mickey would be running around the room with Cathy, aka Mia Culpa, this big big guy and this smaller blond girl full-on making out, not caring one way or the other about public displays of affection, and none of us really did either. I'd get into fake professional wrestling matches with Red Head Ted and cracked-voice Bryan after I got sick of arguing with them about the importance of drummers in bands. Neither of them believed me, always going on like, "Drummers really aren't that big of a deal, Shaquille, you know? I mean, you're good and everything, but I could just get a drum machine and...." And upon hearing the words "drum machine," I'd rip my shirt off and tackle the person talking. Both those guys were pretty small, and they were younger than me, so it was really no problem pinning one, if not both of them, pinning the shoulders then pointing in their faces and yelling, "Take it back! Drummers are important! Say it! Say it!" I'd be laughing the whole time and they'd finally go "OK! Drummers are important! Let me up now!" And I would and then one of them would immediately start up again, "But, seriously though: With a drum machine..." and the wrestling would resume.

Somehow, tanks of nitrous would always show up at these parties, and me and Renee would go off into whatever room the inevitable thick pony-tailed nitrous salesman plied his trade, and we'd suck down our balloons and through lowered voices we'd laugh and ask, "Is yours working?" "I think soooooooooo...." and you'd feel the compression of time and that frozen nanosecond where the world stops and there was nothing to do but laugh...and we'd make it back onto those living room dance floors, stumbling and giggling, propping each other up but never, never losing the rhythm.

We'd make it back to The Enchanter House. How, I don't know, but Renee and I would wake up sweating from the early morning, 90-degree temperatures, hungover yet still drunk, giggling about every stupid thing from the night before, the party post-mortem. "You were so funny last night..." "Did you see ____ doing this and that?" "Yeah, that was ridiculous. I'm hungry! Feed me, Shaquille." "I can't move, dude! I can't, fuckin', think!" "Don't swear, but remember when..." You'd wake up like it was just a nap from the party, still a little drunk, and then Sunday slowly dragged the whole thing down until night time. I could barely hold my drumsticks for practice, but skipping rehearsal was never an option because it was all we had, no matter how much fun or how hungover we felt, you had to ignore it and do it and do it right.

Each week, each party, our numbers kept growing. In the haze of a post-nitrous high with Scott, we observed a packed party after we played our set and he asked me, "Do you think it's gonna last much longer like this?"

"I don't know. Maybe."

Renee always insisted that it would. "Definitely. At least through the end of the summer. Before we move away."

Donald had his ten-year-plan, and Mickey just laughed when asked this question. "Jeez, Little Buddy, I don't care. We're moving soon anyways, right?"

We even got a write-up in the Sprawlburg Springs *Rabblerouser*, our ineffective weekly newspaper, from Rollie St. Bacon, the legendary, long-retired rock critic who said he relocated to Sprawlburg Springs "to escape all music, art, and any trace of what's left of culture in this once-great nation..." But sometimes, he'd be inspired to write in his inimitable post-beat style, like this article I've kept titled, "Who Are The Enchanters and Why Does It Matter?" (I hadn't met him—and I don't recall even seeing him at any of these parties—but he did meet Renee briefly, who described him as "a polite mumbler.")

Here's an excerpt of what he wrote about us: "...Do you jerks even remotely REALIZE how lucky you are to live in the same town as The Enchanters?!? Most of you do not, still feigning contentedness with your twelfth-removed hand-me-down realities as you scrape away your worthless lives on land that grows nothing spontaneous, nothing that hasn't been cleared through at least twenty levels of corporate boardrooms before ground is broken—and you finally have something to call your own—and your reaction is to ignore it and laugh it out of existence. Tsk tsk, because what Renee Eisner and Co. have achieved in such an incredibly short period of time is nothing short of monumental, and, in the long run, historical, because it's no small achievement to take a worthless little burg like this one (perfect for fogy retirees like myself and nothing else) who thinks she's Something Cosmopolitan (har har har), and create a wholly original music scene with no club support and virtually no media coverage (cue self-important pat on the back here)...and if this continues, this could be the MOST IMPORTANT thing I've seen since seeing the Germs back in '79 (which didn't even feel that important really at the time) and maybe even Altamont in '69...yeah, they're THAT good, kids..."

I enjoyed the article quite a bit, proud to be in a newspaper, with even some action shots of us jumping around and knocking each other and everybody else onto the floor. I brought it home with me from work all happy to show it to the rest of the band, thinking they'd be proud or something.

"Don't show that to me," Donald said. "They always get it wrong."

"How could they get it wrong if they haven't even written about us before?" I asked.

"Just don't show it to me." Donald said.

"Yeah, me too," Mickey said. "It'll just confuse me and give me bad ideas."

Renee said, "Here, I'll read it, just to see where he got us wrong." She grabbed the *Rabblerouser* from me and read, huffing every few seconds, rolling her eyes and shaking her head. When she finished, she said, "Mercy! That's a bit of an overly strident tone, don't you think? And how do you expect to convince people when all you do is insult them?"

But I liked the article, and by that point, I wasn't surprised by how contrary the rest of The Enchanters were about anything that could help us in some way.

Somebody else who liked the article was Morgan Pringle, the

guy who booked shows over at Latent Republican Hipster Music Club World, because that was around the time the Enchanter House phone rang at least once a day with messages begging us to please, please play shows over there. And that's when I knew something was really starting to happen.

## chapter two

The first message Pringle left on our machine was greeted with no shortage of self-righteous and vindictive laughter.

"Hey this is Morgan Pringle of Anarchy Now! Productions," the machine's speaker spoke in the disinterested stoner tone of college radio disc jockeys, "and I'm trying to reach The Enchanters about setting up a possible show here at Latent Republican Hipster Music Club World."

"Haw! Haw! Haw!" Donald laughed, looking down over the answering machine and mocking it as if it was Morgan Pringle in the flesh. "Well, look who wants us to play his shitty-ass club! Bwah haw haw!"

"Yeah," Mickey agreed in the same mocking tone. "Lah! Dee! Dah!"

Renee stared at the spinning microcassette and the blinking light of the answering machine. A slight smirk spread across her mouth, dimples emerging like she wanted to say something, but held back.

"We've seen all the press coverage you've been getting," Pringle continued, sounding bored with the very idea of talking to us, "and we were thinking it would be cool to do like a month-long residency every Monday this September, so give me a call and we'll take it from there," and then he added a "thanks" like an insincere afterthought before hanging up.

"He'll have to do *much* better than that," Renee sighed.

"What, he thinks we're some jerkoff suburban punk band or something?" Donald laughed. "Yes, Renee, much better indeed."

The night before on the local news, The Enchanters were the main focus of an "investigative report." I taped it and we watched it over and over again that week as Pringle kept calling and calling, leaving a neverending narcoleptic barrage of messages, practically begging us to play (in an uberhip, noncommittal way, of course) as we laughed at him and laughed at our very own news report.

Of course, we refused to speak with the media, and there's a great shot of Donald yelling "[BLEEP!] off!" and leaping over some hedges to avoid the camera focusing in on him as he was getting out of his car and going to work, the first nail in the collective coffins of our straight job employment.

I kept the VHS recording of the story in my box of "ENCHANTER CRAP," and I like watching it at least once a year, if only for the laughs of watching people overreact to something deep down we thought was just post-teenage kicks. Here's a transcription:

**Channel 8: Kids in Krisis: A Special Report, July 20th, 199-**

***Marla Opsahl, Reporter:*** *"...and as of right now, the lifeguards have told us they expect to have Scrappy the Waterskiing Squirrel back in the water after two days of rest, recovery, and resuscitation. Reporting live via satellite from Dolphin Beach, I'm Marla Opsahl. Back to you, Bob.*

***Bob Weech, Anchorman:*** *Thanks, Marla. Our thoughts and prayers are with that tough little squirrel. In other news, our top story tonight is on a homegrown youth culture overtaking Sprawlburg Springs's teenagers. But does it go too far? Action 8's Investigative Reporter Michelle Chioji looked into the strange new phenomenon surrounding the mysterious rock group called The Enchanters...*

[Shot of Scott dressed in the full Enchanter uniform.]

***Michelle Chioji:*** *Just when you thought you'd seen it all with shocking teenage fashion, get ready for this.*

[Close-up sequence shots of the different accoutrements on Scott's body—six-pack rings, football helmet, orange skin, pink penny loafers as the Billy Joel hit *It's Still Rock n' Roll to Me* plays.]

***Michelle Chioji:*** *This is Scott, age seventeen. This ridiculous get-up means he's a fan of the mysterious musical group The Enchanters, and one of a growing legion of fans of a totally new genre of music with the unusual name Protomersh.*

***Michelle*** [off-camera]*: What does "Protomersh" mean to you?*

***Scott*** [looking down at the driveway away from the camera]*: It*

*means whatever I want it to mean, but today I think it means...*
*oh, I don't care. It just means ignoring the conservative media*
*and not following the dead subcultures of previous generations*
*and making something that can't be used to sell automobiles to*
*schmucks.*

**Michelle Chioji:** *Is that why you're dressed like you are? Aren't*
*you just following your friends?*

**Scott:** *You're right.* [He removes one of his six-pack ring necklaces.]
*Here Michelle. I want you to have this. It's a token of the love I've*
*felt for you since I was fourteen.*

**Michelle Chioji** [Voiceover as the camera shows her politely trying
to decline the necklace]*: Is this just the newest version of Elvis*
[slo-mo shot of Elvis shaking his pelvis]*, or the Beatles* [slo-mo
shot of The Beatles on Ed Sullivan]*? No way, says Sprawlburg*
*Springs Top Cop Ed Halbig.*

**Police Chief Ed Halbig** [Seated at his desk, a triple-chinned,
leather-faced good ol' boy with skin almost as orange as Scott's]:
*This music these Enchanters play drives kids insane.* [Cut to
Michelle Chioji sitting on the other side of Halbig's desk nodding
sympathetically.] *When we stop these secret parties, there's*
*always nudity, fights and lots of vandalism.*

[Cut to random scenes of vandalized garages, cars, and homes
from the Oak Meadow Hunt Club Preserve Trail subdivision,
wherein the viewer sees smashed windows, slashed tires, and
graffiti like "JOCKS ARE ENCHANTERS ARE FAGS."]

**Michelle Chioji** [Voiceover]*: According to Chief Halbig, scenes like*
*these are all too common.*

**Chief Halbig:** *There was indecent exposure, vandalism to property,*
*lewd and lascivious conduct, and if it continues, before we know*
*it, there will even be harassment of tourists! We can't allow this*
*to continue. We don't want The Enchanters playing in this town.*
*Their music has negative effects on the community.*

**Michelle Chioji:** *Who are these Enchanters, and why are they*
*making such disturbing music? None of the members of the*
*group would talk to us.* [Cut to Donald getting out of his car at
work, seeing the cameras, covering the lens then running off to
duck behind some hedges while yelling, "[BLEEP!] off! I'm an
artist! I don't have to explain myself to you liars!" Cut back to
Scott staring right into the camera, not unlike a trash-talking
professional wrestler.]

**Scott:** *The Enchanters are better than you. They have no interest in justifying themselves to people too dumb to get it. It's like anything truly ground-breaking that happens in this world, from Jesus to the Velvet Underground. Confronted with world-changing greatness, the average person reaches for their tar, feathers, nails, hammers, crosses, lynching ropes, and that's just what you're doing to The Enchanters. Thirty years from now, their music will sell maple syrup.*

**Michelle Chioji:** *How'd you get your skin all orange like that?*

**Scott:** *Oh, shut up.*

**Michelle Chioji:** *What can you tell about these secret parties?*

**Scott:** *What are you talking about?*

**Chief Ed:** *We're trying to infiltrate this underground house party network where these Enchanterniks play secret parties announced to their cult just hours before they start. This is more than just some rock band, Michelle. The Enchanters make people get naked, make people lose their inhibitions. This kind of thing must be stopped before somebody gets hurt.*

**Scott** [staring longingly at Michelle Chioji]: *I just like music. Do you like coffee? Do you wanna go out some time? My treat?*

**Michele Chioji** [Standing, live, with the traffic of Apple Avenue zooming by in the background]: *Bob, Chief Halbig assured me these secret Enchanter parties are getting closer and closer to being shut down because they're starting to know where they're at [sic], and as you can see from Scott's appearance, the Chief should really have no problem finding out who the Enchanter fans are. Reporting live from downtown, this is Michelle Chioji for Action 8 News.*

And so much for the liberal media. For a solid week, watching this video was our post-practice entertainment. We crammed together on the couch, Mickey working the VCR remote, rewinding the piece over and over again.

"Well my fellow Enchanterniks," I asked after the first time we watched, damn near pissing ourselves with laughter. "What do you think?"

Everybody laughed, and Donald especially loved Scott's role in the spectacle. "He's really understanding us!" Donald beamed and cheered every time Scott appeared on the screen. "Everything out of his mouth is perfect! He's the perfect spokesperson for us!"

Renee's only response, besides yelling "Oh my goodness!" at every stupid thing they said about us was to add, when the laughter subsided, "Watch. Because of this so-called exposé on our scene? And its sensationalized focus on fashion? Our audience is going to be much dumber."

She was right, of course. The parties were hard enough to pull off, and thanks to the news, we were discovered by a whole new audience with freshly applied orange skin (the kind with the "e-z removal" so there was no trace of it by Monday morning at 9AM), slumming tragically hip types looking to be noticed by everyone, as if anybody gave a damn because they were so busy focusing on themselves. The secret concerts weren't well-kept secrets anymore. We didn't even bother bringing our instruments because we knew the cops would show up before we got to play, before any bands got to play.

The taped news report was no longer funny. July dragged into the kind of taint-chafing August humidity that made even a simple trip to the mailbox a sticky sweat ordeal. We were supposed to play some backyard party near Commuter State, and when we got there, the cops had already arrived, seven cop cars parked haphazardly along both sides of the narrow side street, and it was still daylight. We just drove the van right on by and didn't look back.

"We're fucked," was all Donald said on the way home. "We now have no place to play. How much longer 'til we move?"

"We have about half the money we need," Renee said, staring out the passenger window at the same old sad scene of Cimarron Boulevard. "But it was just starting to get good, don't you think?"

Two days later, Mickey returned to the Enchanter House from work with an announcement.

"They fired me," he said. "Because of the color of my skin."

I wanted to laugh, but really it wasn't that funny, because my own employment was tenuous at best. He had to use the money he saved up so he could just exist from day to day. Cathy helped in some ways, but when she wasn't around, Mickey's consumption of wine and cough syrup doubled, and while it didn't affect his bass playing, it did make hanging out with him even stranger. Like, he spent lots of time looking at those holographic 3-D image pictures that only appear after you slowly pull them away from your face and your eyes adjust to the mishmash of colors. He thought they were the greatest things in the world, forcing them into my hands when I returned to work, all like, "Look at this one, Shaq! Just look at it!"

I'd take the picture, hold it in front of my eyes and unenthusiastically remark, "Oh look at that. It's a teddy bear!"

"Yeah! Isn't that killer?" Mickey did this for hours on the big blue bean bag, listening to the white noise of Lou Reed's *Metal Machine Music* until he passed out and drooled.

Donald's hours were reduced to two weekday lunch shifts over at Happy Time America Food and Drink World.

"I think they're afraid to just go and fire me," Donald said when he returned from work with the news. "They couldn't even admit it was because of the band or my face or anything like that. I think they think I'd show up there with a gun or something if they fired me. Like I'd be so disgruntled to never have to dress like Uncle Sam again for senior citizens." No matter the real reason, Donald used this time to practice guitar. From the early morning until it was time to practice with the rest of us in the early evening, Donald's amplifier was loud and unrelenting, the notes a constant frustrated search for something more original than what we were already doing.

My job lingered like an unwelcome guest. Dan the Aspiring Improv Actor started calling me "Mater," because he thought I looked like a tomato with my face paint, and the nickname spread throughout the kitchen to everybody except Bobby the Dishwasher and Ron Cozumel, but Ron Cozumel wasn't pleased with my performance as of late. He called me into his office after a lunch shift in which I was obviously hungover and making the Shitton of Meat Sandwiches lackadaisically.

"Shaquille, I'm just gonna lay it on the line," Ron Cozumel said, standing behind his desk and leaning into his fists as leverage. "You're screwing up royally. Royally! You gotta turn yourself around, straighten yourself out."

"All right," I said, half-listening, trying not to focus on any one thing in that ugly yellowish office because of the spins.

"I'm serious here, Shaquille. I really don't want to fire you, but I will if this keeps up. This band you're in is destroying your life."

I gave a quick snortlaugh and said, "It's not destroying..."

"No it is," Ron Cozumel continued, stepping back from the desk and fiddling with his watch. "Be careful."

I said I'd try harder, knowing deep down I wouldn't.

"Mater!" Dan yelled from the middle of the kitchen. "We need you and your nice red skin to make us a sammich, duder!"

"Fuck off," I mumbled, shuffling off to the line, wanting to quit right then and there, but who else would hire me, looking like I did?

Renee's job was OK for the time being, because the boutique shampoo industry is a little more liberal than food service and convenience stores, but only a little. We still needed another two months worth of savings to at least get out of town, but there was little hope of any of us getting more employment, and besides, nobody wanted to take on anything more that would get in the way of practicing.

So we were stuck. But Pringle kept calling, asking us to play his club, and the more he called, the more his persistence made us think. Because our practices around that time, while as intense, crazy, and sweaty as always, lacked any clear sense of purpose, because there wasn't one. We had taken things as far as we could take them in Sprawlburg Springs. There was no place else to go, no place else to play. Except Latent Republican Hipster Music Club World. We still practiced for its own sake, but there was nothing to look forward to.

"*Sanford and Son* is on," Mickey announced at the end of one of these practices, unplugging his bass and packing it up into his case. On the surface, the practice was like any other: the sweat sprayed, our bodies lunged and crashed, but it felt like we were just going through the motions, except there were no "motions" in an Enchanters practice except striving for spontaneous combustion.

"Wait stop please," Renee spoke in the microphone. "No *Sanford and Son* tonight. I have an announcement. I think we should play these shows at Latent Republican Hipster Music Club World."

"I agree," I said, throwing my sticks behind me and standing up to stretch and pluck the moisture from my sweat-stained green T-shirt.

"Of course you agree," Donald said, wringing out the sweat from his orange T-shirt until the moisture dripped and formed a puddle on the linoleum floor. "You always agree with your girlfriend."

"And you always agree with your brother," I answered, annoyed, and it took Donald back that I even said anything since I usually just ignored his snide remarks.

"Pringle's not interested in us beyond how we can help him," Donald continued.

"That's right," Mickey said, nodding his head. "Not interested."

"But we need a place to play, something to look forward to," Renee said, still into the microphone. She always spoke in the microphone when we practiced, and it always gave her an authority the rest of us couldn't reach. "Things are different now. We clearly—clearly!—cannot play these concerts in people's homes anymore. This is the only option we have, and it's our only chance to get the money we need to get out of here."

"Pringle's a phony, a jerkoff, and he's not trying to help us, at all, and—"

"But he will be, intentionally or not," Renee said.

"Will you stop yelling into the microphone?!" Donald yelled, removing his guitar and dropping it on the floor by his feet.

"No."

"Well I think we should play those shows because it's our only option," I said, stepping around the sparkly red drum set and walking through the confrontational space between Renee and Donald. I had to piss, and by that point, *Sanford and Son* was sounding really ideal, compared to these futile arguments we always had about every little thing.

Mickey followed me out of the practice space, and Renee and Donald argued for another half hour while Mickey and I sat in the living room silently watching *Sanford and Son*, bonding in that quiet way unique to the rhythm section of bands, when you know the argument ain't yours to fight, and you've already made up your mind anyway, so it's hard to take as seriously as the so-called "driving forces" of the band do. Renee was clearly audible over the microphone: "We need this...no...it's important...where else can we play...we need something to look forward to...this is our job now....what else is there?" Mickey stretched out on the big blue beanbag and held 3-D pictures inches over his face.

"Hey..." Mickey yawned from under a stack of images,

"Who cares, man. We should just do those shows. We need a new venue."

"Well go tell them that's how you feel so they know it's now 3-1 and we can end this dumbass argument already."

"OK." Mickey went off to the practice space. Finally, Renee's annoying microphone was silent, and aside from a few random curses from Donald, the matter was settled. We would meet with Morgan Pringle in person the next day and work out the details.

We cancelled practice the next evening (a rarity) and piled into the Midnite Fantaseas van, headed for our tiny downtown and Latent Republican Hipster Music Club World. The interstate opened up in the post-rush hour blitz of late-leaving commuters eager to get home and early-going fun-seekers zooming whoknowswhere, their early-evening optimism unmitigated by experience, which should have told them there's nothing here, or maybe they had the good times in this town the rest of us never could. Maybe somewhere past all these billboards and apartment complexes, through the heat and the spectacle, these dudes in their customized trucks found whatever it was we wanted, and gave no thought to being anywhere but right here, right now, on the interstate, breezing along past off-ramps leading to streets named after Confederate war heroes.

Sometimes, the interstate was all right. When the light hit the lakes at the perfect angle and the waves glittered like a roomful of chandeliers, when the sky was nothing but cobalt and a burnt egg yolk sunset. The act of going somewhere, past scenery you knew so well, with laughing friends and the windows down to let in the almost extinct smell of orange blossoms. It's always an optimistic time of night, and oftentimes, the high point of the entire evening, because there's no room for disappointment, no place for expectations.

I drove, of course, with Donald in the passenger seat, both of us drinking cans of Buck Urine Lite packed in identical red, white and blue beer cozies reading: "Vote with Your Feet: Reagan '84!" Our windows were down and we all wore aviator sunglasses ("Because we need to look cool on the interstate," Renee insisted). The Minutemen's *Double Nickels on the Dime* kept us relatively quiet, except Donald, who punched me in the arm after a musical epiphany came out of the speakers (which, on that record, happens almost every second) and said, "See? Why can't you do that on drums?"

"Why can't you do that on guitar?" was my logical response.

"Because I suck," was all Donald could think to say. "What's your excuse?"

"I don't know what I'm doing," I shrugged. "I just hits 'em."

"And hits 'em you do, Little Buddy," Mickey called out from the far backseat. I looked through the rearview mirror, and Renee was staring through the purple curtained window at the scenery, smiling. She caught me staring, looked at me through the rearview mirror and said, "Isn't this nice?"

I smiled, feeling like we were on a field trip in school. Donald belted out *Jesus and Tequila*: "My life, Jesus and Tequila, I'm satisfied, and I can't deny it..."

Then we all joined in: "Remember, Jesus and Tequila; I'm satisfied, and I can't deny it..."

At sunset, Latent Republican Hipster Music Club World was dim, desolate and isolated, like we'd climbed into an attic. Light beams reflected dust particles into the brass rails that kept drunks from stumbling into the square lower level that was just five feet below. Tables with unlit candles and drink special displays slept on exquisitely varnished hardwood floors next to these three rails; where the fourth rail might have been was where you stepped down to the lower level straight ahead from the entrance, for a more intimate view of the band. The bar stretched the length of the club, which may have been half a football field but it was hard to tell because I was always drunk when I was there. But it was twice the length of the stage on its opposite side, laid out with thin cheap brown carpeting haphazardly stapled to the back brick wall full of 8 X 11" framed and autographed glossies of now-dead Impulse! and Chess Records artists, a reminder that this place used to be called the "Jazz and Blues Club" before it had pretensions of self-conscious swankiness. Neon blue martini glasses with little neon green olives hung around here there and everywhere in case you forgot what it had become.

The only sign of life, if you wanna call it that, was this horrible fusion jazz music noodling over the PA. "Hull-loooo?" Renee called over the lower level of the club, leaning over the rail like a kid bon voyaging from a cruise ship. The whole scene felt like one of those *Twilight Zone* episodes where the whole world is abandoned and nobody knows why.

"Where are your helmets?" Morgan Pringle emerged out of the darkness from the other side of the room. He descended the steps and approached us in a hurried pace, like somebody late for a very important meeting, star-tattooed arms swinging rapidly, the silhouette of the obligatory trucker's hat upon his head making him look a little bit taller and square headed than he actually was.

We just stared at him. I had no respect for the guy. For all his swagger about being "the only punk booker in town," he never booked anything particularly interesting, or, more to the point, anything that wouldn't be a "big draw" for him and this limp-dick jazz club.

He ran up the stairs to shake our hands, and I saw him immediately for what he was, one of those jerks who thought punk rock was about being a Good Citizen, a secret club for pseudo-misfits who desperately wanted to fit in in high school but were too damn dorky, so now they're making up for lost time by turning punk into just another clique in the smorgasbord of adolescent drah-muh. Conforming nonconformists. Anti-snob snobs. They disgusted me to the very core of my being.

It was the wifebeater T-shirt, with arms covered in hackneyed tattoos (stars, Celtic runes, symbols, cartoon characters), the clamdigger jeanshorts, the thick wallet chain dangling down the right side of said jeanshorts to his knees, white low-cut Chuck Taylors, the little ears pierced and covered with rings and cuffs, the big brown beard, all of it rolled into everything we hated, everything phony.

"We're not punk," Donald informed him, turning down his offered hand with a dismissive wave. "We're Protomersh, and helmets are passé, like this smooth jazz bullshit."

"Language!" Renee whispered loud enough for everyone to hear. "Hi, Mr. Pringle," she said in her "professional" voice as they shook hands, speaking to him like an overly polite teenage boy meeting his girlfriend's parents for the first time. "It's a pleasure meeting you. Sorry about Donald, sir, but he's naturally quite upset because you've never been around to see us play, and it has been nearly impossible to play any concerts around town."

"And your bouncers pick on us every time we come and watch the lousy bands you book," I said, also refusing the handshake.

Pringle stepped back and stared at us through dead fish eyes. "Well, as for the jazz, I have no control over that. I just book shows here. As for getting thrown out, you shouldn't throw food at bands. That offends me, not just as a punk rocker, but as a human being."

"Oh, blow it out your ass!" Donald yelled. "Let's go. I have no interest in having anything to do with this self-righteous turd gobbler!"

"Donald!" Renee said in exasperated tones. "Please. He's trying to help us."

"Fine," Donald said, stepping back, inhaling, then exhaling. "What do you want with us?"

Pringle nervously rattled his tongue piercing around his teeth before speaking. "Do you want to play here or not?"

Donald sneered then started to speak, but Renee covered his mouth and spoke over him, with an indulgent smile as if to say, "Guitar players! What *ever* can you do?" "What would you like to offer us?" Renee asked.

"I want to give you a month-long residency here every Thursday in September," Pringle said, focused on Renee and Renee alone, like how servers in restaurants tend to only make eye contact with the person at the table they think is the most pleasant. You headline, you pick the bands, we'll do the rest. How about it?"

Light was no longer beaming through the windows, and the random car honks and sub-woofer bass of Apple Avenue leaked into the club.

"What's in it for us?" Donald demanded, stepping back from all of us to stick out his bird-like chest.

"Where else are we gonna play, bro?" Mickey asked, followed by an immediate loud-whispered "Shut it, douche!" from Donald.

"Can we discuss this as a group, alone, for a couple minutes?" Renee asked Pringle, smiling.

"Just give a yell when you know," Pringle said, readjusting his trucker's cap, then, standing and walking back to the dark side of the club.

The four of us turned our chairs toward each other and conspired, leaning in and whispering like we were planning a bank heist.

"Fuck this guy," Donald said. "He's a lying shitheel. I don't wanna play here."

"Well I do," Renee said. Mickey and I nodded in agreement. "Whatever his motivations, there's nowhere else to play, and this is our only way out of here."

"You're outvoted," I said. "Again."

"All right, all right!" Donald said, annoyed with losing another argument. "But let's milk this for all it's worth. If we're so important to him, we can make some demands. Otherwise, we don't play."

"What do you mean?" Renee asked.

"I mean like guarantees," Donald said, scooting in his chair even closer to us. "You know: Contractual riders? Like Van Halen, how they got all the brown M&M's removed from their backstage candy jars?"

"Guarantees," Mickey said, looking up to the ceiling and smiling, "Yeah...fuckin', I have some ideas."

"So let's make a list," Donald said, leaning back, hands behind his head. "We could definitely use this to make sure we have enough cash to move to Brooklyn, right?"

Renee had two pieces of scrap paper in her purse: one for us, and a copy for Morgan Pringle. On the back of an old crumpled party flier, Donald wrote the conditions for the performances of our residency at Latent Republican Hipster Music Club World, with contributions from all of us:

ENCHANTERS LIST OF DEMANDS
1. WE WANT A $75 GUARANTEE FOR EACH SHOW
2. FOUR BOTTLES OF RED WINE (THE GOOD STUFF)
3. $5 ADMISSION FEE
4. FREE CUPCAKES TO THE 54TH PERSON WHO WALKS IN THE DOOR
5. MICKEY GETS TWO FREE MASSAGES BEFORE AND AFTER THE SHOW BY A SWEDISH MASSEUSE (FEMALE) (CERTIFIED)
6. TWO EXTRA LARGE PIZZAS, ONE HAWAIIAN (HAM AND PINEAPPLE), THE OTHER WITH SPINACH AND GARLIC
7. ONE CHOCOLATE CAKE WITH THE WORDS: "THIS CAKE IS FOR THE ENCHANTERS AND ALL THEIR HARD WORK ON BEHALF OF THE PEOPLE OF SPRAWLBURG SPRINGS" WRITTEN IN CALLIGRAPHY ON CORNFLOWER BLUE

ICING

8. ALL-AGES ADMISSION
9. NO MEDIA
10. NO SKINHEADS
11. THE BOUNCERS MUST WEAR STRAP-ON DILDOS. NO EXCEPTIONS
12. WE WANT A LIFE-SIZED ICE SCULPTURE OF RED FOXX FAKING A HEART ATTACK
13. BEFORE WE PLAY, WE WANT THE P.A. PLAYING JEFF FOXWORTHY'S "YOU MIGHT BE A REDNECK" ROUTINE ON REPEAT
14. OUR FRIENDS GET IN FOR FREE

Obviously, there was a whole lot of giggling as we made this list, and outright laughter when Donald read them off, and it all sounded fine, except Mickey said, "Hey, let's get $100 instead of $75. Let's really stick it to him."

"Nah," Donald said. "We don't wanna get greedy."

"Yes we do," Renee said. "It'll get us out of here that much quicker."

So Donald scratched out "$75" and wrote in "$100" instead. We beckoned for Pringle. Donald handed him the piece of paper. "If you don't agree to these," he said, "we don't play. End of story."

Pringle read the list, smiling as Donald stood over his shoulder. "Well," Pringle said in a tone that, in hindsight clearly betrayed that he was trying his best not to laugh, "I can see I'm dealing with some hard bargainers."

"You're goddamn right," Donald said. "So is it a deal or not?'

"Well...OK," Pringle said, looking our list up and down, "but here's the deal: My bouncers don't wear strap-on dildos, there will be no massages, no sculptures of Red Foxx, and, thank God, no recordings of Jeff Foxworthy, but we can realistically give you the rest, and let's up the guarantee to $300, if not more, because you'll be filling this place up. Deal?"

Pringle extended his hand to Donald, who was as taken aback as the rest of us at the prospect of getting paid $300 to do what we did; $300 to play our music. That's like getting paid to spit a loogie in Glenda Hood's face.

There was a long silence, but even Donald had to admit it

sounded fair. "Deal," Donald said, shaking his hand. We quickly parted ways, but not before assurances we would call when we knew which bands were playing on what nights, and that was that, and it was back to the purple van and back to the Minutemen, with a renewed sense of purpose.

It was now dark beyond the interstate, with nothing but light reflectors along the center strip of the highway to guide us home. We went back to the Enchanter House, and, in a celebratory mood, got drunk and listened to records.

For the life of me, I can't remember what we talked about that night until just before we passed out, except we didn't talk about the one thing on all of our minds, that we would soon be leaving Sprawlburg Springs, and, this time next year, we would be making music—sweet, sweet music—in Brooklyn.

When the wine was gone, Renee and I fell into her bed, and Renee slurred, "Shhhhaq...you're the funniest...I luuuuuv yewwwww."

"An' I...I...luv yewwww, Rrrrenee," I managed to expel through a voice knocked uncoordinated from wine and excitement.

"Ah, shaddap." Renee sounded like an old Warner Brothers cartoon when she said that, pushing me away with her arms, then they fell on the mattress, and she passed out. I soon followed. It was the only time—drunk or sober—we said we loved each other.

# chapter three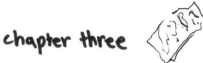

We used some of the moving money we kept stashed in this faded off-white "Patagonian Masters" cigar box to invest in creating and copying two super-nice 11x17 fliers.

The first flier was a crudely drawn still-life sketch I made with a black licorice-scented marker of tomatoes, eggs and rocks one night after practice, below which I wrote the caption, "Hit Me. See if I Care."

The second flier was a sherbet orange representation of the Sprawlburg Springs normally brown city flag—only, instead of the city's seal in the middle (a green Casselberry tree sprouting out of a gray parking lot encircled by intertwined palm fronds), we replaced it with a picture of Andy Kaufman standing next to five-time professional wrestling champeen "Classy" Freddie Blassie. In straight lines angled upward, we wrote the when's and the where's and the names of the bands we'd be playing with in stark black lettering.

We asked all of our friends' bands to play with us, all of whom enthusiastically agreed. When Renee called Scott and asked if The Cabrini Green Preservation Society would be interested in opening up for us during the second Thursday of our "residency," she had to hold the phone away from her ear because he wouldn't stop wailing for joy. I was seated on the big blue beanbag on the other side of the room and I could still hear the, "Oh my GOD!!! I...I...oh my GOD!!! Yes...oh yes...we'll definitely...fuckin'...oh my GOD!!!" It was like that with all the bands we asked.

In the heat, we drove all over town with the a/c cranked, pasting fliers everywhere we could, and quite a few places we couldn't. Abandoned strip malls where skaters practiced and passed around brown-bagged bottles of malt liquor, boarded-up, long-forgotten fast food restaurants like "Admiral Chuckles Seafaring Restaurant Ahoy World" shaped like tugboats plopped on land, bus stop benches where nobody ever waited, ugly gray concrete light posts, all of them covered with a thick coat from our trusty white buckets of wheat paste then plastered with our artwork/advertising. The Brothers enjoyed hanging the fliers the most; they'd run out the side of the van before I had gotten to a full stop, Donald in a full sprint with a stack of fliers, Mickey ambling behind him with the wheatpaste, always looking over their shoulders like they were a couple of spies called The Twig and The Tomato, then Mickey would paint the walls and the backs of the fliers held out by Donald, who would then flatten them one next to the other until there were two rows of fliers and the writing was impossible to miss from the street. Then they'd sprint back in and I'd drive them off to the next good spot pointed out by Renee, our shotgun-riding sentinel.

"Are you all right?" Renee asked as Mickey and Donald were fifty feet away on another clandestine flier mission on a row of concrete lamp posts. "You're not saying much."

"I'm fine," I answered, reaching across the seat to hold her hand. "I'm excited, and it's hard to put into words. All of it, like, it's happening, isn't it? It's really happening?" It was all moving so fast, I needed the reassurance.

Renee smiled, more with her green eyes than with the rest of her face. The orange from the tanning cream had faded to a light red with a sweat glaze making her look demonic, but more in an impish, adorable way than anything that was, well, demonic. She squeezed my hand and said, "Yes. I do believe so."

She leaned back in the seat and stuck the back of her free hand across her forehead and moaned, "Oh God, it's ever so hot out here. It's *so* tiresome. When we finally get out of here, we simply *must* play in snow. OK?"

I nodded, trying to remember what snow even looked like, felt like. I hadn't seen it in over ten years. Renee, Mickey and Donald had never seen it, except on TV. "Very good," Renee said. "And it *is* happening, Shaquille, and it is fun, and it is exciting, and crazy too, right?"

Yeah, it was crazy. When we took our fliers to the one independent record store in town, Obscure Pop Culture Reference CD and Record World, the ordinarily snooty clerks lost their cool, begging us to put out a record. Strangers shook our hands and said, "Thanks." When asked "For what?" their answer was invariably, "For making this town interesting." Security guards chased us out of malls, out of bank buildings, even out of Rehnquist Station— Sprawlburg Springs's attempt at snatching tourist dollars by taking a long unused train depot in the center of downtown and converting it into tacky theme restaurants, bars and T-shirt shops, with everything "olde-tyme" like the brick roads, horse-drawn carriages, men with straw hats and handlebar mustaches pushing popcorn carts, licensed, pre-approved street performers like sax players belting out only that Wham song *Careless Whispers* for four hours a night. Rehnquist Station was everything a typical middle class dumbass family could ever want from a tourist destination during the daytime, and at night, everything a typical Sprawlburg Springs single dumbass male in black silk shirts and too much hair gel could ever want. There were "Post No Bills. This is Private Property!" signs all over Rehnquist Station, but we said fuck it and put our fliers there anyway because it was an outdoor space full of streets and people.

All the yards turned brown from the heat wave. It hadn't rained in weeks. Outdoor water usage was restricted to an hour in the evening, and while it baked outside, we practiced, and practiced and practiced, and despite the rotating fans we squeezed into the practice room, we couldn't cool down, and learned to live with the heat and the sweat and made the songs even crazier until we weren't even sure if we were playing the song we had intended to play when it started. Between songs, we would wring the bottoms of our shirts until they spilled puddles onto the floor like we had just taken them out of the washing machine. When that happened, we took off the shirts, and Renee danced around and sang in her bra, and on more than one occasion, I just wore my boxers, and we even played naked a couple times. But nobody noticed or cared. The elements, the bruises, the ringing ears, Donald's hairy ass—none of it distracted us from throwing everything we had into the songs, into these shows, into getting out of town for good.

Renee and I had a tough time sleeping at night because the practices were so intense. Wide awake, the adrenaline shot through me, and my heart rattled in my ribcage like a trapped frog. My ears rang in loud high-pitched squeals, like the Emergency Broadcast System was transmitting in my eardrums. We were too tired to mess around, and too amped to sleep.

But this limbo of insomnia was good for our relationship. It gave us time to talk about us, because we were too caught up with the band and what was left of our jobs and going around town acting like goofballs to really hang out and talk. Reclined in bed, over the sounds of the ceiling fans prop plane rotations, over the nightly hearing damage we were doing to ourselves, we stayed acquainted in the darkness in ways beyond just being a drummer and a singer in a swinging musical combo.

"What do you think will happen with us when we get to Brooklyn?" Renee asked.

"I don't know. What do you mean?"

"I mean—I'm happy now, and you're happy, right?"

"Uh-huh."

"Well, I imagine the press will be all over us for interviews, and we'll be the toast of the town fairly quickly, and things will move very fast—much faster than here—and I sometimes wonder if you'll just leave me for any harlot New York City groupie seduced by your libido-stirring rhythms."

"No, Renee," I said in a reassuring tone. "Not just any harlot groupie. It would have to be a very special harlot groupie to take your place, my darling."

She punched me in the arm. Between her and Donald, my arms were always covered in purple bruises. "I mean it, Shaquille. I took a big chance dating you. I risked the band, I risked my career in show business" (As she spoke, her affected snob tone was in full effect.) "I broke a golden rule of mine about not dating fellow band members, and I don't want to waste my time if all I am to you is somebody to goof off with until somebody better comes along."

I wanted to laugh at everything she said, but I held it in in the same way I held in my farts when we shared the same bed together. With great effort, I sighed and answered, "No. No way," and then I let out the laughter, but it wasn't laughter at Renee, it was laughter at myself, and my mouth tried keeping pace with my mind as I said, "I can't even begin to tell you how bored and depressed I was before this band happened. Before I knew you, I was miserable. You can ask anybody, only, I didn't really know anybody. And now? I'm happy. Are you happy?"

"Well yeah, but—"

"All right then. And I'm having fun. Are you having fun?"

"Oh sure, Shaquille. Tons of fun. But—"

"But nothing. Everything's fine and there's nothing to worry about."

Then it was silent except for our breathing until Renee said. "I guess you're right, Shaquille. I'm getting ahead of myself here. We shouldn't worry about any of this stuff until we've actually made it to Brooklyn."

The rest of those nights, we'd just giggle at every stupid thing out of our mouths. The sleep deprivation made us even more convinced we were the two funniest people who ever lived. We knew each other better than anybody else by that point, and what was funny to us was incomprehensible to everyone around us, even Mickey and Donald.

Like, one night, we rented the movie *Kiss Meets the Phantom of the Park*, and for days after watching it, all it took to get either of us in total hysterics was for one of us to act out the scene where members of Kiss explain to the teenagers the secret to their superpowers—the medallions around their necks—and one of the kids asks, "And without your medallions?" Peter Criss, the drummer with the kitty-kat makeup, answers, in the thickest New York accent, "We'd just be oahd-nary human beins." We rewound that Peter Criss line eighteen times in a row, and I even used it on my outgoing answering machine message for a couple of days.

"Hey, Shaquille? And without your medallions?" Renee would ask in the middle of a rehearsal.

"We'd just be oahd-nary human beins."

BWA-HAW-HAW-HAW! we'd laugh while Mickey and Donald stood and stared all befuddled like we were living breathing nuclear calculus equations.

We spent hours in bed arguing, just to have something to do, about stupid shit like Mr. Pibb versus Dr. Pepper, Fred Sanford versus Jack Tripper, crates versus barrels, Mick Taylor versus Ron Wood, Werner Herzog versus Whitey Herzog, anything to murder those long hours until the laughter and the futility made the exhaustion too much to ignore and we finally fell asleep flat on our backs, just as the birds were tuning up to yell *Wake Up, Assholes!* by obscure punk rock legends The Queaf Machine.

Reporters were leaving messages almost every day for interviews. We never returned their calls, and if one of us happened to pick up the phone when they called, the procedure was to hang up immediately.

"Our music says it all," Renee huffed after hanging up on an especially persistent reporter. "There's no need to elaborate with quips."

According to Morgan Pringle, Latent Republican Hipster Music Club World was suddenly getting regular visits from health inspectors, the Food Commission, the Liquor Commission, the Fire Marshall, and grave warnings from the Police Department saying they would be around for the Enchanters show to make sure there was no underage drinking, the venue wasn't overfilled, and every little thing was within the rules and regulations. To his credit, Pringle and the club he booked for didn't back down, no matter how spurious their motives were. Apparently the club was getting lots of calls from reporters about us, and of course, the club's guesses about us were just as good (or bad) as the reporters', but Pringle kept begging us to just do one press conference so everybody could shut up and leave us alone.

Walking out of the Perimeter Square Centre Circle Mall, Scott and Jonathan were jumped and beaten up by a gang of six muscle-thug fraternity dudes in the parking lot who thought they were faggots because of how they were dressed. That evening, dozens of cars in the Perimeter Square Circle Centre Mall were vandalized: doors keyed, tires slashed, antennas snapped. We were rumored to be involved with it, even though three-quarters of us were at work when it happened and one-quarter of us were loaded on mescaline and wine at the time of the destruction. Luckily, except for the first concert I played with them, The Enchanters had escaped being recognized by the police at any time since in those three (only three!) months, always managing to escape before the house parties were shut down.

In the middle of all this insanity, which at least made one feel important, I'd have to trudge back to work through filters of exhaustion, hangovers, and the neverending rhythms stuck in my head and body, to do a job I know longer cared about for people I had no interest in ever being around. Not only had I taken the road less traveled, I was way the hell out in the thick brush, lost and eating wild berries that just might be hallucinogenic and/or poisonous. And I didn't care. Because I was happy. So happy, in fact, that two days before we were to play the first show of our residency, I punched out Dan the Improv Actor and got myself fired but good from Cleveland Steamerz Good Time Bar and Grille World.

I just snapped. We were slammed at work, and I could barely keep my eyes open. The squid filled my stainless steel table in jagged white mountains. The more I cut, the more the uncut pile grew. It's a miracle I didn't slice off a finger. My head throbbed and my arms were sore from all the drumming.

"My girlfriend says all she needs is a big dick and nice shoes," Brantley said between slices of baby tomatoes.

"Well at least you can get her nice shoes with your paycheck," Mary said, followed by much laughter.

"Pussy." "Beer." "Pussy." "Beer." "Pussy and beer." "Beer and pussy." "Yeah." "Fuck yeah." So the talk went until Kevin, the second-in-command in the kitchen yelled, "Shaquille! We got a Shitton of Meat Sandwich we need on the fly, brother!"

I dropped my knife, washed my hands and rushed over to the line cook station. The meat was precooked, the baguette premade, the toppings in front of me each in their own square plastic storage containers. Cake work. When the meat was laid out over the bread and topped with cheese, onions, and marinara, I closed the sandwich, poked it with an American flag toothpick and yelled, "Pick up!"

I immediately turned around and walked ten steps toward my squid-cutting duties when I heard Dan speak in his best mentally challenged voice, "Duh...thaaaank you, Maaater for the sammich!"

The words hit my ears, and I froze while everybody in the kitchen laughed. I thought of Scott and Jonathan, beaten up in the mall parking lot. I thought of all the insults. Faggot. Devo. I thought of all the objects thrown at us everywhere we went. Beer cans. Fast food. And we just endured it, thinking this was the price we paid for having the balls to dress like we did, to try and live our lives the way we wanted to.

I froze and pivoted on my heels, walked the five steps back to the line, and stared at the fat fucker. "Ya think you're funny, douche bag?" I yelled, sounding remarkably like Donald. "Huh, Mr. Funnyman?"

Dan was more than a little put off by this. "Damn dude, it was just a joke. Ya want some pot? It might be good for your skin."

That's when I slugged him in the jaw. One punch. Two punches. Then I stopped counting and just kept swinging, my fist crashing into the fashionably bushy bristles of Dan's black soul patch and goatee. He fell two steps back into Kevin, and while everyone was still stunned by what I did, I ran in and kept hitting him everywhere I could, yelling, "You think you're funny cocksmack? Huh, Mr. Improv?"

Then it was over. Ron pulled me off of him and dragged me out the back door. It happened so fast. I couldn't see straight. There were a couple of "What the fuck is your problem?!?" from macho voices in my face, easily rebutted with Ron's "Shut up! I'm taking care of this! Get back to work!"

Somehow, I didn't even get punched, not once. Mary and Alicia had white towels wrapped with ice pressed against Dan's face. Ron dragged me into the humidity and to my car. He threw me against the side and just stared when I slammed my back into the driver's door of my beloved Tempo.

"What's the matter with you ? Dan was kidding. He's always kidding." Ron finally said.

I wanted to cry, but managed to keep it in. "He's not funny." I said, catching my breath.

Ron ran his hand through his thinning scalp, looking back to the restaurant, then up to the sky, then back to me. "I have to fire you, " he said. "You know that, right?" I nodded. "I don't want to fire you, Shaquille, but I see no other alternative. Do you?"

I shook my head "no." I had nothing else to say about it. I made my point.

"You can't fight every single person who gives you crap for looking like you do," Ron said. "You know that, right?"

I shrugged. "I gotta fire you," Ron repeated, more to himself than me. "There's no getting around that one. I don't want to, Shaquille, I just want you to know that. You're one of the smartest people I now, and I don't think you even realize how smart you are, but what you did in there? Was stupid. You're making it difficult on yourself, more difficult than it has to be. But you probably knew that already. I just wonder if there's ever gonna be anything good, in the long term, coming out of it."

I wanted to tell Ron that there already was good out of it that more than made up for the relatively minor bad, and that, for once, I felt free and important, like I was doing exactly what I was put on this earth to do, and how rare is that? But instead, I extended my hand to shake and said, "Thanks, Mr. Cozumel. For everything. And I'm sorry it didn't work out."

He shook my hand, shook his head, looked down, started to say something, but cut himself off and just said, "We'll mail you your check," and he walked back into the kitchen. I drove away and did my best not to think about it, which was easy enough. Our show was in just two days, and the next day, we had finally agreed to hold a quick press conference just so we'd be left alone.

With all the preparations, there was no time to pause and reflect on my newfound unemployment, just move move move. I told Renee before yet another rehearsal, and all she said was "Good. Now you have more time to practice those drums. It was bound to happen..."

We agreed to the press conference only because it was too ridiculous to pass up.

"When will we ever get another chance to hold a press conference...in Sprawlburg Springs anyway?" Renee said, and the matter was settled.

We sat behind a table on the stage of Latent Republican Hipster Music Club World while the flashbulbs popped and the

press asked us questions from the bowl area from twenty-five folding chairs sprawled across.

"I'm not saying a word," Donald announced every few minutes, as we made the late morning hideous traffic in the rumbling purple van, me at the wheel, of course, en route to our date with the local media.

"I never have anything to say about it, so why would I wanna talk now?" Mickey said.

"Me too," I threw in, not sure if it really mattered to them.

"Fine," Renee said. "I'll do all the talking. Shaquille, please hurry. We're running late."

"Good," Donald said. "Make the pussies wait."

We managed to get there only fifteen minutes late. Pringle whisked us inside. Flashbulbs exploded before our eyes could adjust from the sunshine outside to the dim inside of the club. Next thing we know, we're behind a wooden table on stage in a row of seats, from left to right: me, Renee, Donald, and Mickey. We sat there and squinted, feeling very confused.

"So what do we do now?" I whispered to everyone.

Renee sat down last, wearing lemon-colored pants with avocado green splotches and a Duncan Hines brown blouse buttoned conservatively to the top.

"There's no need to worry," Renee said, pulling out a folded-up sheet of notebook paper from her left front pocket.

None of us wore our helmets, and we hadn't reapplied our bright orange skin cream in a couple of days. We were trying to look nice. I even combed my hair. We wanted reporters to think we actually cared about how we were representing ourselves to them.

Renee sat down and cleared her throat into the microphone directly in her face. She smiled at the reporters below her, and read a brief prepared statement. "Hello. We are The Enchanters. As some of you have heard, we're playing a concert here at this venue tomorrow." (Ripples of polite laughter ensued from the reporters.) "We do hope we see new faces there. The fifty-fourth paying customer will win some cupcakes." (More laughter.) "That was not meant to be funny. It is true. Anyway, um," Renee continued, scratching the bridge of her nose and looking away from the written statement before reading again, "We hope everybody likes us and there are no incidents provoked by outside forces. Me and the fellows here," she said, pointing to the three of us, after which Mickey and I waved and Donald sulked, "have been practicing and practicing for this, so we hope it's a special night for everybody. Thank you." We stood to leave, but then Renee stopped herself and said, "Oh wait. Sorry. Any questions?"

The questions were fast and not unfurious, and Renee handled them all like a real media whiz.

"Will you be starting a riot tomorrow?"

"Oh gosh, no! We just hope everything's terrific and people get inspired to start bands like we did."

"What kind of drugs do you use?"

"What a silly question. Why do you equate creativity and original thinking with drug abuse?" This answer made Mickey and Donald shift a little bit in their seats until Renee added, "And what would it matter if it did? We're responsible ay-dults."

"You never talk to your fans. Why do you hate them?"

"We don't talk to our fans because we're very shy. Especially these boys. It's the secret to our vast success."

Even if the rest of us had wanted to speak, we couldn't have gotten in a word over Renee's constant rapid-fire responses. And the reporters were charmed. It was something in her delivery, the matteroffactedness of it, that had the reporters laughing in spite of themselves. Renee had that effect on people.

Once the reporters used all their powers of journalistic analysis to realize we weren't terrorists, the questions went from fastballs at the head to softballs lobbed into the strike zone. This gave Mickey and me some chances to open our mouths.

"We're moving to Brooklyn soon and we're gonna live in a loft and I'll get to be the bartender when we put on shows," Mickey announced.

"My name's Shaquille and I'm the drummer!" My comment was ignored.

Even Donald finally got into it, when somebody asked, "Are The Enchanters really crazy or are you just putting us on?"

In his best Keith Richards mumble, Donald said, "We're just puttin' ya on," and smiled, standing up to leave. But there was one last question, from the legendary and retired rock critic Rollie St. Bacon.

Through the soft lights in our faces, I could barely make him out down in the press corps. He stood out. His gray hair looked pasted and greasy across his scalp, like he hadn't gotten around to washing it in quite awhile. He had a bushy gray mustache riding the sides of his lips that went down to his chin. He wore a beat-up old leather jacket over a faded black and blue GERMS T-shirt. He looked a little haggard, in marked contrast to the pretties from TV and the manicured uglies who were the other reporters.

"Rollie St. Bacon here," he yelled, and Donald looked out and sat back down. "Hey, what's up?" Donald waved. "We like you."

"This is the only man who gets us," Renee announced.

"Well thanks," Rollie said, smiling. "My only question is this: How do you stand it here? I mean, are these shows going to be your, ya know, proverbial, Big Ticket outta here?"

"That was two questions," Renee said, smiling, then standing up to leave.

"But thanks for the nice words, Rollie," I added, because he was the only writer I read. "If there were more like you, we'd stay here."

We smiled and waved goodbye, Renee even shook Pringle's dead-fish hand and said, "Thanks! That was fun!"

"Boy, that was silly, huh?" Renee said as we ran back into the van and sped away.

"Yeah. Retarded." Donald answered. "Makes me doubt what's reported as news."

That was all we said about it on the ride home because we started arguing about which wine went better with cough syrup: cabernet or chablis.

The papers barely reported it, mentioning the shows in a brief two paragraph story deep in the back of the front page, focused on how we weren't looking for trouble, with a counterpoint from Police Chief Halbig finding our claim very hard to believe. The TV stations didn't even think our comments were newsworthy. We presented a contradictory image to what they wanted, which was, presumably, a lot of swearing and insults and "punk rock" behavior. But we weren't punk rock. We were the next step beyond it. Protomersh, which was probably, ultimately, just another label for the same old style of wild music that brings the waking dead back to life since, well, forever, but we wanted to believe it was different, and lots of people, for good or ill, agreed.

That night, Renee and I lay in her bed, catching our breath

after sex.

"You know," she said. "After tomorrow, a lot of things are gonna be different."

"Yeah, I know," I said.

"But it's gonna turn out fine, I think," she said.

I cuddled up to her shoulder and closed my eyes, breathing in the wine of her breath, the sweat of her skin, the vanilla air freshener of her room. Going to sleep like that, I realized that everything had already turned out fine, regardless of what happened at these shows. *I'm only livin' to be lyin' by your side* sung out through my head and heart. There was nothing else for me but Renee and The Enchanters, nothing outside of this but a stupid town owned and operated by stupid people who saw nothing in the natural beauty of this place but an investment to destroy and build endless tacky shit.

*Tomorrow*, I thought before sleeping, *it'll all change.*

chapter four

We arrived at Latent Republican Hipster Music Club World early enough to load in our equipment, and there were already kids in football helmets and orange skin lined up outside the front door and down the sidewalk as Apple Avenue's rush hour traffic rumbled by and slowed down to stare at them under the sunshine. Nobody in line looked familiar, but they saw us and yelled, "Hey! It's The Enchanters!" while cheering, yelling, and clapping. Lugging Mickey's bass amp, Renee and I smiled and waved with our free hands like game show hosts.

Gone were our helmets, and orange skin, and all that hoohaw. We wanted to scale down our fashion, or, Renee did, and we just followed her lead.

"I'm bored with playing dress up," Renee said on the afternoon of the show. "It's so passé, so...*July*." So, instead, we wore jeans and white T-shirts with handwritten slogans across the front in black lettering. Renee's shirt read, "SAYONARA SUCKERS." Mickey's read, "THANKS. THANKS FOR NUTHIN'." Donald's read: "EAT A BAG O' DICKS, FELLOW CITIZENS." Mine read, "THREE CHEERS FOR FRIENDSHIP!" Besides this, the only slightly unusual thing about any of us was Renee's green lipstick.

It was strange having fans instead of friends. You'd look at these people as they looked back at you and you wondered what they were expecting. They had seen the news reports and heard the legend without hearing the music, not seeing us because they never knew where to see us, and then, there we were.

A couple of big bouncer Mr. Clean types stood outside the front door. This customized red pick-up truck with tinted windows stopped in traffic right in front of the club. The window rolled down, and out peeked a skinny leather-brown blond hick in a black tanktop. The wankeries of the Allman Brothers meandered out of the truck like a broken-winged bird trying to fly but going nowhere fast.

"Y'all a buncha faggots!" the hick yelled. Of course. He punctuated this with a spit of chewing tobacco onto the sidewalk.

Without hesitation, the two bouncers sprinted up to the truck and pulled out the hillbilly douche in the passenger seat, right through the window, held him in the air like a baby and yelled, "Did you say something, Jethro?!" and threw his ass into the truck's cab with a nasty clang as it sped off and away. Everybody outside cheered. I had a real good feeling about the night.

Inside, the staff of bartenders, bar backs, servers and security ran around us as we stacked our equipment next to the stage against the brick wall. Everyone kept stealing glances our way. Everything felt hectic, exciting, and uncertain. The other bands—Chloroform and The Sherilyns—were already setting up their equipment onstage. The members of Chloroform were dressed in black bowler hats with bushy mustaches, monocles, tweed double-breasted jackets, and Sherlock Holmes pipes. The Sherilyns were dressed in bikinis and top-heavy Farrah Fawcett-Majors hairdos with tons of green and blue Mardi Gras beads.

"It's about time all of you stopped dressing like us," Donald said to the six of them as they tuned their guitars, untangled their wires, and set up their drums.

Melissa Chloroform turned from adjusting the knobs on her amplifier and smiled at us. Through her mustache and monocle and what was left of her orange skin, I tried remembering what she looked like that night just three months before in that Florida room before my first show with The Enchanters. On top of everything else, her skin was clearing up. So much had changed so quickly, and here we were at, of all places, Latent Republican Hipster Music Club.

"Gee, thanks for remembering all the little people," Melissa said. "Can we come visit you in Brooklyn?"

"Of course you can," Renee answered, also smiling. "You can even play in our loft space."

It took three trips to the van and back to get all our equipment unloaded and into the club. Morgan Pringle stamped our hands with a black circle A anarchy symbol, which meant we had "all access" to anywhere in the club and told us, "Everything's backstage like you wanted it." Through the beard, the piercings, the trucker cap, he smiled and added, "I think what you're doing is important, and I'm glad to be a part of it."

We were semi-circled around Pringle as he said this, and it was hard to not feel flattered by his words, except for the undeniable fact that he all but ignored us and our scene for three solid months when it was impossible to ignore.

"Well, better late than never I guess," Renee said, and we walked away.

"GodDAMN, Shaquille!" Donald said, hand on my back. "This is gonna be GREAT!" I had never seen Donald so exuberant. I jumped on Mickey's back and yelled, "Ya hear that, Mick? Great! Great!" Mickey was startled, then whinnied like a horse, and took off running around the club, with me on his back blowing kisses at the big-boobied bartenders who had been so snooty to all of us in the past.

Before retreating to our backstage for that dead time between arrival and the start of the show, those empty hours that anybody who has ever played in a band knows all too well, Pringle insisted on taking our Polaroid. We stood and smiled against the brick wall just beyond the stage, in front of this amazing picture of Keith Moon carrying Iggy Pop on piggyback—both of them at low points in their careers—degenerates on the town going psycho. I love that picture. It hangs there between me and Renee's head, both of us flanked by the brothers.

It was the best picture ever taken of us, maybe the only

picture taken of us. Just before the Polaroid snapped, Renee grabbed my ass so I'm jolted straight while yelling "Hey!" and her lips are curled into that look of mischief I loved so much about her. Donald and Mickey are laughing at my reaction. There's an innocence and unselfconsciousness about it I like. Ultimately, the picture makes us look like we've arrived, but we have no idea how, or where, we've arrived. Somehow it got into my "ENCHANTER CRAP" box.

We did a brief soundcheck, a cover of a song we used to fart around with in practice from time to time, the very obscure *Clubnite* by the very obscure South Florida band Teddy and the Frat Girls. We thought it would be funny, because the song is just one chord strummed over and over again while the drums pound unrhythmic quarter notes and the female vocalist, one Cookie Mold, yells at the top of her lungs.

As if the staff of Latent Republican Hipster Music Club World didn't have enough to worry about, we wanted them to think we were nothing but an annoying and incompetent punk band. We turned our amps up all the way. Donald sat in a chair with his legs crossed like a classical guitarist. Mickey lay on his back and stared at the ceiling. I stood up and bashed the snare drum and crash cymbal while Renee screamed, "YOU WORE BLACK LEATHER! YOU TOOK MY NUMBER! YOU LEFT ME HORNY! CLUBNITE! I GAVE YOU QUAALUDES! I HELD YOUR COCK! WE SPOKE IN DIPTHONGS! CLUBNITE! MY BEST FRIEND BLEW YOU! I SAID I KNEW YOU! LITTLE BOY WHORE! CLUBNITE! 1 2 3 4! 1 2 3 4! LET ME OUT! AHHHHHH!!!!"

When it was over, the soundguy just shrugged and said, "It sounds fine to me, I guess," to which Donald replied into the microphone, "What do you mean, 'Fine'?" We're The Enchanters! We're a band for the people!"

The other soundchecks went fantastic as well. We jumped around and danced to Chloroform and The Sherilyns as they, like us, finally had the privilege of hearing their music through monitors. They weren't used to seeing us out there since we always hid "backstage" while they played before us. Andy-Bob, The Sherilyns's thin and pony-tailed drummer, strutted up to me in the middle of Chloroform's set and threw more Mick Jagger dance moves than I knew what to do with. Renee locked arms with mine and we spun in circles, and I knew it would be a great night, that things would change for the better for us and our town. We all could feel it, how we were all smiling so much as the bands sound checked and we danced.

When that was done, we retreated to our backstage area, only, as usual, there was no backstage. This time, we were in the kitchen of the club. There were two pizzas on the silver cutting table in the center of the room, with four bottles of wine circling them. To the left was our cake, and it even read "THIS CAKE IS FOR THE ENCHANTERS AND ALL THEIR HARD WORK ON BEHALF OF THE PEOPLE OF SPRAWLBURG SPRINGS" in cornflower blue icing. There were no strap-on dildos, Red Foxx ice sculptures, or Swedish masseuses, but other than that, it seemed Pringle respected our contract, even though it was about as legally binding as a pinkie swear.

"Oh boy!" Mickey exclaimed just like a kid, running to the table, making a pizza sandwich with a couple of the slices and shoving it down his throat.

"Do be careful, Mickey," Renee said, uncorking the first bottle of wine. "You mustn't be sluggish for tonight."

"Mi'mf fimf!" Mickey grunted with a mouthful of pizza.

"Well you won't be fine if you keep eating like that, bro," Donald said, uncorking a second bottle of wine.

I uncorked the bottle for me, and then the mania slowed down to the long wait until we played. I sat in a folding chair and looked around. A kitchen. Green linoleum tiles on the walls. Stainless steel sinks and tables. The dripping of faucets. Aside from Mickey's chomping, everything was suddenly silent. Donald sat across from me, slouched in his chair chugging the wine. Renee was behind me, making a set list, crossing out songs and replacing them with others, switching the order around.

The mania had left everyone but me. I wasn't in the mood to be stuck in one place right then. I was too excited, too restless, so I snuck out the backdoor with my bottle of wine for some fresh air, to calm my nerves and check out what was happening outside.

I knew enough not to mingle with the audience before the show, but I still wanted to see what the scene was like out front, maybe just from a distance. The alley was deserted except for a couple really young looking kids—like fifteen maybe—passing a brown paper bagged 32 oz. (40s were *verboten* in Sprawlburg Springs) of malt liquor about ten feet away from the backdoor.

They wore old white football helmets with the circle-A anarchy symbols painted on the sides in gloopy black.

They looked my way and I nodded hello. "Hey man, we're taking back the alley!" one of them said, the one who wore a beattohell army jacket.

"That's cool," was all I could think to say.

"Do you want some glue?" the other kid asked, the one who wore a black trench coat.

"What?" I asked. The kid repeated his question, extending a small tube of model glue. "No," I said. "I'm cool," I added, shaking the bottle of wine I'd only taken one sip out of.

"Do you have any change?" the other kid asked.

"No, I don't." I said after patting down the front pockets of my jeans.

"Thanks, rock star faggot," the kid in the trench coat who offered me the glue muttered, followed by some pshaw grunt laughter from his friend.

"I'm not a rock star," I said.

"Yeah whatever. Enchanter." the kid in the army jacket said.

There was a ladder connected to the back wall of the building leading up to the roof. I climbed it, but not before telling the gutter punks to fuck off. I walked across the flat roof and squatted down to spy on Apple Avenue.

Utter pandemonium. Apple Avenue was closed off for three blocks around the club, with barricades and cops redirecting the traffic. The line to get into the show looped the perimeter of the closed-off street. Police on horseback rode around with Billy clubs bouncing around their sides. Unicycle-riding vendors dressed like sad clowns were hawking "Enchanter Necklaces" and "Enchanter Bracelets"—nothing but six-pack rings—for $10 a pop, and kids were actually buying them. Some guy dressed like Friar Tuck carried a giant crucifix on his back and warned everybody with a megaphone: "The Enchanters are under the spell of that Greatest of Enchanters, Lucifer himself, and you who follow them have rejected the Son of God."

Reporters with microphones, chased by cameramen, were everywhere. The noise: car horns, yelling, horse hooves, radios. The stifling heat of the setting orange sun never left; the humidity drenched inside and out. The newly turned-on streetlights illuminated the chaos below.

Sadly, it looked just like any other large rock concert atmosphere, which made me a little depressed. I still wondered what these people expected from us, if anything beyond just a good time. What did all of this mean? To me, to Renee, to Mickey, to Donald? What did we mean, anyway? Was it for this?

I went back down the ladder. The gutter punks were gone. In the kitchen, Pringle was telling the other Enchanters how the show would obviously be sold out, and if that's the case, they'd have to move next week's show to a bigger venue. They were smiling, but they weren't saying a word. Donald's hands noticeably shook as he sipped from the wine. The doors were to open in twenty minutes, so I pulled my chair next to Renee, ate a slice of pizza, and waited.

"Where'd you go?" Renee asked.

"Nowhere. Just out back," I said. I didn't want to make her any more nervous than she already was by telling her what I saw.

"Oh," she said, not really listening, eyes shifting around the kitchen. "How's the pizza?"

"It's good."

"I can't eat right now." Renee said. "I want to throw up."

I didn't feel nervous at all. I don't get nervous when I play out. I guess I just don't care. Everything else horrifies me, but performing for people doesn't scare me in the least. I don't know why. I just channel the nervous energy into the performance.

The noise from outside slowly filtered into the club. I tried imagining the male fans inside, making hanging brains out of their nuts in emulation of us, just to get in the spirit of things, admiring each other's bulged nut sacks popped from their flies: "Hey dude, killer hanging brain." "Yeah thanks, I made it myself." Missing the humor of it completely. Within the hour, the once near-quiet club had gotten very loud, and that energy seeped into the kitchen and energized us all. I don't know how many times one of us said, "Well, this is it, huh?" and the rest of us agreed.

"And this time next month," Renee said, "we'll be in Brooklyn."

Mickey took a giant slug from his bottle of red wine, swallowed, shook his head rapidly from side to side four times, and exclaimed, "I could play for hours right now. We should play for hours."

"Fuck that," Donald said, hands still shaking. "We're not a jam band. We'll play for twenty minutes then we'll leave."

"Now, Donald," Renee said, now standing. "We'll just see what happens. It won't be twenty minutes, and it won't be four hours. We'll just do what we always do."

Hearing lots of people making noise in the club amped me. Their energy seeped into the kitchen backstage, into our skin. I was so used to playing in front of twelve to twenty-five people that 500 felt like playing to a football stadium. I paced around the table, bouncing on the brick red tile floor. Everyone felt it.

"We're gonna fuck this crowd!" Donald announced, no longer nervous, pacing in a line instead of a circle like me. "We're gonna spew all over their stupid faces!"

"Donald," Renee said. "Must you talk this way?"

"Yes!" Donald answered. "Today, I must! I can't believe this is happening."

"Maybe we should stay," Mickey said. "Instead of starting over in New York. We'd be too big to get messed with anymore. We could make something good here."

"No, Mickey, this is it." Renee said. "We're just leaving on a good note, which is how it should be."

And on it went, us excitedly talking and thinking like, yeah, maybe we're gonna rise above this and really make it happen. We weren't the first to get hassled for doing something new, and those people with the guts to try always somehow prevailed just by the sheer energy of it, because once a good idea is in motion, it's only a matter of time before it spreads to everybody and by the time those in charge notice, it's too late and it's already there, and it can't be stopped.

It took a while for the 500 people to get in because we had also refused to allow people to bring in tape recorders and video cameras, and we later learned that lots of people were attempting to do just that. We were determined to remain forever enigmatic, a product of the imaginations of the listener, a group identity that would be refracted through the hearts and minds of the people who liked us. "The more room people have to reinterpret The Enchanters themselves, the better it'll be for everybody," was something Renee said from time to time.

"Come on, let me go watch the show!" I begged and pleaded

by the exit to the club. "This is historic, man! Historic!"

"No. Stay. No. Stay." My fellow Enchanters repeated at various times, and I really did want to be out there. The Sherilyns were starting to play, and it wasn't long before they were booed left and right, along with sarcastic audience requests to reveal their tits beneath their bikinis, and I'm sure Bryan's between-song insults weren't helping. He'd yell things like, "Wow, we've never played for a bunch of faggoty-ass faggot Sprawlburg Springs fagabeefy local yokels before! Gosh, what an honor!" and "Please, I beg you, just this one request: Don't rape me after the show! Just please go home and stick it in your $10 six-pack rings, err, I mean, Enchanter necklaces, and pretend it's my butthole." And, in *his* best Mick Jagger voice, "I think I busted a button on me colostomy bag and I hope it don't fall down. You don't want my colostomy bag to fall down now do ya?" They played *Sweaty Hands*, my favorite song of theirs, a song whose only words were "Sweaty hands, whenever I see you I get sweaty hands," repeated endlessly and played for about twenty minutes. (Later, Bryan would come backstage covered in cupcake icing, no doubt a gift from the fifty-fourth member of the audience. "What kind of a jerk gets free homemade cupcakes, and instead of eating them, throws them at the performers?" I asked, to which there was no answer. But at the same time, The Sherilyns had managed to rid themselves of almost all of their Mardi Gras beads in exchange for many audience members showing them their titties, so perhaps everybody was just playing along.)

Chloroform went over a little bit better than The Sherilyns, although you could hear the chatter of idiots during their quiet parts, the kinds of idiots who saw this as nothing more than a way to score some swinging singles action—the chatter of dudes hitting on girls who may or may not be there to see bands. Melissa did a lot of jumping into the crowd, knocking drinks out of people's hands, very confrontational with the newbies, as were our other fans who had been there since the beginning. It was like they were trying to initiate the new arrivals by insulting them, resentful for some reason that they were moving in on what they took to be theirs.

I hate saying this, but no matter how good a band is that's opening up, a small part of me is in a rush for them to be over so I can get out there and play. It's the best high, no matter how indifferent or unreceptive the audience is. So when Morgan Pringle peeked into the kitchen and said, "Chloroform is finished. You can start whenever you're ready," adrenaline, pure sweet adrenaline, flooded my brain and body like an electric current. I never felt more alive than that moment.

"Let's go!" I yelled, leaping out of my seat.

"No. Let's wait," Donald said, grabbing my arm. "Let's make 'em wait a little."

"Yes, let's build the suspense," Renee said between steady swigs from her almost drained wine bottle. "Maybe we can get an 'EN-CHAN-TER! EN-CHAN-TER!' chant going."

Chloroform agreed to set up our equipment so we didn't have to look like our own roadies (God, we were *such* prima donnas), and when the five of them came into the backstage area, the wait was no longer bearable, so we formed a circle, ran in place, arms around each other while Donald yelled, "OK! Let's give these fuckers the sound they've needed to hear their entire lives! Now!"

"KILL!" Mickey yelled.

"KILL!" I yelled.

"KILL!" Donald yelled.

"Do I really have to yell 'KILL' like that?" Renee asked. "Let's just play a good show."

"That audience kinda sucks," Melissa said, walking into the backstage kitchen, looking strangely indifferent to what was happening, removing her mustache and monocle. "Just so you know."

And with that send-off, we ran out of the kitchen, almost knocking over Morgan Pringle, who approached the kitchen door to find out when we were gonna play. We sprinted past him and stormed the stage, wine bottle and drumsticks in my left hand, Renee's hand in the other.

"Are you ready, Shaquille?" she asked as we walked this way through the narrow walkway that led to the stage.

I answered with a full-on French kiss on Renee's mouth, broken up by Donald's shove and a "Save it for later, pussies! It's time to KILL!!!" and there we were in front of 500 onlookers.

# chapter five

I remember doing what I thought of as a Nixonian kind of wave when we took the stage, and I took one second to stare at our instruments: the guitars leaning against the amplifiers, the drumsticks resting across the snare drum, the microphone in its stand. Have you ever been to a show and looked at the instruments just before the excitement begins? Without the players, they're so inert, innocuous, almost like decorative objects, and if you didn't know any better, you would never suspect these cords and knobs and strings and drumheads were conduits for something great: salvation, deliverance, self-affirmation, or even something as simple as Fun.

We were smiling because the whole absurdity of us playing our music in front of 500 people was ridiculous, because we never expected to play for more than 25, not in Sprawlburg Springs anyway. I plopped down on my drum stool and gave the bass drum three test taps. Mickey answered with four test strums of each bass string while Donald tuned and Renee had her back to the audience looking at me and smiling, just like that first show, only this time, I thought it really was for me. The golden sparkles in the drums reflected the red, yellow, and purple stage lights like diamonds. Our friends were up front, cheering and heckling somewhat good-naturedly, lest this "fame" went to our heads.

"Wow! You're like an ugly version of Blondie!" Scott yelled from the front and center, frizzy hair bouncing in rhythm with his laughter.

"Blondie? More like Orangie! Haw haw haw!" Balding Norman laughed.

"Hey! Hey singer! Show us yer tits!" Hirsute Sally demanded not unlike The Sherilyns' hecklers, "Can I lick the orange off 'em?"

Afro Mark threw a bunch of lit firecrackers between Renee and Mickey, who stood to her left. "BAM BAM BAM!" the explosions popped amidst smoke and flashes, and Renee did this hilarious dance with her feet like a Wild West boot scoot when the sheriff takes target practice with the bad guy's boots, then Donald ran from his amp where he was tuning his guitar and dove on top of the fireworks after they exploded like they were live grenades.

I dove behind the drums, peeking out between the rack toms, drumsticks stuck together like I had a machine gun. Already, we were giving these strangers what they paid to see, only they didn't know this is what they paid to see: four goofs with instruments.

"Hello?!" Renee yelled into the microphone. "Can you hear me?!" The audience plugged their ears and growled, "Yes!'"

"Can you—ow! Jeez!" The microphone shocked her mouth and she stepped back and massaged her lips while the audience yelled, "Yes, we can hear you!" Past our disciples, the audience in their fresh undented helmets was growing impatient. A beer can plopped on my snare drum. I whipped it back. It flew back and narrowly missed my face. I left it alone on the stage floor.

"Good," Renee said, from a safe distance away from the mic. "OK, well, we're The Enchanters..." and Latent Republican Hipster Music Club World exploded into screams and applause, and arm-crossed expectancy from others. Renee blushed and said, "Gee thanks!" With a big dimpled smile she added, "And we're from Sprawlburg Springs."

Now the whole audience cheered, and I felt all warm inside when she said that, because, for once in my life, I felt a twinge of civic pride in the place where I lived.

"This first song is called *Sprawlburg Springs Au Prutemps*."

The cheering subsided, and the chatter was gone. We were faced with the kind of silence reserved for those parts of the library where only Asian engineering students study. All you could hear was the buzz of the guitars through the PA.

Mickey looked down at his bass, and started in with four slow open E string thuds, joined in by Donald, making his guitar sound like a WWII fighter plane plummeting earthward, then two quick snare and floor tom hits, and Renee sang, and BOOM. We were off again to this world we had made. I looked out into the audience, past the bright stage lights, my arms swinging and legs kicking, our friends dancing up front as the song became more and more frenzied. To the right was the front door, and you could see tourists with cameras and bright tacky pastel clothing peeking in through the doorway. Some of the newbies who made it into the show ripped off their six-pack rings, ripped off their clothes, and became as one with the mania.

I was floating around the room. Renee was flying too. Mickey and Donald joined us. The four of us flew in circles, spinning while watching ourselves play our instruments. Our friends floated off the ground too, those kids from the Florida room just three months before, horizontal and outspread like skydivers at different heights. Some were crying. Others were laughing. There was no control, and the song kept going. None of us expected this, even those of us who knew what to expect by this point: kissing, nudity, fucking, crying, laughing, dancing, all the elements of the usual Enchanters show, and yeah, that was all happening, but floating? No.

Renee and I faced each other, locking arms and spinning in circles, the lights and sound blurring, breaking apart, reconfigurating. I looked down and saw the "a-ha" looks on the faces of the newcomers, the epiphanies, the gestalt. This was the best show ever and everybody knew it.

OK, maybe not everybody. In the middle of all this happiness, I could see just as many people who appeared confused by the whole thing. Their mouths were agape in disbelief bordering on disgust. Quite a few had their hands over their ears. They stood there dressed like all of us, but they clearly had no idea. They weren't floating, weren't even trying to float. What more were they wanting, expecting?

The songs flowed seamlessly from one to the next. The hard work and hassle was paying off with a mostly appreciative audience. I was back behind the drums, bashing away, the crowd waxing and waning, cymbals shining copper under the lights. The room smelled of smoke, sweat, and wine. Even Mickey was smiling, looking up at the audience, head shaking and bobbing. Donald was even crazier than usual, sliding like a baseball player from one side of the stage to the next, burning holes into the knees of his jeans.

Renee dove into the throng, putting her hands together over her head with knees bent like how they dive in old cartoons. She was lifted, standing straight on shoulders? backs? hands? She slowly rose above the packed-in audience, right hand upraised, carrying the microphone like a liberty torch, the left hand cupping her ear like a wrestler looking for applause, and she rose higher and higher until I could see her from just above the knees. She faced the front of the club. I played those drums and cymbals like I was a percussive octopus, watching Renee, and the fundamental rightness of that moment couldn't be avoided. She turned to me and our eyes met and she smiled. I had never seen anybody so happy. The green eyes and deep dimples and curly black hair radiated joy, reflected off all the spinning and blinking stage lights. Not just happy, and not just victorious, but completely aware this was all any of us ever wanted, and goddamn, not only that, but this was my girlfriend up there.

I looked down and listened to make sure the song was still together, because I hadn't been paying attention. When I looked up...well...I have no fucking idea. I mean, I know what I felt about what happened next, but I wondered how she felt, because we never talked about it, never wanting to talk about it, what it was like to go from all that happiness to sheer fucking panic, the kind of panic that happens when fights break out all over the room for no apparent reason.

From where I sat, this is what happened, as near as I can tell: The people who weren't getting what was going on were really starting to get annoyed with the scene. Neopunks in their wifebeater T-shirts stood side-by-side with rednecks, united by annoyance. They didn't agree on much, but they agreed that The Enchanters sucked the big one.

A bunch of these dudes (dudes, natch) started yelling at, of all people, Donald, things like, "Y'all suck!" "Y'all are faggots!" and "Get off the stage, you have no musical future!" Donald gave it back to them in kind until somebody threw a shoe at his forehead. The black vans sneaker knocked him out of the trance of the music. "Who threw that!" he yelled into the mic while the rest of us kept playing, and Renee towered over everyone like a big coil-haired goddess.

Nobody stepped forward so Donald jumped into the group of serious hecklers and swung madly, forgetting to remove his guitar so it bounced around behind his back. Mickey saw Donald flailing off the stage and took off his bass to help his brother. From there, the whole thing turned into a real raw rumble.

The smiles evaporated and lots of people caught in the middle of it fled out the front door. Renee dropped forward, right arm still extended, hanging there at a 45 degree angle before hitting the floor, falling like a torn down statue. I dropped my sticks and ran off the stage to try and get her out of there. I shoved people away and tried picking Renee up and she screamed "My leg!" Scott was there and helped get her up onto the stage and with great effort we did it. Her T-shirt was stretched out and she couldn't move her right leg. Her eyes were widened in fear, lips trembling.

It all happened so fast. The bouncers stepped in and broke up the fights, carrying people out in headlocks. The police arrived and made arrests.

"We need a fucking ambulance now!" I screamed into the microphone. "Our singer's leg is broken!" I was ignored by everyone, caught up as they were in their own worries, except Mickey and Donald, whose fights had been broken up and they ran over to where we sat.

Renee was crying, tears falling off her face as she protected her leg with her arms from the riot in front of her. Finally, a small crowd gathered and joined in the pleading "We need an ambulance now! Stop the fucking fighting! We're all friends here! We should be...so stop it! Now!"

An ambulance finally arrived and Renee was taken away in a stretcher. The three of us followed her outside past sympathetic faces and flashbulbs.

"You're gonna pay for all the damage you did here tonight!" Morgan Pringle yelled in my ear. I was too stunned to react. We grabbed our gear, quickly, in one trip with help from Scott, Alison, and Norman, shoving through people running from cops swinging Billy clubs, the shoves and shittalk of fights, kids on curbs crying and catching their breaths, wondering how they'd get home since their rides fled the scene.

The ambulance left without us, and we left once our equipment was loaded into the loud purple shag van, driving around dozens of very scared and crying kids who, like us, were wondering what the hell went wrong.

I couldn't process it, could only drive and drive until the mess on Apple Avenue was way behind us like something that couldn't have happened the way it did, because we were trying to make music for kids to enjoy and nothing more.

# part four: aftermath

"It takes a long time to get what you want
no matter how hard you try, it just won't
come but you keep on tryin', and you don't
give up and it's really silly, and it's all in
vain and if you don't stop you're going to
go insane cause it takes a long time to get
what you want no matter how hard you
try, it just won't come but you keep on
tryin', and you don't give up and it's really
silly, and it's all in vain and you could
be doing other things you could be doing
what you want, but you keep on tryin' and
you don't give up and it's really silly and
it's all in vain and if you don't stop you're
going to go insane it's all in vain and if
you don't stop you're going to go insane
it's all in vain and if you don't stop you're
going to go insane insane! insane! insane!
insane! it's all in vain, and if you don't
stop you're going to go insane."

**The Descendents**

# chapter one

Why. Fucking. Bother.

More than anything, that was the thought keeping me awake at night in Renee's empty bed.

I just lay there in silence, trying and failing to sleep off the myriad chemicals we were ingesting to help us forget what happened, and failing at forgetting too.

I mean, really: Why start up a band? Sure, everybody can do it, but should anybody do it? Forget the superficial reasons like, "Chicks dig it, man," cause they don't, at least not any more or less than they might dig something like say, wealth and/or athleticism, and if girls are your big motivation, you can save yourself a whole lot of time, energy, and futility by simply working out and saving up your cash for a nice car. Christ knows you'd tolerate less bullshit so your third drumstick gets a little play.

Why practice? Why play shows? Right from that first practice, they know you're a sucker for this. From the shittiest shithole-in-the-wall club owner to the biggest promoter, they know you can't do anything else, don't want to do anything else, and they pay you accordingly. In their eyes, you're just another stupid band, and quite expendable, and don't you forget it, so why fucking bother because there's a line out the door of bands who are just as minor league as yours. And their hair's nicer too, more fashionable, which automatically makes them better in the music biz's myopic eyes.

Fun? Well, you're getting warmer. But so is miniature golf, right? Why not do that instead? It's healthier. You don't see too many kids who have to drink wine and cough syrup to heighten the thrill of sinking that hole-in-one down that emerald slope, fluorescent orange ball ricocheting off the back wooden enclosure, skidding then spinning right to the lip, and you wonder if there's enough momentum to carry it hole-ward bound, and yes, Sammy, there is. Nice shot.

And it is fun, until you're living it twenty-four hours a day and the money's non-existent, and your van's broken down in one of those dismal, unfortunate parts of the country devoid of tolerable music scenes (most of the Southeast, the Southwest, Appalachians, the Ozarks, the Rocky Mountains, and the Plains), or when you've driven 15 hours, crammed in a van with four other dudes who, like you, haven't bathed since whoknowswhen, just to get to some piss-smelling club in the ghetto part of town just to play for 5 people: the bartender, the doorman, the earnest and apologetic scenester who set up the show, his girlfriend and the douchebag soundman. When you call your family for money and they ask you the quite logical question, "Why are you wasting your time with this?" After night after night of drunks yelling, "FREEBIRD!"; night after night of club owners saying, "Sorry, man, but this is all we can pay you,"; night after night of a capitulation of all the creature comforts inculcated into your middle class DNA, you're unsure how to answer them.

Or you play for a bunch of jaded indie jerks who stare at you with slouched backs and critique every little thing you do until you want to doubt yourself and this thing you took the time and effort to create. The hangovers pile up, your skin turns gray, the last thing you wanna hear in the van is music—any music— all the crappy fast food settles in your gut, you're convinced your girlfriend back home is doin' it with somebody else, just as convinced as she is that you're doin' it every night with somebody different. Frownland cowards always stare at you 'cause you don't meet their criteria of "normal," so they're expecting trouble, even if all you're interested in is using the toilet. Your old friends settle down, start careers and families, and you drift apart from them, play with their kids, eat their food, enjoy their backyards, and you wonder what you've missed.

It's just music. Granted, it's not warfare or coal mining. But still, it's so much futility and absurdity just to play some drums on a stage.

But after all this, as you lean against your rusting van after your half-assed soundcheck through a substandard PA from a semi-competent yet fully arrogant soundguy and watch the sun set over a very strange town very far from home, you think: Yes, in spite of all this, I'm certainly not bored. So I must be having fun.

But more importantly than fun, the reason is Liberation. For the right to do what it is you think you were put on this earth to do, you'll tolerate the rest. It beats overbearing bosses, selfish customers, boring water-cooler small talk, and monotonous commutes any day. Just to play that 30-40 minute set, no matter where, is reward enough, no matter the conditions or compensation, or lack thereof.

# chapter two

Renee was in the hospital for two days with a broken left leg and a sprained hand. They had to run a bunch of tests on her head to make sure nothing bad happened from the fall. Even though we packed Latent Republican Hipster Music Club World, Morgan Pringle saw fit to charge us for every little thing that broke—ceiling tiles, pint glasses, mic cables, mic cords, mic screens, tables, chairs, ashtrays, exit signs—and he was kind enough to simply go along with club policy and mark up the fines way more than what the broken items were really worth. Despite Pringle's highway robbery, we still had about 40 percent of what we earned that night, all of which went toward Renee's expenses. Luckily, she had insurance from being a manager at The Great American Shampoo Shoppe in the mall, so it wasn't all bad, at least on that end.

Mickey and Donald's faces were scraped and swollen from the fighting. They kinda looked like they had rocks shoved into their cheeks. I was the only one who emerged unscathed.

With Renee en route to the hospital, and told there was nothing to be done until the morning, drunk with nowhere to go but to somehow sleep this off, the three of us got into this huge argument. I was driving, tapped into something inside that kept me together, sane, as the van belched down the highway, away from all that happened.

"Why weren't you helping us fight?" Donald demanded. They were both in the captain's chairs behind me.

"I was trying to help Renee. She was way worse off than you."

"We were all worse off," Mickey said. "You were just standing there."

"No, Shaquille, I'm talking about after we got Renee out of there," Donald said.

"We?! It was me and Scott!" I yelled.

"You coulda jumped in," Donald said.

"It was over by then," I said. Which it was. Like I said, it all happened in a matter of minutes before bouncers came, then the police, and then the ambulance for Renee.

The argument boiled down to me being unable to be two

places at once, and those guys thinking I should have picked them over my girlfriend, who was unconscious and going to the hospital. Renee! I couldn't think about any of it. I just dropped them off, my parting words to both of them being Bite Me, and drove home, my real home in Lake of the Balsawoods, where I hadn't stayed in weeks, and it wasn't until I got back there and on my own couch, trying to focus on some '80s movie on the Spanish channel about post-apocalyptic ninjas fighting radioactive zombie nuns, did I cry about any of it.

## chapter three

I'd pass out at random hours and dream I was pelted with turnips. Whipped at my head, chest, back, ass, legs. From all sides. They felt like pitched baseballs, but I couldn't fall. Their pointed ends poked into my skin, making the sting that much harder. They came from all directions, from everybody in town. I was surrounded, like being in the center of a dodgeball circle, only everybody had a limitless supply of turnips, nobody I recognized, just your basic Sprawlburg Springs archetypes: mulletheads in black tank tops purchased in cold hard Camel Cash, pink sweatsuit–wearing housewives with sewed-on teddy bears, ballcap dudes in Abercrombie + Fitch leisurewear, the Women Who Love Them, proud sailors with the Old Navy, smug Republican shitdicks, unrepentant New Yorker emigrants, glassy-eyed ravers sucking on pacifiers, Type-A fitness nuts, Type-Z buffet gorgers, TV children, cranky elderly, and on and on.

## chapter four

"Rock Concert Wreaks Devastation at Local Club" was the next day's Sprawlburg Springs *Reaganite* front page headline. I could imagine Renee's pshawing all like, "Rock concert? The Enchanters don't play rock concerts. Who do they think we are, The Eagles?" I had no interest in keeping the paper, but I do remember the picture accompanying the story.

It was Renee wheeled out in the stretcher. The three of us are right behind her as the EMTs push her toward the waiting ambulance. The slogan on our faces, with varying shades of rage and confusion—me, Mickey, and Donald—said in effect, "We're fucked and we don't know why."

But it's centered on Renee. Her springy black hair dangles off the edge of the stretcher as her head is tilted toward the camera. She's looking above the camera lens, that smile when she rose above the crowd long gone from her face, no dimples, everything pulled downward, even those big green lips I had kissed so much. She looks like she's trying to say something, but nothing's coming out and nothing did come out because I was there and once she was on the stretcher she didn't say a word. An EMT hand is on its way to turning her head forward and up. It could have been a great album cover had it been just a little less painful to look at.

Renee wouldn't take calls and wouldn't accept visitors, or so the folks at St. Strom's Mercy Hospital informed me.

I spent the day listening to talk radio. During new breaks, they reported the statistical aftermath: forty-five injuries, twenty-two arrests, and The Enchanters couldn't be reached for comment. The talk of the day from callers was about our show and what happened, like an open forum.

"Yeah man I saw them Enchanters," said one gentleman caller who sounded like the kind of guy who would nonironically yell "Play some AC/DC!" at a live band. "They had no idea how to play their instruments. Just loud and annoying. That ain't music to me."

Morgan Pringle came on and announced that there would be no criminal prosecution of The Enchanters, as much as the club he booked for wanted to, but The Enchanters didn't really do anything wrong, even though both he and the club's management had no idea they would get that kind of reaction from both audience and performers.

The calls were split evenly between Yay Enchanters and Nay Enchanters. Both factions were quite fervent in their beliefs, and completely ridiculous.

"It was like the most transcendent thing I've ever experienced," raved a female supporter. "While they played, I was getting all these ideas, about what it would be like to start my own band, ideas about what I could do with my life."

"It was the worst thing ever," a male hater ranted. "The guitarist spent more time falling over and running back and forth than playing his instrument. The drummer couldn't play sitting down like a normal drummer, the singer just seemed stuck up and couldn't carry a tune to save her life. They were so annoying, no wonder a fight broke out."

"Amazing!"

"Sucky!"

"Brilliant!"

"Retarded!"

"Original!"

"Painful!"

For hours, I listened to this barrage of nonsense until the talk radio host announced a call from one "Mick," and a too-familiar voice came through the speakers.

"Hi, uh, first time listener, long time caller..." (In the background, another familiar voice laughed hysterically at that corny joke.) "But I don't know man, I thought The Enchanters were just OK."

"Just OK?" the host repeated, some neo-conservative dipshit like you hear on all talk radio anywhere in America. "Well Mick, you're the first caller expressing indifference."

"Yeah, you know, they were kinda like a pizza sandwich in how—"

"W-w-wait a minute Mick. What's a pizza sandwich?"

And with that question, Mickey proceeded to go into a detailed explanation of how to make a pizza sandwich, with lots of pointless tangents, which the host would try to cut off, but Mickey just plowed on until the momentum and the ridiculousness of it overwhelmed him and both he and his brother started laughing and couldn't stop. I was laughing too. I wish I had taped it.

Two minutes later, the phone rang.

"Did you hear that?" Donald demanded.

"Yeah," I said laughing.

"What're you doin'?

"Nothing."

"Have you talked to Renee?"

"She's not taking calls."

"I know." There was a pause on the other end. "There's all these reporters outside our house."

"Are you gonna talk to 'em?"

"Of course not. We're coming over. We're having a party at your house tonight."

Before I could answer, the phone line went dead. Apparently, they had forgiven me, and I would have no choice but to forgive them. I already had anyway.

## chapter five

Actually, the party idea was good because it kept my mind off Renee and all that went wrong the night before. The mood at my house was not unlike a wake. Our reason for getting together was very much on our minds, but it wasn't explicitly spoken of until much later in the night, when we were too drunk to restrain ourselves.

First Mickey and Donald knocked on my door. Through the peephole, I watched them weeble-wobble in place, two silhouettes of a pole and a chunky giant. The pole kicked the door and yelled, "Hey let us in, shaka brah!"

I opened the door and Donald ran in past me, howling with four bottles of Merlot. Mickey gave me a bearhug.

"Oh, Little Buddy," he slurred. "I'm so sorry we argued last night. Can you forgive me?"

I grumbled a "yes" as he still kept me locked in his embrace.

"You're one of my best friends, Shaquille, and you're my favorite drummer." He let me go. I could breathe again. "Why does your house smell so bad?"

"Squid."

"Squid? Oh yeah: from your job! That's why we never came over."

We walked out of the front doorway and into the living room, Donald on the couch working the phone, inviting everybody to a party at my house while Mickey put the Germs on the turntable and I uncorked the wine. From my kitchen, while tapping the corkscrew into each bottle (I had gotten quite adept at doing this in just 3 months), I could hear Donald. "Hey Alison! It's Donald!

We're drinking wine at Shaq's apartment so come over. Shaq, you know, our drummer? I'm kiddin', heh heh..." (to this, I glared at Donald) "I know you know *him*, but he lives in Lake of the Balsawoods here's how to get to his house..." And so he repeated to the other 11 members of The Enchanter contingent, all of whom were strongly encouraged to steal a bottle of wine from their parents.

I sat on the couch next to Donald while Mickey sat across from me, rifling through my records. I finally got a good look at their faces. Both were swollen and puffy. Donald's normally pointed nose looked red and inflated, but that could've just been the wine. Mickey's cheeks looked like he had big wads of chewing gum crammed in there. There was a Band Aid under his left eye.

While our little party slowly filtered in, the three of us geeked out on music. Mickey played disc jockey, switching records every couple of songs until the top of my left speaker was stacked with played records removed from their covers.

"Hey Shaq: have you ever heard The Safetypinned?" Mickey asked.

"Uh...no?"

"They were like this Belgian band from 1979. They only put out one 7", like 500 copies. I found it at a garage sale for like a quarter."

"You'd like it Shaq!" Donald said. "godDAMN, put that Roxy Music on...yeah yeah, that one." *For Your Pleasure* and then Donald busted out a flawless Bryan Ferry falsetto, "Do the strand...when you feel low..."

He kept going, standing up and acting it out while we laughed and cheered, the conversation shifting all over the place about bands, bands and more bands: the Vapors, Kinks, Stooges, Black Randy and the Metrosquad, Descendents, the Kids, MC5, Crime, Weirdos, Electric Eels, and on and on, until the Enchanter Contingent arrived, all that excited talk of musicians about the stuff they like and why...and after awhile, as Mickey and Donald argued about which Vapors record was better, *New Clear Days* or *Magnets*, a different debate raged in my head as I silently listened.

It's. Just. Music. Who cares?

But that's the thing: What else is there? This is the only constant in our lives, and these songs, unlike everything else, have never let us down. It's just music, but it's way more than that—it's what puts us in the mood to love, to hate, to feel something, anything, in a world rapidly losing its ability to do just that.

## chapter six

To their credit, nobody discussed last night's debacle, but to their discredit, everybody had to ask me if I had spoken with Renee. Of course, there was never an opportunity to answer everyone at once.

"Hey man, did you hear from Renee?" wide-eyed Jonathan asked while we were in line to use the bathroom.

"Dude: What's goin' on with Renee?" Balding Norman asked while I stood outside on my patio and enjoyed the breathtaking view of the apartment directly behind me.

"Shaquille? I wanted to ask: How's Renee?" Hirsute Sally asked while I was in the kitchen pouring myself more Merlot into a plastic cup that read "MY WIFE SEZ I NEVER LISTEN TO HER... OR SOMETHIN' LIKE THAT."

I told them everything I knew, which wasn't much, even though the not knowing was tearing me up. The hospital could only tell me that she had a broken leg and a swollen hand and it didn't look like anything worse was happening, but I wanted to hear her voice. I wanted to be with her. No matter what happened with the band, as long as Renee was with me, it would be all right.

Well, soon enough, the wine made all of us happy and sappy. A group of six, me included, circled in the living room and sang along to *Parachute Woman* by the Stones. Andy and Tommy were on my couch making out, tweaking each other's nipples. Everybody asked everybody else how their bands were going. Their bands. These kids had bands now, and I knew that, but it hit me how they were independent of us now, and the funny thing was, none of them were dressed like Enchanters anymore. They hadn't reverted to their old modes of dress either. Their skin was normal. They wore jeans. Their only distinguishing thing now was that they wore black armbands that said "ENCHANTERS" in big white letters. And that was it. It was like we were all still friends, but we had taken them as far as they could, and now they would have to take it from there, with or without us. As time passed, I realized this was a sad but liberating feeling, like when your youngest kid moves out of the house.

It wasn't until much later did The Enchanters even come up in any conversation, after hours of dancing and talking about bands, of Cathy and Mickey making out on the couch next to Andy and Tommy, of spilled drinks and dancing, of endless records spun, to talk of leaving Sprawlburg Springs for good.

I was on the wobbly back patio with Donald, looking out into the darkness while white moths flew around the lights on both sides of the screen doors. The wine was going down quick. Behind us was the party, the endless chatter and cigarette smoke, and over it all, *Berkeley Mews* by the Kinks played.

We were silent for a long time, just staring at nothing and brooding, then Donald said, "That was pretty fucked up last night."

I was stunned he brought it up, and all I could say was "Yeah. It was."

"I'm still not sure how it happened."

"Well," I said, taking a sip of wine. "Some people liked us and some people didn't, and the reactions on both sides were extreme. We're extreme."

"And nobody's gonna have us play anymore," Donald said sadly.

"We wanted to move anyway."

"All this—reporters, cops, fights—just because we're making music for kids to dance to." Donald said.

I shrugged.

"We're doomed here," Donald continued. "The three of us, we can still rehearse, but as soon as Renee's healed up, we're leaving."

"To Brooklyn," I said, raising my glass, even though I never thought we'd really do it.

"Yeah. To Brooklyn." Donald said, trying to sound like his usual intense and committed self, but he couldn't feel it either. With Renee in the hospital, incommunicado, nothing felt right about anything except to throw this party and be around friends.

It was silent again until Donald said, "But fuck it right now. Let's not talk about it 'til Renee gets out. This is a party. Let's act like it."

So we kept drinking the wine until it no longer felt like a wake for The Enchanters, but just another dumb party of smart kids doing dumb things. The dudes moved the furniture against the walls and engaged in tag team pro-wrestling. The women removed their tops and jiggled their titties at the building behind mine, making out just for the sake of making out between giggles. Donald shot a bottle rocket off the porch from his buttcheeks. Bryan passed out on the couch and pissed himself. Everything compressed into functional blackoutitude. I threw my plates out the back windows like Frisbees, loving the way they flew and the crackle they made when they shattered. I threw the empty wine bottles out the kitchen window, garbage out the window, moldy leftovers out the window, then I stumbled into Melissa, whose bare breasts stuck out like a couple'a li'l dollops and said, "C'mon baby, less go do it or somethin'..." to which Melissa looked at me, laughed and said, "You're drunk, Shaquille. What about Renee?"

Renee. "Oh yeah," I giggled, stumbling away happy... happy...happy...

## chapter seven

The phone woke me up. I grunted and farted and wailed "Shut up!" in bed, somehow, in my bed, face down above the covers with my clothes on.

Hungover. The worst hangover I've ever experienced. Sweaty, and the veins in my forehead pounded and my stomach was upside down and my bowels tied in intricate knots known only by Boy Scouts and Green Berets. I was still drunk, but it wasn't pleasant. Not at all. I just wanted to die, which was how I felt before the party and now it was worse.

I left my room and stepped gingerly through the living room over empty bottles and cigarette packs. Mickey and Donald were passed out on the floor; and Bryan was on the couch with a huge wet peespot on his yellow pants.

The phone was in the kitchen, under the sink for some reason that only makes sense to guys in their late teens and early-20s who throw parties. "Hullllowww?" I moaned into the phone.

"Hello, Shaquille."

It was Renee. The words jumped out of my mouth before my mind could regulate them. "Hi Renee are you OK I miss you can I come see you now…"

"Yes," Renee said, a little haughty. "I'm free to leave. I need to be picked up in the van."

"Oh, OK," I said, excited.

"Are you drunk?" Renee asked.

"No," I said, "I mean, a little. We had a party here and Mickey and Donald are here and they can come too and—"

"No," Renee interrupted. "Just you, Shaquille. It's very important I speak with you, and do hurry."

I chugged a glass of water and left the apartment over Mickey and Donald's snores. Muggy doesn't even begin to describe the blast furnace humidity outside on the black parking lot. The van never cooled, in spite of all the windows rolled down. Cimarron Boulevard was as ugly as ever.

But I wasn't thinking about any of that. The windows were down and all I could think about was Renee. I remember thinking on the way to the hospital, *Ya know what? For once, I'm really happy.* I thought that maybe Renee and I could really get serious, no matter what happened with The Enchanters. No matter what, we had each other, and we'd been through a lot in three months, but as long as she was with me, I could handle the rest. I guess in spite of what went wrong, a lot went right, and in the end I felt super-lucky.

Two orderlies wearing bright green wheeled Renee to the van in front of St. Strom's Mercy Hospital. Her right leg was extended in a cast that went from her ankle to above her knee. Her left arm was in a brace that went from her hand to just below the elbow. She wore a homemade white T-shirt that read "TIME TO GO BACK TO WORK."

For once, there was no expression on her face as she got closer to the van. I got out and opened the side door to let her in. She looked disheveled and extremely tired. Her face had aged. Not like an old lady or anything, just older, more adult, or adult period. Everything sagged, even the green eyes, even the frizzed out black hair. The orderlies helped her into the van. I shut the door and climbed into the driver's seat.

"I missed you so much," I said, turning around and leaning

in to kiss Renee on the lips, but she turned away and said, "Not now, Shaquille. I haven't said a word to anybody since that show."

I drove away, hands gripping the steering wheel harder than usual. I cut off an old lady in an off-white Cadillac. She honked. I honked back and, without thinking, gave her the finger.

"Oh, that's a brilliant retort!" Renee said.

"Look, are you OK?" I asked, looking at her through the rearview mirror.

"No, Shaquille, I'm not. I have rods in my right leg because it's fractured, and I have rods in my left hand because that fall pushed one of my knuckles back from where it should be. I'm gonna be like this for months." Then she huffed and said more to herself than to me, "It was never supposed to be like this."

"Well...I'm sorry," I said. "Is there anything I can do?"

"No. There isn't." Then, she added, almost like an afterthought, "I don't want to see you anymore."

My heart and lungs went cold. I had her repeat what she said and she repeated it, again with that nonchalant air. "I don't want to see you anymore." Not knowing what else to do, I pulled over into a vacant yet open public library parking lot right off the road.

I held back tears and blubbered, "But...why?"

"Oh, come now Shaquille. You can't say we were exactly serious now, can you? This wasn't some really special love affair."

"Well it was to me," I said, still not crying but wanting to.

"Oh Shaquille, it was oh-kay and everything...and you will always mean a lot to me, but I simply cannot be with anybody after all this, especially somebody in the band with me."

"Well what about the band then?"

"Oh, Shaquille," Renee said, completely weary, as if this were a question asked of her 500 times a minute. "You know what? Fuck The Enchanters." What she said, and how she said it, stunned me; because it was full of a bitterness I had never heard from her before, to say nothing of the curse word. "Yes. Fuck The Enchanters. It's not fun anymore, and it just wasn't supposed to be like this."

I wanted to drive the van off the nearest cliff, but there were no cliffs around, so I got back on Cimarron Boulevard and drove Queen Bitch home, which was definitely how I felt at the time, unable to think about what Renee was going through right then with everything. There was a lot I wanted to say, but I said nothing because of pride and shock and I just didn't know how to express any of it. So the rest of the ride was silent except for the van's mufferless rumble.

I pulled up into The Enchanter House driveway, opened the side door and helped Renee out, then handed her the crutches, and immediately ran back to the driver's seat.

Renee hobbled around the van over a garden of weeds. "I'll call you when I'm feeling better," she said.

I nodded while backing out, not crying until I was halfway down the street, having to pull over every block to clear my vision from the pent-up tears.

## chapter eight

Renee called me a few times while I spent my days in a hazy alcoholic torpor watching muted TV as Lou Reed played out my stereo's speakers. I just wanted to get back together with her, but she didn't want to hear it. Neither one of us was very fun to talk to, especially with each other. We both lost the things we wanted, what we were hoping for, and they were often two different things.

I had to see her, but I didn't want to see her, so I went to see her at the Perimeter Square Circle Centre Mall. I hadn't been to the mall since we broke up. It brought back memories of the good times. My clothes were dirty, my hair unwashed, and my eyes were slits. The shoppers rode past me on the escalator and gave me dirty looks, not like the old dirty looks of youth freaking out squares, but like the dirty looks reserved for homeless lepers. A group of punk teenagers pointed at me and laughed. I couldn't comprehend any of that just then. It was enough to grip the escalator's black rubber rails and try and figure out what I would say to Renee.

"Hey," was my brilliant opening line as I leaned against the creamy white counter of The Great American Shampoo Shoppe. The boutique was bustling with back-to-school shoppers. Renee's teenage girl employees glared at me from between the cruelty-free shampoo bottles they were sticking angrily with their price guns, no longer wearing Enchanter paraphernalia on their uniforms. The bilish wine stench of my breath contrasted with the flowery fruit aroma of all that shampoo.

"Hi. How are you?" Renee spoke in a total professional tone, as if I was just another client. Her springy hair was cut close. She wore a pearl necklace and old lady perfume. Her gray blouse was tasteful and subtle, adorned with nothing but her nametag. Her left arm was in a Velcro brace up to her elbow.

"I need to talk to you."

"Well I'm quite busy right now, Shaquille. Besides," she added, hopping one step back, looking around, then leaning in to whisper, "You're clearly drunk."

"No, I'm just hungover." That was my great counter-argument. "Please."

After much huffing and eye-rolling, Renee followed me to a bench by the penny fountain, hobbling along on crutches.

"Why are you doing this?" I asked.

"Doing what?"

"Leaving me and ending the band." I couldn't look at her as I said this; I just stared at the white skylights far overhead.

Renee sighed and talked to me like a child in need of discipline. "It's just over, OK? You need to move on. The band was fun, and we had some good times, but, I don't know. I'm getting older."

"Older? You're 23!"

"Yes. And I don't want to be 24 and still singing *Nugget (I Loves You)*. I mean, that would just be pathetic. Besides, I want to focus on my career now."

"Career? With the shampoo?"

"They told me if I keep up the good work, they're going to make me District Supervisor, in charge of 25 stores in the area. I'd get a raise and the company car."

"So you're just like them," I said, looking around at all the shoppers. "The whole band meant nothing?"

"I outgrew it," Renee announced, and I looked at her. She was older in the face, dimpleless, eyes focused but dim. "Bands are for kids, and I'm not a kid."

All I could think was that all of it was a lie, and I was stupid enough to believe it when Renee herself didn't believe it, and never did, or so she now claimed. Either way, the depression was replaced with anger, with myself, with Renee, with everything and everyone around me. I believed in it and I always would, even if I was the last to do so. I just got up, said "I'm leaving," and left her to sit on the bench next to the fountain's gurgles and the splashes of kids tossing pennies from the second floor.

For weeks, the vandalism around town exploded, all of it graffitied absurdities like "THE ENCHANTERS ARE THE REASON FOR THE SEASON," and the even more ridiculous "THE ENCHANTERS WILL NEVER DIE."

But we had died. I didn't leave my apartment unless it was absolutely necessary, preferring the boredom of television and the a/c to anything the world offered. There were calls, familiar voices asking me to play drums for bands they wanted to start, but the calls were left unreturned. I just couldn't. Not then. Not there.

Time passed. One, two months. I got a job as barback over at Faux Irish Bar World. I hated every minute of it. I worked hard, hoping the exertion would take my mind off the band, off Renee, but it hung there heavy in my head, especially surrounded by annoying drunk idiots while sober and working. I hate drunk people when I'm not drunk.

I'd be washing pint glasses, wiping down the bar, changing kegs, and at least twice a week some schmucky dude, always a dude, would come up to me all drunk like,

"Hey man, you were in that band. What were you called again?"

I'd tell him. They always wore backwards ballcaps and white T-shirts tucked into their acid-washed jeanshorts.

"That was some fucked up shit, brah!"

"Thanks."

"So what happened? You work *here* now?"

I'd nod and shrug, and the dude would go back to his drinking, but not before saying, "Yeah, fucked up. Y'all didn't act like normal bands."

Dude always meant compliments like that as insults, but I always felt flattered after hearing comments like that. Maybe we did something right after all.

I'd visit Mickey and Donald from time to time when I knew Renee wouldn't be around. The Enchanter House was more like a crackhouse. The Alexander brothers were always loaded. Mickey still watched bad TV and he was always really sappy to me from the wine, all like "I miss you, Little Buddy. I miss the band. Cathy dumped me because she said I don't do anything interesting anymore. Why'd it have to end?"

"I don't know." I said. "Most people weren't ready for us. We weren't ready for us. This town can't handle risk."

"This town…" Mickey grumbled. "We were gonna move to Brooklyn…Brooklyn."

Donald was a real mess. I'd hang out at what was once the Enchanter House, where all this fantastic music was created, and now a steady stream of raver kids in bright track and field suits came and went, bringing with them all sorts of shitty drugs—Xanax, roofies and even heroin. Where there was once fun, thoughts, ideas and determination, there was now lethargy and mindless chatter about absolutely nothing. This new crowd… they went to raves, listened to horrible music, offered nothing but hackneyed self-destruction under some bullshit chic veneer that had all the depth of a junkie's piss puddle seeping out of his stinking pants. God, it was boring. Uncreative too.

I'd sit over there and Donald would snort heroin off a book on guitar chord progressions and scales right in front of me. He'd smile a little bit, nod off, then scoot away into his room. Everything was secretive about him now, like he knew he was fucking up but didn't care. He stopped playing guitar, and he never wanted to talk about what happened, unless he was high on ecstasy, then he'd call me in the middle of the night all like, "Shaquille you gotta come over right now and I know it's late but who fuckin' cares, now's the best time to play it'll be perfect because we really had something and you you're so…good…and it would be amazing if we could just play right now because ya know you're so…good…at the drums Shaquille the best and I want you to know that because I really mean it and that's how I feel and you're drumming it's just so…"

"Good?" I'd kindly fill in the blank for his speeding sappy mind.

"Yeah! Good! Great! Awesome! I love you Shaquille!"
Click.

The energy of all of us, the energy that created and sustained the band, dissipated into nothing, and with nowhere to channel that energy, there was nothing left but self-destruction.

Obviously, it was a real depressing scene, so I stopped going to The Enchanter House.

I just worked and didn't say a word to anybody, which was naturally disconcerting to my co-workers, but I just didn't care. It was just like, "Fuck everything and everyone." These phony Irish-accented whores behind the bar, these gel-haired creeps in front of the bar, all these gutless and flaky phonies. I looked around for new friends, interesting people, but it was like Hendrix in my head moaning, "oh...there ain't no life here nowhere..."

## chapter nine

As much as I tried, I couldn't numb myself to the vapid realities of living in Sprawlburg Springs. The Enchanters had taken it as far as it could go, and crashed hard on a very low ceiling, so I could either take the Donald approach of tuned-out hedonism, or I could be like Renee and disown it all and just work a job, or I could leave.

I wasn't ready or willing to give up with bad drugs, and the job wasn't something I wanted to do for much longer, and like I said, there was nothing else out there for me, so I decided to save up some money and move to Chicago. I did some research. It was a relatively affordable big city, and it was the Midwest, a place for some unknown reason I equated with sanity, with levelheadedness, with everything Sprawlburg Springs could never be in a million years. Yeah, it was much colder, but I didn't care about that.

If I saved up for about six, seven months, I could have had the money, but then I was fired.

"Hey Enchanter! Gimme a beer!" this regular (regular alcoholic, that is), yelled at me while I quickly washed pint glasses in the tub of water below the bar.

The regular's name was Eddie. He smoked cigars and always wore T-shirts that read "Got Cooze?" from Coozes, that bad chain restaurant where scantily clad ex-cheerleaders serve mild buffalo wings to Republican losers too chickenshit to go to bona fide tittie bars. He wore pastel green oxford shirts with a couple buttons undone to reveal mounds of salt and pepper chest hair. He had a giant head and his balding blackish gray hair was combed in a near-pompadour. And he was loud. And belligerent while drunk.

"I can't serve. I'm not the bartender," I said, even though we both knew I probably could.

"Aw bullshit! Just open up a bottle and give it to me! Now!"

I refused. Eddie called Seamus, my boss, over, and told him how I was a rude asshole. I explained that I was just barback and not supposed to serve anybody. Seamus fired me on the spot. I didn't say a word. I just left. Fuck 'em. I didn't care. In the parking lot, I walked past Eddie's purple Iroc-Z, pulled out my Ford Tempo car keys, and nonchalantly keyed the passenger side from front to back tire as I kept walking, pausing only long enough to admire the long scratch work left behind.

I went home, downed a bottle of wine and promptly threw it up on all fours leaning into the toilet. My head spun. My teeth had a thick puke grit on their backs. I wanted to just die, and that's when the thought hit me.

You can leave. Right now.

The thought made me sit up in bed. Yeah...I could leave. Maybe not Chicago, not yet, but there was a college town about a hundred miles north that could take me in, and I wouldn't need much money. I could lay low and figure it out from there. I could sit under live oaks, teach myself guitar and drink sweet tea. I could sit on ramshackle student ghetto roofs and drink malt liquor and stare at the stars. I could skinny dip in kelly green apartment pools. I could play drums in another band. I could be in a real "scene," surrounded by self-important kids with piercings and tattoos, obsessed with soy and other nondairy products. I could find another girlfriend, some thrift-store emo diva I could turn on to vastly superior music. She could be better than Renee even. I could drift from day to day to day and let the hours take me where I need to go. Where new friends would know my business fifteen minutes before I knew my business. A lush and gentle kind of purgatory, surrounded by fellow Big Dreamers. Accomplish nothing, but feel inspired by what I'd see each day, just to wake up each day and smile at my surroundings instead of cringing, wincing, shuddering and gagging.

I passed out on the bathroom floor thinking this, and for the first time in months, I smiled.

# chapter ten

It was mid-November, and it was still hot and sticky, just like it was before The Enchanters started. I threw in as many of my belongings as would fit into the car and shitcanned the rest. I closed my bank account. I had $47 to get me there. After I filled up the gas tank, I had 34 bucks.

I didn't call anyone. I just wanted to leave. I could call later when my head was clearer and I had enough time and distance from Sprawlburg Springs. Cimarron Boulevard at night came and went and I smiled at it, knowing it would be a long time before I looked at it again, and when I did, it would be through wiser eyes, eyes smart enough to realize these roads are everywhere.

Through the rear-view mirror, I saw my football helmet stacked on what little I kept of my possessions. Without thinking, I reached onto the backseat with my right hand, left hand on the wheel swerving across empty lanes, snatched the helmet by the facemask and threw it out the window. It bounced a couple times on the concrete before rolling into the brown grass of the median.

Glenda Hood and her landfill floated into nothing behind me. The Stones played *Dead Flowers* on the tape deck and I sang along with Jagger's kountry twang:

> "*Send me dead flowers in the morning*
> *send me dead flowers by the U.S. Mail*
> *say it with dead flowers to my wedding*
> *and I won't forget to put roses on your grave*
> *and I won't forget to put roses on your grave.*"

The lights of the town were gone, and there was nothing but white reflectors in the middle of the road to lead me through the void. My escape was hasty, I was hungry, and I had no money. But I was an Enchanter. And that's all that mattered.

# acknowledgments

I figured this book would be done by the end of summer. That was ten years ago.

Now, nine apartments, thirty-nine jobs, twenty-three drafts, three computer crashes, twelve disk corruptions and two burglaries later, it's finished.

Like Dee Dee Ramone accepting his induction into the Kinetic Republican Ex-Hipster Music Hall of Fame in Cleveland, Ohio, I wish I could just thank myself. Or, like the back of The Damned's first album, I wish I could say "Thanks to no one" and be done with it, but gosh, that wouldn't be right. Too many people did too much at just the right time.

So...first off: Thanks to my family for knowing how (and how not to) help, and for always believing in me, even when I clearly had no idea what I was doing.

Big huzzahs to Jonathan and Zach for starting *featherproof* books and asking to put this out. It's an incredible honor to be a part of this, and if we don't outsell Iron Johnny Updike, it won't be for a lack of time and effort on your parts. Even more huzzahs to Zach for the cover.

Thanks to all the Florida kids, most of whom have scattered across the country (if not the South Pole, like Mike Mulvihill), especially Mark Geary, Bryan Hoben, Major Jarman, Ed Ballinger, and Lynora Good, all of whom read very early drafts and were kind enough not to rip it to shreds.

Besides disabusing me of the cartoonish delusion that good writing stemmed from being drunk, living in squalor and acting like a jagoff, the Fiction Writing Department of Columbia College Chicago taught me what I'm capable of as a writer and as a teacher, and continues to inspire and push me to the next level. Special thanks to John Schultz, Randy Albers, Ann Hemenway, Mark Davidov, Betty Shiflett, Penny Memoli and Irvine Welsh for their valuable advice and encouragement.

The spirit of this book owes a substantial debt to the shows, parties, and great times I experienced from my friendship with the people who make up the unclean rock 'n' roll scene centered around *Horizontal Action* magazine. Thanks for all the fun, and cheers to all the mutants I've befriended in Chicago, Milwaukee, Detroit, Seattle, Austin, Atlanta, and (ironically enough) Orlando these past four years.

Mark Dunihue MacKenzie (aka Mac Blackout) came through on short notice to provide the fantastic illustrations for this book. Besides playing guitar in the Functional Blackouts, Mark is one of the most authentically creative and unique people I know, and hopefully soon his fliers, album covers, and paintings will get the recognition they deserve.

Elizabeth Crane, Todd Dills, Joe Meno, Shawn Shiflett and Sam Weller were all nice enough to read the book and write some kind words in the midst of their busy schedules. They're all great Chicago writers, and you should check out their books if you haven't yet. Dills, from Chicago's premier literary broadsheet, *THE2NDHAND*—along with Rachel Shindelman—had the unenviable task of copyediting this haughty grammarian's worst nightmare.

Jimmy Hollywood and Uncle Ted also provided blurbs. Jim produced the FB's first album, and plays in two of Chicago's best bands, the Baseball Furies and the Tyrades, and he has always been a great friend. Uncle Ted from *Horizontal Action* has taught me almost everything I know about fishing and BBQ.

Extra special thanks to Sara Bassick, the sweetest, funniest, most beautiful woman I know.

Finally, I wish to thank my Uncles Bill and Mike, my Grandmother, and Chris Saathoff, all of whom died in the past 2 years. My uncles taught me about being true to yourself, my Grandmother taught me the importance of family, friends, and Irish humor, and Chris reminded me of the inherent joy in jamming econo with your friends. This novel is dedicated to their memory.

-**Brian Costello**

Chicago, Illinois

August 23, 2005

# about the author

Brian Costello grew up in Unincorporated Seminole County, Florida. He now lives in Chicago where he teaches Fiction Writing at Columbia College Chicago. He drums for the Functional Blackouts and hosts "The Brian Costello Show with Brian Costello," America's First and Only Live Talk Show. His writing has been published in *Bridge*, *THE2NDHAND*, *Sleepwalk*, *F Magazine*, *Hair Trigger*, and many others both online and off, including *The New England Journal of My Ass*.